Plaintive Vow

Splintered Empire Book One

Erin Robinson

Editing by Yvette Rebello at yreditor.com

Proofreading by Chelsea Adams at Starlight Editorial

Cover by Maria at Steamy Designs

Dedication

For the women who have made themselves small to accommodate for others—you deserve to show off exactly who you are, and anyone who says otherwise couldn't be more wrong.

Contents

Author's Note

This is an adult dark mafia romance. It contains graphic on-page violence and death. For full list of content warnings, please visit the author's website at authorerinrobinson.com/content-war nings

Prologue

BLAIR

S omething clatters against the front door.

Instinct has me scrambling out of bed, reaching for the knife that's stashed away in the bedside table before I can figure out if I've imagined it or not. Daniil stowed weapons around the house when he helped me move in, but I figured they would be just as redundant as the rest of the precautions he put in place.

There are alarms on all the doors and windows, weapons hidden but easily accessible throughout the house, and he made sure I had his phone number memorized backward and forward. Not just his number, either, but his friend's, too.

Thinking about Andrei is enough to send a shiver down my spine. If I was ever in a situation and needed his help, I'd be better off praying for divine intervention. That man hates me more than he has any right to, and I'm going to avoid ever seeing him again if I can help it.

I push aside the stack of notes that I tossed in the drawer before I finally crawled into bed and passed out last night. The only light streaming past the lace curtains that I love so much is from a streetlight, and it isn't doing shit to make it any easier to see.

The last thing I need is to slice my own hand open before I even know what's going on.

Frustrated, I grab my phone for a light, only distantly registering the time. I have to wake up for work in an hour, and with the adrenaline pumping through my veins, there's no way I'll be able to fall back asleep any time soon.

Another series of loud bangs echo from the front door, and suddenly all those safety measures don't feel so ridiculous.

Why did this have to be the one night this week that Daniil had to work?

With my phone in one hand and the knife in the other, I creep toward the door, trying to keep my steps light as I do my best to maneuver around the stacks of unpacked boxes and scraps of bubble wrap, cursing myself for not cleaning up before I went to bed.

Tentatively, I push aside the curtain and peek out at the patio, nearly collapsing with relief when I take in the familiar silhouette leaning against the railing. I put the knife and phone down on the entryway table before I sigh, doing my best to bury the frustration and lingering adrenaline.

"I hate you," I mutter under my breath as I disengage the alarm and undo all three of the locks. Cracking open the door, I glare at Daniil. "You have a key. Why are you knocking?"

"Hey, Blair," he drawls. His voice sounds tired, which isn't unusual considering it's three in the morning, but I've never seen him be anything but energized and alert. Daniil's always ready for anything, and even after an all-nighter all he needs to keep going is a cup of coffee and a quick smoke break before he's good to go.

Most of the time I envy him for that, but right now it makes me narrow my eyes as I try to figure out what's going on. It's dark, but his hair looks messier than normal, and when he sways slightly, I can make out sweat beading on his forehead.

"Are you okay?" I reach out to take his hand, but he flinches away. He twists to glance over his shoulder, the movement enough to reveal the dark red stain spreading across his shirt, barely concealed by his jacket. I nearly choke on the wave of panic that hits me. "Are you bleeding?"

Seemingly satisfied that no one's behind him, he nods and stumbles through the door, slamming it shut behind him. "I might have been shot." He stumbles over his feet, crashing into me. It takes a moment before I'm able to stabilize us both, my throat tight.

"You don't *maybe* get shot, Daniil. You either were or you weren't!" My voice is high, and he smiles at me weakly.

I won't be able to hold him up for long. He's too heavy, and my legs suddenly feel like rubber under our combined weights.

"Well, then I guess I got shot."

Oh, shit.

I put his arm around my shoulder, trying to maneuver him to lie down on the floor. He smiles at me weakly, and as soon as his head is cradled against my thighs, his eyes flutter shut. I try to push his jacket back, but I can't get it off his shoulders with him lying down.

What the hell am I supposed to do?

"Shit!"

I might know how to talk someone through first aid for a gunshot wound, but now that I need it, all that knowledge is gone, never to be seen again. My hands shake as I press down on the spot on his arm where most of the blood seems to be coming from.

Daniil flinches, and I hiss out an apology I'm not sure he can hear.

I can't call 9-1-1. That's the only thing I *do* know.

Keeping one hand firmly pressed against his arm, I try to pat him down for his phone. Andrei will know what to do, and I hope like hell he's awake.

It takes me three tries to get my fingers to cooperate and dial Andrei's number, and the ringing sounds like both an alarm and a chorus of angels singing.

"Your ass better be bleeding out in a gutter. Do you know what time it is?" Andrei barks as he answers, and it's the greatest sound I've ever heard.

"Yes," I breathe, sniffling against tears that I refuse to let fall. "I'm going to text you an address, and I need you to come here. Right now." I swallow thickly. "Please."

There's a brief pause, and then the sound of shuffling.

"On a scale of one to ten, how bad is he?"

I use two fingers to try to find a pulse in Daniil's neck. It's there, and it's strong, but he isn't awake, and it doesn't take a genius to know that's a problem.

"Please, just come."

"Christ," Andrei mutters, and I feel like I'm going to choke on my tears. I cradle the phone with my shoulder, using my other hand to press against Daniil's wound. I can't tell if the bleeding is getting worse or not.

"Andrei, please, I don't know what to do." My voice cracks and, feeling a combination of terrified and useless, I let the tears fall, adding to the dark stains on Daniil's coat. Andrei grunts as he hangs up. I type out the address, trying not to think about the way Daniil's blood is all over my hands, smearing across the phone screen.

"You better make it out of this, because we both know Andrei will never believe this isn't my fault if you don't."

Apparently, Daniil's regained consciousness, because he has the nerve to huff a laugh, as if he didn't show up in the middle of the night, bleeding all over the new floors. We only moved in a week ago, and now I have to figure out how to get blood out of the pretty hardwood flooring.

He clenches his jaw, brows drawn together as he breathes through the pain.

"He likes you more than you think, you know. He'd probably help you bury me."

"Yeah, right."

Andrei's never made his feelings for me a secret. For fuck's sake, the only time he ever even smiled at me was the first time we met, and that ended in him kidnapping me at gunpoint, keeping me hostage for three days, and threatening to kill me until I agreed to work as an informant for him. It's the kind of thing that's hard to look back on fondly, and even if I could, it would probably be a hallucination that my brain makes up to compensate for what a giant idiot I was.

"I'd rather not talk about burying you any time soon," I whisper, arms shaking from the effort of keeping pressure on the wound. "You're going to be fine, and if you ever do this to me again, I'll kill you myself, consequences be damned."

Before our first date, Daniil promised me that he's not one to put himself in harm's way. He's a lawyer, for crying out loud. He doesn't deal with the nitty gritty details of working with the Bratva.

The whole reason he's in Colorado in the first place is because Andrei's supposed to be cleaning up some sort of mess in their drug smuggling business, and people keep ending up in jail. Daniil's job is to help mop up the legalities for their men.

He told me that he doesn't even carry a gun most of the time.

He rolls his eyes, managing to look handsome despite the fact his brown hair's plastered to his forehead with sweat, his usually tanned skin pale. Somehow, it only makes his dark eyes stand out even more. If I wasn't so fond of him, I'd hate him for how he's able to look so put together all the time.

"No, you won't. You love me." He smirks, like the ass that I know he is. Confident, full of himself, and infuriating beyond words.

"No, I don't. Not right now."

He lets out a strained chuckle, and I want to slap him across the face. "Yes, you do." His eyes slip from my face and down my body, like he's just properly looking at me now, and he flashes a filthy grin. "You aren't wearing a bra."

Another tear slips free while I glare at him. I have never hated another person more than I hate Daniil Krutikov right now. He's bleeding on my new floor, disturbing my precious sleep, and he has the wherewithal to notice whether I'm wearing a bra or not?

He's lucky that Andrei's on his way. If something happens to Daniil, Andrei will make me wish I was dead, but Daniil's quickly burning away the good will my affection for him has bought.

"It's three in the morning, and I have work in less than an hour, you ass."

He shrugs, hissing with the movement. "You're still pretty when you're mad."

"Shut up," I seethe.

Fortunately, the door slams open before he gets a chance to dig himself a deeper hole. I flinch away, looking up to see the barrel of a gun sweeping the room, Andrei's broad shoulders block the doorway like he's waiting for someone to rush past him. His cold gray eyes take in the scene, observing the unpacked boxes and blood like they're opponents to be conquered.

"There's no one else here, just us," I rush to explain. "He showed up like this."

Andrei looks at us for a moment before putting his gun away. "Well, you didn't tell me that on the phone, did you?" he practically growls, rolling his shoulders. "You hardly told me anything." He pins me in place with a glare, and I glare right back. "Daniil, you good?"

His head rolls sluggishly toward the door. "Did you kick the door in? It was unlocked."

Andrei shrugs, looking like a pissed off dog as he stomps forward. He grabs Daniil around his shoulders, and lifts him into a standing position. I look around him at the splintered remains of the doorframe, closing my eyes and taking a deep, steadying breath while my heart pounds anxiously in my chest.

I like this house, but these two are working so hard to make it as miserable as my last apartment.

"Where's the bedroom?" Andrei asks, eyeing the unopened stack of boxes disdainfully.

I sigh and open my eyes. Daniil's good arm is propped up over Andrei's shoulder, and he looks miserable.

"Up the stairs, second door on the left."

I shake out my arms, not sure what to do now that Daniil is in far more capable hands. I look around the room, trying to ignore all the damage that's been done in a matter of minutes.

When Daniil bought this house, I thought it was a step toward something more stable than what I had. I was sick and tired of the drafty windows, the noisy neighbors, the thin walls and locks that only worked some of the time. This house is supposed to be a new start for me, and maybe the start of something a little better for Daniil and me.

When Andrei's work here is done, Daniil's going to have to leave Colorado and go back to Chicago, but I hope this house means that he'll make an effort to not use that as a reason to set an expiration date for us.

"What do you need me to do?" I call out.

They're already climbing the stairs, and for a moment I'm not sure Andrei heard me. When they reach the top, he looks back at me and I wonder how I look through his eyes.

Pathetic, probably. I'm a fucking mess. Covered in blood, face puffy and tear-stained.

"He should have a first aid kit around here somewhere. Grab that, bring it to me, and then fuck off for a while."

"Don't be rude to her in her own house," Daniil grunts.

Andrei snaps something back, but I'm already sprinting toward the hall closet for the medical supplies that I put away. Daniil thought we didn't need to have a full suture kit, but it looks like we were both wrong about what this house needed.

Darting up the stairs, I practically toss the first aid kit at Andrei, who catches it with infuriating ease.

"Thanks. Now go get some sleep." He almost looks sympathetic as he looks at me. I open my mouth to tell him how impossible that would be, but before I can, he shatters an illusion of him caring by opening his mouth again. "Today's shipment is too big to fuck up, so I need you to get it together."

I straighten my spine and stare at him, refusing to flinch away from his uninviting stare.

"No, you don't."

He looks at me over his shoulder, gaze so sharp that I feel pinned in place. "Pardon?"

"You don't need me."

"Last time I checked, I only had one useless dispatcher on my payroll, and that was you. Go put yourself together so you can do your fucking job."

Frustration that's been bubbling inside me for the past eight months boils over. I want to find something to throw at him, but I don't want to distract him while he's taking care of Daniil.

"Tell your idiot driver not to take the interstate and to stick to the highways instead," I say. I've told him this a hundred times already, but he refuses to listen. "He's moving drugs, and we all know it, but if he takes the slower route, there's less traffic. If a cop pulls him over, it'll take longer to get backup, and the cops sit on their asses, scared they're going to get shot. Not to mention, it's next to impossible to be stealthy about following someone when there are no other cars on the road. It throws off the troopers, and it throws off DEA agents, too. The cartels do it, and I've heard them call off entire operations over it.

"Or, even better, wait a day. Switch your driver and the car that they're using, because both of them are under surveillance. Because if the fucking State Patrol has any intel, they probably got it from public sources. Facebook, or Discord, or some other social media. They aren't fucking clever; your drivers are just stupid."

I clench my fists, hating how the drying blood makes my skin feel tight. "Your drivers are the fucking problem, Andrei. Find some who can keep their mouths shut and they'll stop getting busted all the time. And if that doesn't work, then you have a rat."

I take one more glance at Daniil, throat squeezing when I see his eyes closed and head flopped against the pillow. "I can't fix that, so I'm taking a sick day. You dragged me into this so I'd make sure things get missed, right? You want to make it easier to get charges thrown out in court because I didn't document something, or I took too long to get cover so your driver gets let off because the State Patrol could get charged for false imprisonment. If you listen to me, he won't get pulled over at all, and I'm redundant."

I turn on my heel, wanting nothing more than to lie down as the adrenaline fades to impotent worry. "I'll be downstairs. Please let me know when he wakes up."

Andrei grunts as I turn the corner.

"And you're going to get my door fixed!"

I stop in the hall bathroom to scrub the blood off my hands, turning the water as hot as possible and scrubbing until my skin feels raw. I can't tell if Andrei's intentionally being quiet, or if I'm just feeling numb after everything that's happened, but the silence lurking in every shadow feels like it's going to suffocate me.

I wander through the first floor, trying to find somewhere that isn't haunted by my dread. I make it as far as the living room before I stop dead in my tracks. Daniil's blood is drying between the floorboards.

I can't leave it there. I just can't.

I grab a bucket and sponge and turn on the lights, staring at the stain in the bright light for the first time.

With a grim sigh, I twist my hair into a loose braid, get on my knees and start scrubbing.

Daniil's going to be fine.

He won't leave me to deal with all this shit alone. If he cares about me at all, he's going to fight with everything he has to make it out of this, and he'll be *just fine*.

I *need* him to act as a buffer from the nightmare that Andrei turned my life into. When Daniil's around, it's all a little bit easier to stomach. Sure, my family doesn't talk to me anymore, and, sure, I'm working so many hours that I'm slowly killing myself. But when Daniil's there, Andrei doesn't feel like a looming giant that I'll never be able to get away from. When Daniil's with me, I'm not as worried about finding myself alone with that creep Pavel again.

A shiver works its way down my spine at just the thought of him. The last time I was face-to-face with him, his dark eyes reminded me of the obsidian display that I enjoy looking at in the museum.

They were the last thing I remember seeing before I woke up in a hospital with a dislocated jaw and three broken ribs.

Daniil's stuck to me like glue since then, but it doesn't erase the fear that I'll run into Pavel again.

By the time I pour out the bloodied water, the first rays of sunlight are peeking through the scattered clouds, making my little kitchen look far cheerier than I feel. I'm emotionally wrung out, and all I want to do is to crawl into bed and pass out, but there's no chance of that happening when I still don't know if Daniil's all right or what the hell happened to him.

I'm staring out the window above the sink when Andrei knocks on the wall, getting my attention and nearly making me jump out of my skin. He looks worn, and his dark hair looks like he just got out of a wind tunnel. I wonder if he was asleep when I called, or if he was just annoyed that he had to deal with us before sunrise.

I can't say I blame him.

"Daniil's fine. He's awake and waiting for you." He sounds as tired as he looks.

"He's okay?" I cling to the counter, feeling like a puppet whose strings have been cut.

"Yeah, Blair. He'll be fine. He only needed four stitches and a band aid." He runs a hand through his hair, an aggravated sigh passing through his lips. "He's a melodramatic asshole, but he could've handled this on his own."

I nod, looking toward the stairs. "Thank you, Andrei." The only acknowledgment he gives me is in the way the corners of his eyes tighten, but I know better than to expect anything more from him.

Andrei Voronov is a man of few words. When he says something, he means it, and if he's silent, it's because he's busy listening and watching. Nothing escapes his notice, and half the time it feels like he knows exactly what I'm thinking, even if I'd never dare voice it.

"I'll swing by later with some antibiotics." He sighs, looking around like he can't wait to get out of here. "Then I'll fix your door."

If I didn't know any better, I'd say he looks upset, but I'm sure it's just a lingering worry. Or maybe he's still mad about being here. Either way, I don't like seeing it.

I head toward the stairs, stopping long enough to squeeze his forearm.

"Are you okay?" I ask him.

He swallows, shaking my hand off and taking a single step toward the front door. "I'm fine. Go talk to Daniil." He hesitates for a moment like he wants to say something else, then shakes his head. "Tell him that he needs to call Maksim later. I'm not cleaning this mess for him." Without another word, he walks out the front door, taking care to close it gently even while it still sways on a broken hinge.

I wait until I hear the roar of his car from the street then dart up the stairs, knowing I won't be able to relax until I see Daniil. He's spread out across the bed, looking more annoyed than he does pained, but the white dressing on his shoulder has me blinking back tears.

"Are you okay?"

He smiles at me, and it's enough to get me through the door and climbing into bed next to him.

"Yeah, babe. I'll be okay."

I tuck myself into his side, trying to hide the way my hands shake.

"Don't show up bleeding in the middle of the night. You scared me."

He threads his hand with mine and presses a gentle kiss against my hair.

"I'll do my best."

"Do I even want to know what happened?"

He tenses, and I tentatively look at his shoulder like the small movement will be enough to tear out his stitches. "Probably not," he answers in a dismissive tone that tells me he really means *absolutely not*. "Try not to sweat it, huh? Andrei's got me all patched up, and now I get to spend all day in bed with you." He smirks, and I'm right back to wanting to smack him upside the head.

"You know what we're going to do with that time?"

His eyes dart down to my lips. "What's that?"

"Sleep, you ass. You got *shot*."

His chest rumbles under my head as he laughs, throwing his head back against the pillow. I bite my lip to keep it from trembling. I could have lost this. Lost *him*. Daniil will probably never tell me what happened, but whatever it was could've been so much worse.

Running a hand through my hair, he settles, looking down at me. "You're right, that was rude of me. I'll work harder to avoid it happening again."

I close my eyes and take a deep breath, taking comfort in the familiar scent of his cologne, even though it's tainted by the lingering smell of antiseptic. My mind's running a thousand miles a minute, and panic beats an unforgiving rhythm in my chest. Now that I'm not freaking out about Daniil, I have to worry about the weight of what I told Andrei.

When I open my eyes and look at the end table, all the notes I'd scribbled down, every piece of information I've gathered on the planned drug busts today and for the next few weeks are gone. Presumably tucked away in Andrei's pocket.

"If Andrei pulls his head out of his ass, he won't need me anymore," I realize with an airless breath.

If Andrei decides to listen to me, if he uses my notes and realizes his issues are deeper than I can fix, then he'll know I've never been crucial to his success here, and I've gone beyond my usefulness. If anything, I've been slowing down their progress so that I don't have to face the other side of this arrangement.

I haven't pushed Andrei to realize the truth because I don't want to be left alone again.

There's no reason for Daniil to stick around in my life if I'm not helping them. And there's no reason for Andrei to let me continue living. I'm just a walking liability.

Oh, god.

"Good. If he finally listens to you, then maybe we can wrap things up and head back home." Daniil shrugs, and I close my eyes, bracing for the inevitable pain. The arm wrapped around my shoulders shifts, pulling me closer against his chest. "I was hoping you'd be open to moving back to Chicago with me."

I stare at him. Even in my wildest fantasies, I thought he'd ask about having a long-distance relationship, but moving to Chicago with him?

"You want me to come with you?"

His grin is amused, but I feel like he just shifted the ground I've been standing on.

"Of course I do. I love you, yeah? Leaving you behind doesn't really work for me." I blink, dismayed as he closes his eyes and settles into the bed, relaxing.

Easy for him to say.

His whole life is back there. All he has to do is figure out what to do with this house, and he'll have nothing to worry about. I'd have to leave behind everything and everyone I've ever known and jump straight into the murky waters he's offering without so much as a life vest. I'd have no choice but to cross my fingers and hope everything works out.

Then again, what would I really be leaving? My family doesn't talk to me, and it's not like I have any close friends. I don't love my job, but even if I did, there are dispatching jobs all over the country. The only person who'd notice if I disappeared today is Daniil.

There's this house, but do I even want it if I'm going to be alone again? Daniil has his own home back in Chicago, so it's not like I'd need to keep this one.

"Just say yes, babe. Don't overthink it."

What do I have to lose? My peace of mind?

I take a deep breath, then exhale slowly.

What do I have to gain?

I look at Daniil. He's smirking like he's just waiting for me to give in.

I could gain a lot, but I have to take a chance on him to find out.

"Okay. Let's do it."

CHAPTER 1

Blair

FIVE YEARS LATER

I trace the recipe card again, triple-checking it against what I have laid out on the counter. I don't think I'm missing anything, but it doesn't hurt to be careful. If I forgot something, it wouldn't be a big deal to pivot and make something else, but I need a win tonight, even if it's just a nice dinner.

Niko's playing upstairs, happy and content. After an afternoon running around the park, he's all tuckered out. If I'm lucky, he'll fall asleep tonight without any problems, regardless of whether or not his father's home.

The house is as clean as it's going to get when there's a toddler helping, I have everything I need for dinner, and it isn't even that late yet.

I feel like a Super Mom.

It's not enough to keep me from looking at the clock on the stove every few minutes like it'll fix the rest of my life, but I try to savor the little wins while I can.

Evenings have a habit of creeping forward as slowly as possible before they slam into me like a brick wall, and bracing for it wears on me just as much as the hit.

I close my eyes, taking a deep breath and forcing my shoulders to relax.

I can't do anything to change what's happening outside of this house, so I have to find a way to be grateful for the things that I *can* control.

The pitter-patter of little feet startles me out of my quiet meditation, making me smile. No matter how miserable I am, Niko never fails to cheer me up.

"Mama!" he cries, and the warble of his voice is enough to have me tensing all over again, whipping around to make sure he isn't hurt. "Mama! I need help!"

For a moment, all I can do is blink at him. He's holding out his hands, fingers spread wide like I need help seeing what's wrong. His hands are stained a blue so dark it almost looks black, and the same color is smeared across his face, even streaked through his golden blond hair. A pit opens up in my stomach, and I'm not sure if I want to laugh or cry.

If it was a bright blue, I'd at least be able to reassure myself that it's from his markers, or maybe he got into his finger paint, something that's washable and non-toxic. But of course the small tornado that I call my son wouldn't do something as simple as that.

His brown eyes shimmer with unshed tears as his chin wobbles.

"Hey, it's okay," I soothe, pulling him against my chest. I almost regret it when I feel how wet his hands are against the back of my shirt. "Let's go get washed up, and we'll figure this out, okay?" He nods, tucking his head under my chin as I carry him toward the bathroom, taking great care to ignore the blue handprints and smears that decorate the walls along the way.

Forty-five minutes later, my plans of a nice dinner have been abandoned, and Niko's humming happily to himself as he tears into his microwaved chicken nuggets and boxed mac and cheese. I stare at my plate, reminding myself how much worse it could have been. I can handle ink, but if he'd found one of Daniil's weapons?

Through the relative peace and quiet, the sound of front door unlocking is as loud as a gunshot. I brace myself just as Niko takes off, sprinting toward the front hall. It doesn't matter how many times he's been told to wait for either Daniil or I, it's like talking to a brick wall. He's too young to understand that our world is dangerous, and he's too eager to see his father to learn caution.

Niko's dinner is instantly forgotten, and I have to take off after him before he can try to open the door on his own.

I manage to pull him to me just before he's able to slam into the black door, immediately wiggling to get loose as I pull him back. Experience tells me that it's Daniil, but life's taught me to rely on what I can see, not what I think I know.

As soon as Daniil's through the door, he drops his briefcase and the band of tension around my chest loosens. He crouches, arms spread wide open in greeting.

"Papa!" Niko shoves back against my chest and slips free.

"Niko!" Daniil's hair is a mess and his tie is loose, but he's full of enthusiasm as he wraps his arms around our son, lifting him into the air. There are matching smiles on both of their faces. It's their standard greeting, and it fills me with a sense of longing, just like it has every other time they see each other after a long day.

I stand at the edge of the room and swallow thickly, feeling like a voyeur as he carries Niko further into the house. It's apparent the moment he actually notices Niko's face, because he stops dead in his tracks, his whole body going tense. His eyes dart to me, looking almost panicked.

"Uh, hey."

"Hey."

He looks between Niko and me again, mouth gaping while he processes.

"Babe, why's our son a Smurf?" Niko's still smiling, but he's caught off guard at the way Daniil's frozen on the spot.

Frantic googling told me that rubbing alcohol might remove the stains, but I'm not sure I should be slathering him in it. It was bad enough when we tried it on his hands. It worked pretty well, but we also found a paper cut that he didn't know about yet, and I'd rather he be blue for a while than miserable. As it is, his hands and arms only have a slight blue hue, but his face and hair still look like he's turning into, well, a Smurf.

My smile feels brittle as I pat Daniil on the arm, nodding toward the living room. "That's a great question," I say. "Why don't we all sit down and eat while we talk about it?" Daniil nods, still staring at Niko's face. "What do you think, baby?"

Nikolai smiles, but it doesn't meet his eyes. We talked while I tried to bathe him, and even though he knows it's better if he tells Daniil what happened himself, he never wants to disappoint his dad.

When they head toward the dining room, I stop to make sure the door is locked, taking a moment to glare dolefully at it before I follow.

Daniil has pulled the glass of wine I had next to my plate in front of him, watching as Niko goes right back to his dinner. This night might have turned into a mess, but at least someone's happy with his hobbled together meal.

"Niko, do you want to tell Papa what happened today?"

He shakes his head, guilt lining his features as he refuses to look at either of us. Daniil's lips are pursed, and as much as I want Niko to own up to his mistakes, that might be too much for him right now. He's still fresh off his hysterical fears that he's going to be blue forever.

"That's okay. We can talk about what happened when we got home from the park."

That perks him up right away. His lingering shame is replaced with a fierce glare at Daniil, who simply takes a sip of my wine, swiping a chicken nugget off my plate without a care in the world.

"You said that when I call, you'll answer!" For as defeated as he was, all of Niko's anger revitalizes him, and if Daniil didn't look so confused, I'd laugh at them both. Instead, I take back my wine, keeping it close. Daniil wipes the crumbs off his fingers and looks at me for a moment before he focuses on our son.

"And unless I'm at court or in a meeting, I do. If I can, I'll call you back. You know that."

"But you didn't! We called, and you never answered."

Daniil stiffens, face turning pale for a moment. It's the only sign that he knows he's fucked up before he gathers himself, pulling his phone out of his pocket and looking at all the missed notifications.

"I'm sorry," he says with a sigh, running a hand through his hair. "I must have forgotten to turn it back on after my meeting." I hold back an eye roll.

It's a fucking Saturday. There was no meeting.

I twist my ring around my finger, wishing for the millionth time that I was as stupid as he thinks I am. Niko crosses his arms in a pout.

"What does that have to do with"—Daniil gestures vaguely toward him—"all of the... blue?"

Niko goes back to poking at his plate, all his anger leaving him in a rush. "I found your paint," he mumbles.

"What?"

"I found your paint," he repeats, a little louder and more sure of himself. "It's blue and has a gold sticker."

The confusion clears from Daniil's face and is immediately replaced with an alarmed dread. He looks at me like I have the power to change the past. "He found my fountain pen ink?" I nod, giving him a carefully practiced smile.

If I were a pettier person, maybe I'd point out that leaving out an open jar of *permanent ink* when we have a curious toddler is the sort of stupid that most parents learn to overcome before their kids are old enough to get into their things. I try to school my face so Daniil can't read my thoughts, but the way the corners of his mouth tip into a frown tells me I'm not as successful as I'd like to be.

I drain the rest of my wine.

"But it's okay, because Mama said we'll figure it out." Niko nods with determination. "Right, Mama?"

"That's right, baby."

Daniil blinks before his shoulders fall in resignation. "Now, finish your dinner so Papa can put you to bed." Without any further prompting, Niko's reabsorbed in his dinosaur chicken nuggets, resuming the nonsense melody he was humming to himself.

I push my mostly untouched food toward Daniil, who pokes at it like he's trying to figure out what to say.

"So, what's the damage?"

I close my eyes, trying to picture everything that is going to have to be scrubbed, painted over, and replaced. "There's ink all over the walls outside your office, you need a new rug, your chair is a disaster, and I didn't look too closely at your desk, but I'm willing to bet that's stained, too. And I hope you weren't attached to having a white bathtub, because that's a lost cause." I have a feeling we'll be finding blue in unexpected places for years, but there's nothing to be gained from pointing that out yet.

"Oh, and we already talked about him not going into your office without you, so don't get mad at him for it."

"What was he doing in there, anyway?" He asks around a chicken nugget.

We've told him numerous times that he isn't allowed in Papa's office when he isn't there to supervise him, but he's so antsy when Daniil isn't home, and I can only keep my eyes on him for so long before he wanders off.

"He missed you at nap time." I shrug.

Most of the time, getting Niko to take a nap is easy. It's getting him to settle in for the night that's a consistent challenge. He needs to know his dad is there or he doesn't want to sleep, which is difficult when Daniil is often gone in the evening. Sometimes Niko needs the same assurance before he'll take a nap.

Today was one of those days.

"And apparently while I tried to get dinner ready, he decided to find comfort in your office."

He rubs a hand along his jaw, still nearly clean shaven at the end of the day. He looked tired when he got home, but he's a different kind of worn down now.

It turns out parenting is hard sometimes. Who would've guessed?

By the time Niko is sound asleep, I'm exhausted and longing for the day when things between us were simple. I wouldn't change having Niko for the world, but I wish he hadn't been born *after* Daniil decided that status was the most important thing to him.

Before that, we weren't perfect, but we had the little things. Washing the dishes together, hanging out before bed, or even just brushing our teeth side by side at the end of the day.

For a brief moment, that quiet companionship is there as he reads Niko a story and helps me clean up the kitchen. And as I watch Daniil leaning against the headboard, reading a stack of papers held together with a binder clip, it's easy to forget how tense things have been between us. When it's like this, loving him is as easy as breathing.

The fine lines on his forehead are relaxed, only showing when he lifts a brow at whatever he's reading. Like usual, he's foregone a shirt, lounging in just his boxer briefs and the reading glasses perched on the end of his nose.

He's always been a handsome man, but seeing him with his defenses down, when he's dropped the persona that he puts on for the rest of the world, he's one of the most stunning men I've ever had the pleasure of beholding.

It doesn't seem fair that he looks this good at the end of the day. With his guard down, his dark hair rumpled, and all the fancy suits put aside, it's hard to tear my eyes from him. Like this, he isn't the powerful lawyer that struts around town like a peacock. I don't have to share him with anyone else.

He's just mine.

I should consider myself lucky that he shares my bed more often than not.

He takes a brief glance at me, an easy smile splitting his face before he puts his papers on the nightstand, abandoning his glasses on top of them.

"Have I ever told you that you look good in my clothes?"

I pinch the collar of the old T-shirt I'm wearing, pulling it away from my chest. "This old thing?" He nods, the corners of his eyes curling up as he does. "Maybe once or twice, but I'm not opposed to hearing it again." As I approach the edge of the bed, he slips his hands around my hips, pulling me onto the mattress and against his chest. I laugh, and the soft way he looks at me causes butterflies to flutter in my stomach.

"Well, in that case, you look stunning, babe." He kisses me, pulling back only enough to say, "And you should wear my clothes all the time." He lays his lips over mine, deepening the kiss, and a knot of anxiety winds around my chest, smothering the butterflies.

I press my hands against his chest, pushing away despite his strong hold on me.

"I actually wanted to talk to you about something."

He draws back with a brow raised, annoyance written all over his face. I pull myself free, crawling under the comforter. "Are you still going to be able to make it to the aquarium tomorrow?"

He hisses in a breath between his teeth as his shoulders tense, and it's all I can do to not throw my hands in the air in frustration. "Niko's been talking about how excited he is for *days*, Daniil. You promised you'd come."

He squeezes his temples between his thumb and forefinger. It's like just thinking about it is giving him a headache, and I'm tempted to drop it and leave him to live with his regrets when our son is older and doesn't want to spend time with us anymore.

"I know, I know, but... He's *blue*, Blair. It isn't like I don't want to hang out with you guys, I just think it would be better to wait a while. Until he's not... funny colored."

"Everyone looks blue at the aquarium; it's part of the charm." He shakes his head, and I pull my shoulders into a firm line. "Well, Niko and I are going. If you would rather spend another day fucking Emiliya, that's up to you, but I'm not letting you take this from him."

He flinches, and it's like all the air has been sucked out of the room, but I'm not going to take it back. He can pretend that

I'm ignorant of his affair with Emiliya all he wants, but I'd have to be the biggest idiot on the planet to not know.

He doesn't just flaunt it for the rest of the Bratva, he's gone so far as to flaunt it in front of me, and all I can do about it is look the other way and pretend he isn't slowly crushing me.

"C'mon, Blair, it's not that. It's just that—"

"Appearances are important. Trust me, I heard you the first hundred times." He rolls his eyes, and I turn over to switch off my lamp.

Honestly? Fuck him. We both know damn well that I can't do anything about what he does or doesn't do, but if I don't have the thin protection that our marriage offers, there's a real chance that the pakhan, Maksim, would let his son do what he failed to do the first time I ran into him.

Maksim's son, Pavel, was so determined to see his plan to smuggle drugs from Mexico succeed he ignored all of the problems. And when Andrei and Daniil went to Colorado to clean up the mess he'd created, he was determined to lay the blame at their feet.

He wanted them to fail so badly he cornered me on my way home from work one night and beat me half to death. If he hadn't been interrupted, I have no doubt he would have killed me.

And I wouldn't put it past him to try again if he thought it would help erase history.

Daniil can do whatever he wants because I'm stuck, and I refuse to go out of my way and make it easier for Maksim and Pavel to let my son grow up without a mother.

Eventually, Daniil turns off his own lamp, but I can feel him watching me in the dark.

"We aren't going to run into Maksim at the aquarium. You know that, right?"

"I know," he eventually answers.

"And if we did, you could always just blame me for why Niko looks like that." I swallow, closing my eyes against tears. "Maksim already hates me. What more is there to lose?"

The sheets shift as he rolls over, pressing a kiss to the back of my head. "It isn't that I don't want to spend the day with the two of you. I do, it's just... things are a fucking mess right now, Blair."

I don't doubt that.

Daniil makes an effort to hide his work from me, but he's away more nights than he's home lately, and when he *is* home, he's often gone before Niko and I are awake. It doesn't take a genius to know that *something's* going on.

"I know, but Niko isn't getting any younger. He misses you."

I miss you, too, I think, but don't dare say.

The way he pulls me back against him, arms tight, tells me he heard it anyway.

For a couple of agonizing minutes his steady breathing is his only reply. Each one makes me long even more for the days when our conversations were easy and our arguments were only petty squabbles. I'm sick of spending the few moments I'm able to steal with him arguing.

"You're right. I'll go." I try to relax against him, but it's hard. "I love you, yeah?"

I don't know if I even believe that anymore.

If Niko weren't a factor, would Daniil toss me to the wolves? Would he wash his hands of our relationship if it would get him closer to Maksim?

My chest squeezes.

"I love you, too."

CHAPTER 2

Andrei

Ashes float down like snow, blanketing everything in a coat that will linger here for weeks. When I come back, I'll be tracking the evidence of this fire with me in the dust and smell that will cling to my clothes.

I stay back, watching from across the street as firefighters stalk around the ruined remains of my warehouse, dousing the few remaining embers.

I clench my fists in my pockets, taking a breath to get my temper under control.

This is the fourth warehouse that's been destroyed in the past two months, but at least this one paints a clearer picture. It was public information that I owned the other three, but this one was owned by a shell company. And that shell company is owned by another shell company.

It's enough layers deep that most people wouldn't bother doing the work to trace it back to me. Including law enforcement. They'll have to do the work for their investigation now, but I doubt the culprit behind this bullshit did.

That narrows down my list of suspects significantly.

It also means I don't have to worry about cops trying to talk to me tonight. As long as they don't see me here, anyway.

With that in mind, I slip back down the alley and make my way to my car.

Already, the acrid smell of smoke is stuck to my clothes. I make a mental note to ensure I get the smell out of the seats before it gets a chance to settle in and make a home there.

I spend the whole drive home trying to figure out how to approach my next steps.

What I *should* do is go home, toss my suit in the trash, and get some rest so I can deal with the rest of this shit in the morning. It's not like I can actually prove who started the fire. Not yet.

If I try to make accusations at this point, I'd end up looking like an idiot with my pants around my ankles before I end up in a shallow grave.

At least this warehouse was empty, unlike the last one.

That doesn't mean I can afford to have more attention on me right now, though.

I've been fortunate to keep my nose clean as far as the law's concerned, but I'm under no illusions that it'll stay that way. And if someone keeps shoving me into the law's spotlight, I have no doubt my luck will run out sooner rather than later.

But pissing off the pakhan by accusing his son? I'll be dead before I'm able to get a single step off his property.

Pavel's been an issue since he officially became part of the Bratva at nineteen, but his attempts to follow in his father's footsteps are dragging us into a pit we'll never be able to escape even faster than Maksim has been able to.

He's been whispering in Maksim's ear about his grand ambitions with very little thought about the execution or consequences of his actions. Add that on top of Maksim's bloodthirsty, ruthless approach to anything relating to business, and we're all going to end up in prison or destroyed in a matter of years.

I can't do shit to stop their runaway train, so I have to focus on covering my own ass in the meantime. Even if that means I have to bite my tongue and let Pavel have his pointless destruction.

Shoving my suit into the garbage, I toss my phone between my hands, trying to focus on the issue at hand and ignoring the rest until it eventually boils over. It burns at my ego, but I'll have to keep pretending that I'm an idiot for now.

Glancing longingly at the bottle of vodka sitting on the kitchen island, I shake my head. I'm sure I'll have to be up by sunrise, and it's already nearly three. Getting drunk isn't going to fix it. I look back at my phone screen.

I know something else that will comfort me, but it's just as stupid.

Then again, knowing that something is a bad idea has never stopped me before. Pulling up a contact, I press call before my conscience can tell me off.

"Kak?" Daniil barks, sounding tired. It makes me smirk, but it's wiped away when I hear a woman's voice in the background. "It's work. Go back to sleep," he soothes, voice dripping with affection that has my blood pressure spiking.

I roll my shoulders and look up at the ceiling.

"Are you at your place or Emiliya's?"

I'm not sure if I'm asking because I really want to know, or because I want to take my frustrations out on him.

"Fuck off, Andrei." I hear the sound of a door closing. "Don't ask me that shit when I'm around Blair. You know how she gets."

"What, she doesn't like hearing about your mistress? Imagine that."

"Mudak," he mutters under his breath. "What do you want?"

"Someone torched another warehouse."

"Shit," he sighs, and I just know that he's running his hand across his forehead. "Was it in use?"

I squeeze the bridge of my nose, willing away the headache that's brewing at the back of my skull. "No. Not unless you count construction supplies, anyway."

"At least there's that. Was it staffed?"

"Skeleton crew for security, but they all fucked off before anything happened."

Daniil laughs. "You need new employees, my friend."

"Considering what happened at the last place, I'd be worried if they had bothered to stick around." The fact that there aren't bodies to deal with is the upside.

"Sounds like it was clean and easy, so why are you calling me?"

Because I hate myself.

I've already called Alexei, another member of the Bratva, so he can have his lackey, Lev, can sort through the footage, and I don't have to worry about cops tonight. It was just property damage, so unless someone connects me as the owner of this warehouse as well as the other buildings, then this is a problem with little consequence. But it still pisses me off, and hearing Blair's voice, even when I know she's in *his* bed, helps make it easier to deal with.

"Just wanted to give you a heads up. You're probably going to have a couple detectives at your office in a couple days asking questions." It's a thin lie, but it's the best I can come up with right now.

He laughs, dark and bitter. "A text would've worked, too. But, hey, we both know why you really called, yeah? Did you get what you wanted, jackass?" I grunt, but it seems to just piss him off even more. "You need to get over this bullshit crush, Andrei. She married me. She had my kid. And calling me in the middle of the night isn't going to change it."

I hang up, refusing to give him the satisfaction of gloating any more than he already has. He's right, but I don't have to listen to it. I made my bed before I even knew what I was doing, but that doesn't make it any easier to lie in.

***

It feels like I've just fallen asleep when the sound of my phone ringing startles me awake, pressure instantly pounding behind my eyes. I scramble to answer, not bothering to check who's calling before I do.

"*Da?*" I run a hand over my eyes, trying to get my bearings as I look around the room, lit by the first rays of light through the windows.

"You had problems last night. Why am I only hearing of them now?" Maksim's gravelly voice and thick accent wake me up faster than a slap to the face. *Blayd.*

"Forgive me, Pakhan. The building was empty and unoccupied. The structure was the only thing lost, and I didn't think it prudent to wake you."

Should I have called him last night? Probably. Did I want to deal with him after talking to Daniil? Fuck no, but that's not what he wants to hear. The truth is that I wasn't going to tell him anything at all if I could avoid it.

It might not have been my smartest plan, but it's what I had. And, *fuck,* I wish it had worked.

"My office. Thirty minutes."

He hangs up, and when I check the time, the early hour glares back at me dispassionately. His place is a half hour away without traffic, and he makes everyone who enters go through a security screening that takes at least ten minutes. I roll my shoulder to relieve the tension that rushed back as soon as I woke up, and I make my way toward my closet to get dressed.

Maksim's paranoia is already going to make me late. I might as well put on a suit before he chews me out for an hour.

And he does, but at least it isn't for not being dressed appropriately this time.

He flips through the photos that my guy at the firehouse emailed me last night, thick brows drawn together as he inspects them.

Maksim's office is still dark, the obnoxious blackout curtains still closed and only a couple of floor lamps casting the room with a dramatic glow that highlights the luxurious, deep red velvet of the chairs and dark wood of the built-in units. He hopes the effect makes anyone who comes here uncomfortable, but it just makes him look like a melodramatic asshole.

Apparently, he never got the memo that trying to look like a supervillain just makes him look pathetic.

Crossing my legs at the ankle, I take in his graying hair, wrinkled face, and tobacco-stained fingers. Every time I see him, he manages to look more weathered. Idly, I wonder how much longer he'll be able to stick around before someone takes care of him.

Maybe that's why he's letting Pavel take the reins on so many projects.

"Any idea who did this?" He slaps down another photo, glaring at me from under his brows.

"I have some ideas." I shrug. I try to keep the corner of my eye focused on the open door. It wouldn't be unheard of for someone to be eavesdropping. It doesn't matter if it's Pavel or one of the household staff. I have to assume that anything I say here will end up being the subject of gossip by the end of the day either way. "Pests don't stay in their holes for very long. Whoever it was, they'll come crawling out soon enough."

Maksim leans back, running a hand through his thick hair.

"I don't need more of this shit, Andrei. The feds have been circling as it is. We have too much going on and too many eyes on us. So fix it, or I'll have someone fix it for you. Understand?"

Maksim's definition of fixing things tends to rely less on subtlety or tact, and more on blowing everything to smithereens. And besides me, most of the men he calls on to clean things up for him follow suit.

If he wants this handled without attention, then he'll have no choice but to let me handle it myself.

I nod, standing when he waves a dismissive hand toward the door. As I leave his home, I don't spot anyone, but I still resist the urge to pull out my phone until I'm in my car and off the property, nodding at the guards at the gate as I pass.

It takes three blocks before I'm sure he isn't having me followed. The old man's not above spying on his own men, and I'm not going to make it easy for him.

Pulling out my phone, my jaw is tight as I call Daniil, waiting impatiently for him to answer. By the time he does, my knuckles are white against the steering wheel.

"Thank you *so much* for calling Maksim for me, you *pizda*. I really appreciate the heads up."

He laughs, and I comfort myself with the soothing image of what it would look like if I bashed his head into a wall. "You woke me up in the middle of the night. I figured letting the pakhan know what happened was the least I could do for you."

I'm seething, ready to rip him a new asshole when I hear children laughing in the background. Not just Niko, but several children.

"Where the hell are you?"

"Aquarium. I promised Blair and Niko I'd spend a day with them." I try to picture uptight, boring Daniil, no doubt dressed in a full three-piece suit, surrounded by happy families and endless displays of fish. Then I picture Blair at his side, smiling at him while they both hold one of Niko's hands.

A perfect little family.

A honk brings me back to the present, and I shake my head to clear the image, focusing on the Prius I apparently cut off.

"Well, tell Niko I said hi."

"Sure thing. Anything else you need from me?"

"Yeah, just a small thing."

"Make it quick, Blair's waiting for me to catch up with her."

"When you get to hell, make sure you're easy to find so I can fucking kill you."

CHAPTER 3

Blair

Niko's practically bouncing in his car seat by the time we pull up in front of Mila's house. Before the car has even stopped, he's struggling to free himself, and when I let him out, he's more of a hindrance than a help, but he's smiling so wide that I don't dare say a word.

It helps mute the dread that I'm feeling; his happiness is a beacon I refuse to disturb.

Daniil stands to the side, scrolling through emails on his phone and only looking up when Niko sprints to the door. We both hang back, watching as he practically skips up the stairs, waiting impatiently by the front door. Taking a deep breath, Daniil slips his phone into his pocket and reaches out to take my hand.

"Let's get this over with," he grunts, face grim, like he's preparing to march into battle, certain that neither of us will make it out alive.

"She's your mother. You only have to be pleasant for ten minutes."

His shoulders roll back, but before he can retort, Niko's standing on his tippy toes and pressing the doorbell. Not even ten seconds later, Mila opens the door with a wide smile, arms open wide so she can hug her grandson.

"Baba Mila!"

They hurry inside, voices a flurry of Russian that I'll never have a shot of keeping up with. Daniil rolls his eyes and steps back toward the car, jerking to a stop when I slip my arm through his.

"Don't you dare," I hiss through my teeth. "You are *not* leaving me here again." I can only sit politely and be ignored for so long before I snap, and I'm not interested in starting a fight with my mother-in-law today.

Honestly, I'm never interested in fighting with her, but there's only so much that I can take when she goes out of her way to make sure I know she doesn't want me here.

I play nice because my son adores her almost as much as he does Daniil, and because I don't need to do anything to widen the gap between me and Daniil.

Not that I think he'd mind if I told Mila to crawl into a hole and stay there, but still. It's the principle.

I plaster on a polite smile and drag my husband through the front door, even though just the looming shadow of this house makes me shiver.

As soon as we step through the door, we're wrapped in the scent of freshly baked pastries and a warmth that can only come from having the oven running for hours on end. Every time we come over, it's the same, but I've never gotten used to it.

I've tried to suggest that Mila open her own bakery before, but she's brushed me off like I'm nothing but a fly buzzing around her head.

Mila looks over her shoulder at us, eyeing me like an intruder before she's able to wipe her face clear of any expression. It only lasts a moment before she's back to smiling, patting Daniil on his cheek with a soft hand.

"*Privyet,* Moma," he mumbles, sounding like he'd rather be anywhere else. I pinch his arm as subtly as I can, and he pulls away, dropping my arm like a hot potato. Mila doesn't hesitate to speak to him, spitting out Russian so fast that not a single word of it means anything to me.

When she runs out of steam, I smile weakly.

"Hi, Mila."

She doesn't even spare me a glance, just loops her arm through Daniil's and herds him toward the kitchen, urging him to sit next to Niko at the table. I lean against the wall, watching as she pushes plates of pastries in front of them, speaking as enthusiastically as she does quickly.

Niko laughs at something she says, responding much slower.

His Russian will never be as good as theirs, but Mila has made a point to only speak to him in her native tongue since the day he was born. I'm sure she's furious that Daniil doesn't do the same, but he had to draw the line somewhere.

Thank god.

If he hadn't, I probably would have had no choice but to ask for a divorce and make him deal with the consequences. Regardless of the state of our relationship, I like to think he'd rather have me around than be left to raise our son on his own.

Daniil's phone lights up, and he makes a dismissive sound before he picks it up and walks out of the room. Apparently, all my practice is paying off, because he passes me in a way that lets me know that I'm nailing my impression of wallpaper.

I'm invisible and not worth paying attention to, just another decoration cluttering up his childhood home.

Mila watches for a moment, looking upset before she redirects all her attention back onto Niko, who's laughing as he munches on the handmade bear claw on his plate.

My mouth waters, but I bite my tongue. She is incredible in the kitchen, but I know the only way I'm going to get my hands on one of Mila's creations is if either Niko or Daniil ask to take some home. And considering how little Daniil wants to be here and the bottomless pit that is my son, the odds aren't looking great.

Maybe I'll drive around town this afternoon and find a bakery so I can get one for myself. It'll be terrible in comparison to the masterpieces that Mila makes, but at least I won't have to hand over my pride on a silver platter to get it.

For the life of me, I can't remember why I insisted on coming along today.

I've long since given up any hope of Mila learning to like me, much less considering me family. I don't like it, but I've learned to bite my tongue and take it for what it is.

"Right, Mama?" Niko asks, snapping me back to reality.

Rather than committing to something I can't promise, I shrug. Mila shakes her head like I've given the wrong answer, but it also causes enough of a lull in their conversation that I feel like I can jump in.

"Mila, I've been meaning to ask. Would you like to come over for dinner next week? Maybe on Tuesday?"

She might do a great job of pretending she only speaks Russian when I'm around, but I know better. Her English is perfectly fine. Mila learned alongside Daniil when their family immigrated to the States when he was young, helping him with his homework every chance she had.

She looks like she's investigating me for some hidden motive for my question, eyes narrowed and a line forming between her brows.

"It would be nice to spend time with you, and I know Daniil feels the same way."

He certainly doesn't, but a little white lie can't hurt, right?

She's the only family he has outside of Niko and me, and even if he doesn't like it, I don't want to watch him throw away his relationship with her.

Mila and Daniil are both stubborn assholes, but so am I, and I refuse to let them one-up me.

Her lips are pursed, and for a moment I let myself hope that she's actually contemplating it. Mila will do just about anything to spend time with her boys, and I'm hoping that my presence isn't enough to deter her. Then she turns her back, returning her attention to whatever it is she has in the oven.

My blood boils, and I look at Niko and tell myself to bite my tongue.

If it weren't for him, I'd snap at her. I'd let her know every awful thing I think, and then I'd remind her that the only reason she ever sees her son is because I have to physically drag him here, just to rub salt in the wound.

But Niko deserves more than that, so I stew silently until Daniil finally comes back.

Turning toward him, I raise a single brow, but as pissed as I am, he looks even worse. His jaw is clenched, and his fists are held even tighter by his sides. He looks pale. I try to ask him what's wrong, but he wraps his arms around my waist, pulling me into a tight embrace before I can.

"Let's get out of here, yeah? I have to make some calls." There's a slight tremor in his voice I'm not sure I've ever heard before.

What happened to shake him up this bad? He was fine before he left the kitchen.

"Something came up, Moma. We have to head out." He doesn't wait for her to acknowledge him before he's pushing me toward the door.

I pry myself free long enough to say goodbye to Niko, but Daniil hardly takes his eyes off me.

"*Zhdat!* Daniil!" she calls, and he turns around for a moment, but he doesn't stop walking while I struggle to keep up with him. She gives me a brief look, grinding her teeth together. "Could you come over for dinner this week? You, me, and Nikolai?"

Like that, all my worries about Daniil's sudden mood swing burn to ash as my anger rushes back in to take their place.

"Are you fucking *serious*?" I hiss, hopefully quiet enough that Niko doesn't hear me. I extended an olive branch, and she's going to use it to beat me away? And of course, she had to do it in the language I actually speak. Where the hell does she get off?

"*Da*, sure, Moma," Daniil replies absent-mindedly, already turning his attention back to his phone. Mila beams, and I'm ready to rip them both a new asshole, but he wraps an arm around my shoulder, urging me to the car before I get a chance. "Blair will pick him up at four."

Four? That's hours earlier than I typically pick up Niko. The whole point of letting Mila baby-sit him is so they get to spend a full day together.

He rushes us out the door before Mila's even finished celebrating, the storm door slamming shut while I dig my heels into the ground, refusing to move.

"Nope. Absolutely not."

I'm not dealing with that woman again until she manages to find a shred of decency in her spiteful, rapidly aging body.

He purses his mouth but doesn't say anything, just keeps pulling me to the car like I'm not fighting him at all.

I slam my door shut behind me, tuning in my seat to glare at him.

"Listen, I know she's unbearable, but I need you to do this for me," he tells me.

I cross my arms, waiting for him to elaborate, but he doesn't.

"No," I object. "I've tried with her a hundred times, and I'm sick and tired of being invisible. And I'm sick of you letting her treat me like that."

He checks the mirrors as he pulls onto the street, not sparing me a single glance. "Yeah, well, I had to move up a meeting that I can't risk being late to, so I can't do it."

"And what part of that means I have to pick him up early? He's going to be furious, and we both know Mila won't back me up when I tell him it's because *you* said so." I'm so sick of being the bad guy. I'm always the one who has to tell Niko that plans have to be pushed back, or that he can't do something, or to make sure he does the many little things he hates.

Daniil's silent until he pulls into the driveway. I expect him to get out or say something else, but he stares straight ahead. Eventually he clears his throat and turns in his seat so he's facing me, tension lining the corners of his eyes as he works his jaw.

"Daniil, what's going on? Why are you changing plans last minute?" He wraps a hand around the back of my neck, pulling against me until he's able to rest his forehead against mine. "Is everything okay?" He closes his eyes and swallows.

"Yeah, babe. It'll be fine." He presses his mouth against mine in a slow kiss. "I have to work late tonight. Someone made a big mess, and I have to clean it up. I just want to make sure you and Niko are home before I leave."

We stay that way, breathing each other in until I nod. He might piss me off and make me miserable more often than not, but I'm not going to pretend that I want to make his life harder. If Daniil just wants to make sure we're home so that he doesn't have to worry while he's working, then I'll find a way to make it happen.

Chapter 4

Andrei

I've spent most of the past week chasing shadows that are leading me nowhere. No matter who I ask or where I look, it's like there's nothing to find. Not any evidence pointing me toward Pavel, and not anything that implicates anyone else, either. I haven't gotten more than a couple hours' sleep at a time, and if one more thing gets added to my plate, I'm going to fucking snap.

Which is why I'm pouring myself a shot of vodka at noon, ignoring my phone as it rings on my desk. If it's Maksim, I'll gladly deal with the consequences later. If it's anyone else, I don't give a fuck.

The crisp, smooth drink is exactly what I need.

I lean back in my seat, taking a deep breath when my phone stops ringing. It rings again almost immediately.

"Fuck." I drag a hand down my face and check who it is, declining the call when I see Daniil's name. Whatever bullshit he wants to pile on can wait until tomorrow.

I don't even close my eyes before the stupid thing starts ringing again.

"*Da?*" I answer with a snarl. "What's so important that you won't let me have a moment of peace?"

"I need you for a meeting tonight," he rushes out, sounding almost panicked.

"You need me, huh? Well, too bad I don't give a shit."

I'm already pulling my phone away, intent on hanging up when he blurts, "I'm meeting with Semyon." I pause, hesitating for a moment before I press the phone back to my ear. "If I meet him alone, odds are at least one of us isn't going to walk out of that room. I need a mediator."

"A babysitter, you mean."

Daniil and Semyon get along about as well as oil and water, but their paths don't cross often enough for me to worry about it. I respected lawyer shouldn't take notice of a mere foot soldier, and a soldier shouldn't have any need for an attorney unless he's in trouble.

Lucky for us all, Semyon—who I have the unfortunate designation of calling my brother—has always had a lucky habit of wiggling his way out of situations before he needs to worry about it.

"You two have no reason to be in a room together. Whatever he's done, just ignore him. It'll go away soon enough."

"I'd love to, but he's crossed a line I can't ignore." Daniil sighs. He sounds frustrated, and it piques my curiosity. Semyon has largely been quiet for the past few months, but when he does cause a mess, I'm typically one of the first to know about it.

"What'd he fuck up this time?"

"Apparently he's been running his mouth again."

"That's nothing new. Why do you care?"

Semyon's the type of person who thinks more highly of himself than anyone else ever will. He'll talk a big game, cause a mess, and he won't care when I'm left cleaning it all up afterward. If it weren't for me, he would have ended up in prison ages ago.

There's a beat of silence. Long enough that I have to check to make sure the call hasn't dropped.

"He was talking about Blair. And from what I was told, it sounds like he was planning on taking her out."

My heart stutters in my chest as my blood burns to a boil.

"He can't. Even Maksim wouldn't let someone kill your wife." I'm trying to reassure myself just as much as I am him. He might be erratic and unreliable, but even Maksim knows that when you start killing your men's families, they don't stay loyal for long.

It's part of the reason I didn't fight Daniil when I found out he was planning to propose. At least their marriage gave Blair some sort of protection when Maksim decided that she was a liability.

In his eyes, once a rat, always a rat. It doesn't matter to him if Blair was only acting as an informant because I strong-armed her into it. Maksim doesn't give a shit if she was giving us information about the cops' plans, or that she was only ever helping me clean up Pavel's sloppy mistakes. He'll always view her as a risk to his entire operation, one who will turn around and tell law enforcement everything she's learned over the years whenever she wants to.

"Well, he made it sound like he was given a thumbs up from someone higher up the food chain."

"That'd be a slippery fucking slope. Who the hell told you that?"

"Does it matter who?" he snaps. "I can't let him talk like that, man, and he agreed to a proper sit-down." He sounds desperate, almost pleading. My jaw aches from how hard I'm grinding my teeth.

Semyon's bark has almost always been worse than his bite. He's always been the type of person who'll do anything if he thinks it'll give him a leg up in this life, but doesn't have the smarts to be trusted with anything serious. Still, I can't help but ask myself if this is different.

Maksim wouldn't give Semyon the okay for *any* assassination, much less for someone associated with the Bratva, but Pavel? He's short-sighted enough that he wouldn't wait for permission. Especially if he thinks it would impress his father.

I don't know if killing Blair would be enough for that, but Maksim wouldn't lift a finger to stop it. If Semyon's serious, then the only recourse would be to meet him face-to-face and either talk him down or end his ambitions in a more permanent manner.

Daniil can talk his way out of a paper bag with most people, but my shit-for-brains little brother? He's too stubborn to listen to anything that anyone has to say. He'll probably just go into the meeting with guns blazing because he thinks that's what'll get him ahead.

"Please, Andrei. I need you there." I've known Daniil most of my life, and I don't remember the last time I heard him say *please.* "You're the only one who has a chance of talking him out of this bullshit."

I don't believe that.

Semyon's only become more untamed the closer he's gotten to Pavel. I can't stand to be around him for more than a few minutes at a time, and I don't even remember the last time we talked about something that wasn't related to the Bratva.

But I'm not willing to risk betting that he's just running his mouth, either.

The thought that something could happen to Blair is almost enough to paralyze me, and if something did happen and I didn't do anything to stop it, I'd never forgive myself.

"Fine. But try to keep a level head when we're there, alright? I can't manage two hot heads at the same time."

"Yeah, no problem," he mutters. "Just remain calm around the guy threatening to kill the mother of my son. Should be easy."

I should have expected that.

I stare morosely at the bottle of vodka for a moment before I twist the cap back on. So much for a calm afternoon.

"When and where?"

"Come to my place around eight. I'll drive. You won't have to worry about my damn mouth, yeah?"

I grunt. I'm sure Blair's worked herself into a frenzy over this. Knowing that she's going to be at home with Niko, worried sick until Daniil gets back doesn't sit right with me. "Do I need to get someone to watch your place while we're gone?"

"No." His answer is decisive. "Blair doesn't know about any of this. Let's keep it that way, yeah?"

I scoff. For a man who claims to know his wife, he doesn't know anything about her. "I know you like to pretend that she's an idiot, but if you're this worked up, then she'll know something's up."

She might not know exactly what, but she'll know there's something to worry about. She's done a pretty good job of putting on her blinders and feigning ignorance, but she's too smart for the box he wants her to fit into.

Watching her try is infuriating.

For a moment, I let myself wonder if the only reason they're together is to keep her safe, if maybe Blair's miserable in her relationship and hates all the shit she has to deal with.

Maksim won't do anything as long as their vows work as a gag order. He thinks she's a risk, but as long as she can't be compelled to testify against Daniil, he'll hold his tongue.

Maybe she doesn't want their marriage. Maybe she feels like she needs it.

Then I remember the way she smiled at him the last time I saw her and shake my head.

She didn't look miserable. She looked like a woman who was in love with her husband, not one who was desperate to escape her relationship at the first opportunity.

"That doesn't mean she needs to know about the specifics, Andrei. Besides, she'll be home with Niko. No one's going to mess with her when he's around."

Sure, no one's going to mess with Niko, but he's only three. He can't tie his own shoes, much less defend his mother. If someone really wanted to do something to her, they'd only have to pick him up and take him away to eliminate any threat to him.

And depending on who's going after her, they'd probably do it just to see her worry about him.

She's nuts about that kid. If she thought someone was going to hurt him, she'd give up anything to protect him.

Even her life.

Part of me wants to argue with him. Insist that he stop being an idiot and get someone to protect her, but what's the point? Tonight's already set up to be a shit show. I don't need to make things worse by picking another fight.

"Whatever, man. Just try not to kill my brother."

"No promises."

He hangs up without another word.

God-damn it.

I grab the vodka bottle, half planning on throwing it across the room. How the hell is Daniil able to simultaneously show so much concern and be so blasé about Blair's safety?

Is he just showing concern because he knows that I'd fucking kill him otherwise, or is he actually worried? It's not like Daniil has a long, storied history of putting Blair's needs before his own.

Before I can talk myself out of it, I call Alexei. He's an asshole, but he's resourceful and owes me a favor. Or six.

"Kak?" he grunts. There's muffled music in the background, and I hazard a guess that he's already at one of his clubs and setting up for the night. I wait for a moment, then hear a slamming door and the music fades away entirely.

"Any chance I can steal Lev for the night?" His cousin typically lingers around him, doing whatever he needs. Whenever I need something from Alexei, it's Lev he makes poke through and delete hours of surveillance footage or give me a hand in cleaning up bloody messes.

"Maybe," he hums. "Depends on what you need him for. I was counting on him for some additional security tonight, so it'll cost you."

Of course it will. Alexei doesn't like to trade in cash, but the favors that he calls in can be fucking expensive. That's why I like to make sure that he always owes me more than I owe him.

He needs inconvenient bodies to disappear from one of his clubs? He calls me. He needs to have people removed with more subtlety than his typical security can handle? I can do that.

But my favors are just as costly.

"I need him to watch a place tonight. Just watch and stop anyone who shouldn't be there from getting inside."

"You want him to house-sit?"

"No. I just need to make sure a couple people are safe. He doesn't need to talk to them, and if he can make sure they don't see him, even better."

I might not agree with the finer details of it, but Daniil was right that Blair doesn't need to know the exact details of what's going on. If there's a way to keep her from worrying about someone coming to kill her, then I need to find a way to make that happen.

He lets out a heavy sigh before he relents. "Fine, but we're even after this, alright?"

"No. But this can count for two. It'll get you closer."

"Fine. Text me the address and time, and he'll be there." He blows out a frustrated breath, and I put the vodka away with regret. "I don't suppose you're free to help out at Virgo tonight, are you?"

"Something interesting happening?"

Nearly all of Alexei's businesses are aboveboard and totally legit. The only exception is Virgo, an unlicensed strip club that manages to stay open almost entirely because of bribes. It's nothing but a front for the Bratva's money laundering.

It reeks of cheap booze, attracts the kind of clientele that know how to mind their own business, and employs the kind of dancers that will put up with a lot as long as they're getting paid under the table.

It's also the kind of place that's perfect if you're meeting with someone and know it'll probably end in bloodshed. Alexei doesn't care whenever it needs to be closed for cleaning, and we can keep messy negotiations out of the legitimate clubs.

It's a win-win.

But when there're meetings, it's always smart to have a couple guys on hand to make sure everyone there knows exactly what did and did not happen inside the back rooms.

"Krutikov has some sort of business and requested the room."

I freeze, free hand flexing to keep myself from forming a fist. "Tell me you don't mean *Daniil* Krutikov." I would beg him if I thought it would make a difference.

"Is there a different one?" He sounds genuinely confused, but it bounces off me as I grow numb to everything but my rage.

No wonder Daniil didn't want to tell me where the meeting is. He's already planned on it ending with someone needing to see Doc, and if I'd known, I would have worked harder to put a stop to it.

I'm going to kill him.

CHAPTER 5

Andrei

The Krutikovs' front door is as black as my mood. I glare at it as I take a deep breath, doing everything I can to rein in my temper. The sound of Niko's laughter rings through the wood, and there's no point in storming in and scaring him.

The fact that he's such a happy, well-adjusted kid is a testament to Blair and Daniil's parenting when everyone else around him is typically a miserable bastard. Myself included.

I close my eyes and picture what I'll do to Daniil when I get him away from his family until I'm able to relax my hands and knock on the door. There's a murmur of low voices, and then the door opens to reveal Blair peeking at me through the crack. For a moment, she looks so fucking happy.

I want to capture that expression and keep it close so I can look back on it whenever I want.

Her smile freezes on her face as she registers that it's me, stepping back as quickly as she can to put distance between us before I can protest. Just like that, all my anger is gone. Like it wasn't even there, consumed by the familiar regret that weaves its way through my veins. My gut squeezes so tight I can't breathe, and I have to clench my jaw as I step inside.

"Andrei," she says, hardly louder than a whisper.

"Hey, Blair."

Niko laughs as he runs away from Daniil, who's stomping after him, head thrown back in a dramatic roar. He's still dressed in a full suit without a hair out of place. Blair moves to lean against the wall furthest from me.

I close the door behind me, the soft click enough to draw Nikolai's attention. His head whips toward me so fast I worry that he's going to get whiplash as he sprints toward me.

"Andrei!" he squeals, his smile all gums and teeth when I sweep him into a hug.

"How've you been, kid?" he takes a deep breath, and I can't hold back a smile as he launches into a full explanation of everything that's happened since I last saw him. I try to come over for dinner at least once a month, if only because Niko makes such a big deal about missing me, but I haven't been over for a while. And when you're only three, I guess four months feels like a long fucking time.

Over his shoulder I watch as Daniil goes to Blair's side and gives her a quick kiss, taking a moment to whisper something I can't hear. She gives him a private smile as her whole demeanor softens, releasing the instinctive fear that's held her tight since she saw me.

Niko's fingers dig into my forearms, dragging my attention back to him. "And Papa says we're gonna have pancakes!" His eyes are glittering with excitement, cheeks flushed as he talks.

I haven't heard a word he's said, but he doesn't seem to care. He just wants to talk *at* me, and I'm not going to deny him the opportunity.

Unfortunately, I can't let him talk for as long as he'd like to.

"Hey," I interrupt, "I have to steal your papa for some work stuff." The joy on his face seeps away, leaving him glancing warily between Daniil and I. "That alright with you?"

His eyes settle on Daniil in the fiercest glare a three-year-old can muster. "You promised we could have breakfast," he whines. To his credit, Daniil rubs the back of his neck, looking ashamed.

"We will, buddy. I have a meeting tonight, but I'll still be here for pancakes."

"You promise?"

"I wouldn't miss it for the world. I promise."

Niko pulls away from me and wraps his arms around Daniil's leg, his hands clinging to the thick fabric of his pants. When they look at each other, it strikes me how similar they are. The same eyes. The same unshakable confidence. The only thing that keeps him from looking like an exact clone of a younger Daniil is his blond hair, a gift he got from Blair.

Niko's shoulders slowly slump forward as the two of them look at each other, having a silent debate before Niko gives up, trudging toward Blair with his arms folded across his chest. Reluctantly, he waves in my direction, and I smile at him.

"You be good for your mama, okay?" Daniil waits for Niko to nod, then grins. "Good. Love you guys."

They call out quiet goodbyes after him as he leaves, heading straight toward his car.

I nod at them as I walk out the door, unable to find a voice to say anything. Niko might not like it, but I'm sure Blair doesn't mind. I wait on the patio until I hear the soft *click* of the dead-bolt behind me, then follow. The moment we're alone in his car, the tension from earlier is a persistent ache inside of my skull.

"So. Virgo, huh? I thought you said you wouldn't kill my brother."

He remains quiet until we're only a couple miles from the club, his hands tight on the steering wheel. He doesn't try to argue with me or justify himself. He just sits in his silence.

"If I had to pick between her and your brother, I'd pick her every time," he eventually says with a sigh. "So would you."

If I thought it would accomplish anything, I'd argue with him, but what's the point? He's right. Semyon might be my brother, but he's just as stupid as he is ambitious, and I've always known he was going to end up in an early grave. He's not worth protecting, and by threatening Blair, he's assured me he's not even worth the breath it would take to defend him.

But Blair? She's worth all that and more.

He pulls into the parking lot, the neon lights above the door reflecting a tasteless red across the interior of the car.

"I'm not willing to gamble with her, yeah? I'll do what I have to in order to keep her safe. And if that means I have to piss you off?" He shrugs. "Then so be it. I know it's a big ask, but I'd rather you have my back on this."

My head thumps against the headrest as I close my eyes, taking a bracing breath. Taking on Semyon two-on-one has far better odds, but it means accepting that I probably won't have a brother by the time the night is done.

Daniil's right—if we pretend that this is just a conversation, then it's a risk. Semyon's stubborn enough that the best-case scenario is him pretending to drop this while he moves forward with his plans. He's a stupid man, but do I want to risk him actually succeeding?

No.

I can't.

I'd rather lose the only remaining family I have than let him hurt her.

"Even if Semyon's no longer on the board, there are plenty of others who would gladly be Pavel's pawn," I say, resigned. "I doubt Semyon came up with this idea on his own. If this is some plan Pavel cooked up, are you going to kill him, too?"

Daniil is well suited for his job. He's clever, arrogant, and direct, but he isn't prone to killing and violence. He's the type of person to use intimidation and blackmail to get what he needs done. Violence isn't foreign to him by any means, but he tends to rely on others to do that if he's able.

"If I have to."

"And if it wasn't Pavel? What're you going to do if this was Maksim's idea?"

For a moment, his carefully practiced façade fails, and he looks like he's going to be sick.

He swallows, shaking his head as he looks at the door to the club with a sense of determination.

"Let's get this over with, yeah?"

I'm grim as I follow him inside.

Virgo is exactly how it's been every other time I've been here. The floors are sticky beneath my feet, and terrible music blasts through the speakers, the bass boosted so hard my teeth rattle in my skull. None of the patrons bother to look anyone else in the eye and dancers wander around the floor, happy to offer a lap dance to anyone who asks, and even more if you're willing to pay for one of the private rooms in the back.

I catch the eye of the guard blocking the door to the private rooms Alexei sets aside for private meetings. With a single tilt of his chin, he steps aside, letting us into the dark, disgusting space. Daniil makes himself comfortable right away, settling into one of the old, cracked leather seats, bouncing his foot where it's crossed over his knee.

I take my time looking around the room, familiarizing myself with everything while he glares daggers at the door, muscles coiled like a spring ready to launch at anyone who walks through. By the time I take a seat of my own, I'm on edge just from listening to the ceaseless tapping of his fingers against the arm of the chair.

If he doesn't find a way to calm down soon, he's going to let Semyon wind him up and get himself killed before he gets a chance to do anything.

"Hey, what happened with that DA you've been working on?" I ask after he checks his watch for the fourth time in two minutes. Semyon will probably be late to his own funeral, and I can't figure out why Daniil expected this to be any different.

It's Semyon's version of a power move. If he makes others wait, then he tells them that they're unimportant to him. He's never understood that everyone has the amount of respect for him that he offers them.

"The guy from up-state?" Daniil squints, and I lift my chin in affirmation. "Guy's a tool. He seems to think that he's too good to meet with me, but I've asked Artyom to look into him." He shrugs, flexing a hand over his knee. "I'll get my meeting, and he'll learn to like what I have to say."

"And if he doesn't?"

"Then he'll quickly figure out why everyone else finds me so agreeable."

Sometimes I wonder what it is Daniil likes most about his job. Is it the power of controlling the outcome, or is it the threats and intimidation? Making sure that he has contacts that are willing to work with him when someone ends up in prison is important, but it's better for him to make sure none of us end up there in the first place. If he has to make sure charges are dropped, or evidence is lost, or ensure that whoever is prosecuting the case decides there isn't enough evidence to move forward, then it helps to have the right carrot to dangle on the end of stick.

I'm willing to bet that having dirt on half the politicians in the state is where he finds most of his fun.

He looks at me with an intensity that I can't brush off. "And what about you? Anything on your mysterious warehouse fires?" I watch as he pulls out a cigarette, lighting it.

"Really? We're inside, asshole."

He lifts a brow and simply nods, waving a hand to urge me to continue.

"If you're asking if Pavel left any real evidence, then no," I sigh. "The camera footage just shows a man in a ski mask, and forensics are coming back clean. All I actually have is that they're using cheap accelerants and know most of the security routes.

But who else is petty enough to destroy my buildings? He's still pissed I didn't let him claim credit for mopping up the mess in Colorado."

Daniil takes a long drag, shoulders falling a fraction of an inch. "You planning on doing anything about it?" There's an ashtray on the table between us and I push it toward him, lip curling when the smell of smoke drifts toward me.

I glance at the door and shake my head. "Not yet." Depending on how things work out after tonight, I'll see what happens. If he's still targeting Blair, then maybe I'll be able to use that as an excuse to take action against him. But until I have something concrete, my hands are tied.

He rolls his eyes, running a hand through his hair. For the first time in his life, Daniil looks ruffled. His hair's a mess, and his tie hangs loosely around his wrinkled collar. It's a total contrast to how he presents himself in every other situation.

As soon as he got out of law school and started making decent money, his collection of suits was his first investment. Probably because when we were kids, he was always the one in worn-out clothes that his parents got at a thrift store. His family immigrated from Russia when we were still in grade school, and outside of Bratva families, he was always an outcast.

We might be far removed from those days, but it feels like he's still trying to make up for it.

When the door flies open, Daniil's hand twitches, creeping behind him as if he's already determined to bring his gun into the equation. I tense, but he stills himself before Semyon looks up, his eyes darting from Daniil to me as he schools his face and his eyes light up with a cruel glee.

His hooded gray eyes, so similar to the ones I inherited from our father, dart between the two of us. It's like I'm staring into a mirror that makes me itch if I look for too long.

I resist the urge to loosen the knot on my own tie.

"Sorry I'm late." Semyon smirks, flopping onto the couch across from us with his arms stretched across the back. "I didn't realize that you'd be joining us, Andrei."

He tilts his head in my direction, as if he's trying to see straight through me.

"Figured it was a good time for a family reunion."

His smirk grows into a full grin, and my skin crawls in a way that only he's able to invoke. Beside me, Daniil leans forward, stabbing his cigarette into the ashtray.

"As touching as this is, let's get to why we're really here, yeah?"

If anything, Semyon just looks more amused. No doubt seeing Daniil worked up is exactly what he wants. I'll have to make sure that I don't feed into his bullshit too, or this is going to end up a lot bloodier than it has to be.

As long as Daniil and I walk out of this room, I'll find a way to make peace with whatever happens here.

"Care to tell me why you've been running your mouth and acting like you have any business even mentioning my wife?" His voice is controlled, but there's an undercurrent of barely contained threat.

Semyon's glee is practically pouring off him in waves, and I want to throttle him.

"I don't know what you're talking about. But if someone wants to see her dead, I'm willing to bet people would be lining up for the opportunity. You know, since she's a security risk and all that."

I squint at him, and his smirk only grows.

"Cut the shit," Daniil snaps. "No one's been talking shit except for you. I don't care who else has the motivation. You're the only one who's stupid enough to think that you can get away with attacking my family. But newsflash, asshole. You can't."

Semyon doesn't flinch. In fact, he doesn't react at all, and a vein of trepidation works its way down my spine. He's looking at us the same way he used to when he hid my toys when we were children. Like the only thing in the world he cares about is that he has a secret he can lord over me.

"I don't *think* anything. I already have a green light to do whatever I want." Despite myself, I tense, and Daniil sits up straighter. "So, do you really want to spend her final days here with me and this jack-off?" He nods his head in my direction. "Or, wait, let me guess. You'd rather be off fucking your whore, right?" He laughs. "Why are you even pretending to give a shit?"

"Not pretending, *suka*. I'm not going to let you touch a hair on her head." Daniil sounds calm, but his knuckles are blanching white where he clenches his hands on his knee.

"Don't worry, Krutikov." Semyon smirks, his eyes glued to mine. "I'll make sure she bleeds when I do it."

Daniil pulls his gun out faster than either of us can react. His grip is tight as he rests it against the arm of the chair, his finger resting against the trigger guard. Only years of being surrounded by violence and anger allows my shoulder to remain relaxed and my face blank, but I'm a brewing storm of anxiety, itching to pull out my own gun.

He's pissed. I get it, but he's playing right into Semyon's ego. He needs to find a way to chill the fuck out in a hurry.

"See, I don't think you're going to do shit, Semyon. Not if you want to walk out of this room anyway."

Semyon looks between the two of us, then at the door where the echoes of the pounding bass and bustle of drunken customers trickle in. "I don't know, man," he says with a click of his tongue. "Isn't your whole thing to make sure we stay out of prison?" Semyon shrugs without a care in the world. "I'd think that causing a scene in an illegal, crowded club would be counterproductive."

"That's the beautiful thing about illegal clubs. There's no such thing as a witness, only a person who knows how to cover their own ass."

"You're right." Semyon laughs as he reaches around his back, pulling out his own gun. "That *is* beautiful." My hand is steady as I pull out my gun, refusing to let Semyon have any sort of advantage.

The sound of Daniil clicking off the safety of his gun echoes through the room; it's so loud I almost think that the people in the main room must have heard it.

"And you." Semyon cuts his gaze to me, eyes shining with manic delight. "Why the fuck are you here? Doesn't Krutikov know that you're in love with his wife?" There's a lump in my throat that makes it hard to breathe, but Semyon's too busy waving his gun in Daniil's direction to notice. "Or are you just *that* fucking dense?"

"He knows," I answer, the words cutting like glass against my tongue. I've never said the words out loud before, but of course Daniil knows.

When he's feeling particularly cruel, he loves to hold it over my head. He thinks it's fucking hilarious that I fell in love with Blair while she was terrified I was going to kill her at any moment, and he made sure I knew how laughable my attempts were to hide the bitter pill of regret when I found out he was going to propose.

Daniil doesn't acknowledge me, but he doesn't have to. He knows me better than anyone else, and I've never had to say a word to make my feelings plain to him.

The fact that I'm in love with Blair is the whole reason he brought me here tonight.

Because he knows I'll do anything to protect her, even break my own heart every time I see her. Even kill my brother for her.

Semyon's grin is pitch black, his eyes predatory.

"That's not why we're here, though. We're here because my job is to make sure you know your place, and apparently you need a reminder of exactly how short your leash is," I say, falling into a familiar habit of ignoring my feelings.

Semyon's lip curls into a snarl. "Your *job* has nothing to do with me." His disgust is palpable but impotent. He's always been a loose cannon, and we both know it. He just wants to live under the delusion that it's something that benefits him. "But my job? I do what the boss needs." Semyon rolls his head from side to side, his whole body coiled like a spring. "And if that means making the little rat disappear, well"—he shrugs—"I'm good at my job."

Daniil tenses, the only warning we get before he fires a single shot at the space between Semyon's feet.

Ah, fuck.

The room is instantly full of the sound of gunfire, swiftly followed by the ringing in my ears that drowns out all other sound. I throw myself behind my chair as the lapse in bullets is taken over by screams and a stampede of footsteps as the patrons and dancers in the main room seek refuge in the nearest exit.

I go to fire, but the stomach-dropping *click* of my gun jamming screams at me over the rest of the chaos. When I pull back the slide, it sticks and I swear under my breath. Fucking *wonderful*.

Now I'm stuck here with two pissed off idiots who are determined to kill each other, and I don't even have a functioning gun.

The cheap chair offers only an illusion of cover, but it's better than nothing. I look over to my side and see that Daniil has the same idea, crouching as he grabs at his side, red blooming through his shirt. He flinches as he presses against the wounds, but I try to focus on fixing my gun.

I'm not even sure if I managed to hit my brother, but at least Daniil's wound doesn't look bad enough to make me panic.

"You've really fucked up this time, Semyon," I mutter through gritted teeth as I try to use brute force to get my pistol to work long enough to get out of this situation. His cackle grates like sandpaper over my nerves, and I cringe. If he's laughing, then neither of us hit him anywhere vital and he may very well have the upper hand.

By the time my gun's fixed, there's a puddle slowly spreading on the carpet around Daniil.

Blyad.

Apparently, it's worse than I thought, and if he doesn't get to a doctor soon, I'm going to have even bigger problems on my hands.

If Daniil were smart, he'd focus on taking care of himself and let me handle this. He'd keep his head low and let me handle my brother. But outside of a courtroom, he's always been a bit of an idiot. He's hotheaded and impulsive, and as soon as Blair gets mixed into the situation, he's even worse.

It's why he rushed their relationship before they had a chance to settle. It's why he proposed to her before he could really grasp the consequences of what that would do for his position with Maksim. It's why he started fucking Emiliya as soon as he realized his mistake.

And it's why he shoves himself to his feet before I can do anything, aiming his gun in Semyon's direction. I lurch toward him, grabbing him so I can pull him back down behind the flimsy chair. He sways on his feet but is strong enough to stay standing while two gunshots go off.

He collapses to his knees, not because of my strength, but because they give out under him. Blood flows, steady as a river, from a hole at the point where his neck and shoulder meet. There's a pained grunt from Semyon, but it hardly registers.

"Fuck!" My hands shake as I check Daniil over for other wounds, pressing a hand against his neck.

I pull my phone out of my pocket with my free hand, but it keeps slipping in the blood. Daniil lets out a wet gasp and Semyon laughs, cruel and pleased as my vision flashes red.

When Semyon was born, I promised my mother I'd protect my little brother with my life.

But our mother is dead.

I don't owe her anything.

I press Daniil's hands against his neck, trying to get him to keep pressure on it, and snatch his gun from where it lies uselessly beside him. Standing, I look at the pathetic heap that Semyon has become, bleeding from his arm. He's grasping at it, eyes darting wildly around the room, his defensive stance relaxing marginally when he sees me.

Acting on instinct alone, I raise my arm and pull the trigger as his eyes widen, my hands as steady as my resolve. I don't wait to watch his body drop, turning back to Daniil instead. I drop his gun and go back to trying to unlock my phone. I can't do anything for him, but I can try to keep him alive for a little longer. If I can just get Doc here, maybe—

"Andrei," he chokes out.

"Shut up," I mutter, trying to get my phone to register the passcode through the blood, but it isn't fucking working.

He grabs onto my forearm, trying to make me put down my phone, but his grip is weak. I look him in the eye, and the resigned look he gives me makes my throat squeeze. I shake my head, but he just blinks back at me.

I can't do this without him. He's been a royal pain in my ass since the day I met him, but he's my best friend. He's the only person I've ever trusted with my life, and I've never had to navigate life without him. He smiles weakly, even when I place my hand on his neck.

I'm no longer trying to keep him from bleeding, just forcing myself to feel every beat of his heart pushing him closer to death.

"Take care of my family, yeah? Better than me?" His voice is weak, his eyes barely open.

"C'mon, man, they need you. Let me call Doc to come fix you up and you can go home and look after them yourself." He grips my arm a little tighter, and it feels like an apology.

He's not going to let me lie to myself, and I want to hate him for it.

Even if the doc was already here, Daniil's losing blood faster than we could push it into him. I just wish that he didn't know it, too.

"Promise me, Andrei. She's gonna need you." He blinks again, his eyes taking a beat too long before he's able to force them open again, looking around blankly but not really seeing.

When I nod, it feels like I'm betraying him. "I promise."

He smiles faintly. "Sorry I was a shit friend."

"You aren't."

He shakes his head, and the heartbeat against my hand is so weak I can barely feel it. "I was, and you know it. I shouldn't have made you feel like shit. Tell her I'm sorry, too," he coughs, a wet sound. "Make her happy, yeah?"

Daniil's head falls forward and I adjust him, moving my hand to his unmoving chest. I have to clear my throat, trying to find my voice.

"I promise, *bratan*. I'll make sure she's happy."

Around us the room is quiet. I have no doubt that all of the people in the main room have fled, and someone has turned off the music.

I hold Daniil until the blood cools, and the chill seeps into my bones.

CHAPTER 6

Blair

My phone stays dark next to me as I chew on my thumbnail, watching the ticking clock. A baking show is playing on the TV, but I can't even pretend to pay attention to it.

Daniil always texts me when he's done with his meetings.

I don't even know if he realizes it, but it's the most comforting thing he's ever done for me. If he texts me, I know that he's okay. He might be working late, but he's fine. He's not in the fray, and he'll come home in one piece.

Even when he's with Emiliya, I typically get some indication he'll be late. Either he'll say something before he leaves in the morning, or his phone is turned off when I call, or—if we've been arguing—he'll tell me not to wait up.

But I called him an hour ago, and it rang through to voicemail, so I doubt he's with her. Besides, it wouldn't be like him to stage a whole production of having Andrei come over under the guise of work so he could meet up with her. If he wanted to, he'd just go to her.

Where the hell is he?

I've only called once, and I resist the urge to call him again.

Maybe he really is just working late, and blowing up his phone will just make things more difficult. Or he's just with Emiliya, but he forgot to leave me any painful hints.

I settle into the couch, trying to let that thought settle me.

The more time passes, the more I convince myself that, yes, Daniil's out getting laid, and when he gets home I'll chew him out, we'll go to bed angry, and we can go right back to pretending everything's fine in the morning.

Do I wish he'd found a way to be content in our marriage? Of course.

I constantly wish I was enough for him, but wishes aren't reality. Instead, marrying me hurt his reputation with the pakhan, and Daniil could never let that lie.

At least he didn't divorce me and leave me for the wolves. It would've been easier for him, but his affair lets him keep his standing while keeping me alive. It's better this way.

At least I'm alive to resent his choices.

I watch as the clock ticks away another hour before I give up and move my vigil to the front room, sitting on the bottom of the stairs and fidgeting with my ring while I wait for headlights to pull into the driveway.

I check my phone again. Still nothing.

I swear, when Daniil shows up completely fine, I'm going to strangle him. Then I'll have to figure out how to bring him back to life, because Niko and I need him. Even so, I'm still going to kill him, and it's going to feel great.

When finally, *finally* I'm treated to the reflection of lights in the driveway, anger has overtaken my worry. Was it too much effort to send a single text message? Or make a quick call? Hell, smoke signals would've worked at this point.

My line of thought stops dead when instead of keys in the door, I hear a knock.

Daniil wouldn't knock. He wouldn't want to risk waking up Niko. Daniil knows that getting Niko to sleep when he isn't here is the hardest thing I do on any given day.

Yet there's a shadow visible through the curtains, standing just outside the front door. I look back up the stairs, a lump in my throat.

Whoever it is, they're here for me, right? If someone was trying to get ahold of Daniil, they'd call him. And no one needs to talk to a three-year-old at two in the morning.

I'm the only other person here, and I don't get visitors.

My mind flashes to Pavel's cold eyes the last time I had the misfortune of finding myself alone with him, shortly after I moved to Chicago with Daniil. It was the first time Daniil brought me around Maksim, and from the promise of violence when he looked at me, Pavel wasn't happy to see me again.

I felt like I couldn't breathe again until Daniil and I got home and the doors were locked behind us.

I've only seen Pavel a handful of times since then, but I've never been able to shake the fear that paralyzes me when I do.

What are the odds that the person at the door is him? He's too important to do his own dirty work now, right? He wouldn't stoop below his rank long enough to put his hands on me again. Right?

If he hadn't been scared off by some passing bystander the one time he caught me alone, he probably would have killed me.

I'm not lucky enough for him to make the same mistake twice. My fear twists in my chest, making it hard to breathe.

The person at the door knocks again, louder this time.

If I let them in, I have no recourse to prevent them from doing whatever they want. I can scream and fight, but it probably won't stop them. I'll just wake Niko up and scare him half to death. I can't let that happen.

I have to do what I can to protect him, even if it kills me.

They aren't here for Niko. They're here for me. As long as he stays upstairs, they won't go after him.

I walk toward the door, fingers fumbling as I try to undo the lock. When it clicks, I take a shaky breath and open the door, half expecting to come face-to-face with a weapon, but I don't.

It's just Andrei, though that does little to soothe my anxiety.

His hands are tucked into the pockets of the leather jacket he definitely wasn't wearing when he was here earlier, and he looks more haggard than I've ever seen him. His dark hair is a mess, and his gray eyes that normally pin me in place look almost haunted. I glance behind him, expecting to see my husband, but instead I just see his empty car parked in the driveway.

"Can I come in?"

"Where's Daniil?"

He shakes his head, looking absently at a point over my shoulder. "Please let me in, Blair." My throat squeezes, trapping the air in my lungs. "Please." His shoulders are set, and I cling to the doorknob for balance, shaking my head.

"Andrei, where's my husband?"

He opens his mouth and closes it, like he's trying to figure out what to say. I stumble backward, wrapping my arms around my torso as I try to ward off the chill of dread. He steps closer, catching me when my knees feel like they're going to buckle.

"Daniil didn't tell me he was on the way. He always tells me when he's done with work, he..." I blink. My eyes sting, but they're dry.

It feels like the room's spinning around me, and I have to close my eyes for a moment.

Andrei uses his foot to gently kick the door shut, taking a moment to lock it before he guides me back into the living room, urging me to sit on the couch. He sits on the coffee table, taking my face in his hands as I try to gulp in enough air.

"He's gone, Blair." His voice is gentle, but it cuts me like a blade to my throat. I'm shocked that I heard him at all over the rushing of my blood and my pounding heart. "Things between him and Semyon got heated, and..." He trails off as I shake my head. "I'm so fucking sorry."

"What do you mean he's *gone?*" I don't recognize my voice, and Andrei runs his hand down my arm. I don't know if he's trying to keep me grounded or make sure I don't run away, but I'm grateful for the comfort, as paltry as it is.

There's conflict written all over his face and I can't stand to watch, so I close my eyes again. It doesn't help. Even when I can't see anything, I still feel like the ground is moving under me, carelessly tossing me around.

"He fought so hard to come back to you guys. He fought so fucking hard, Blair." His voice is full of grief, his typical predatory grace absent as he holds his hands on my knees. My ears are ringing, and I choke on a silent sob, my chest caving as I fall forward, unable to hold myself up. He catches me, tucking my head onto his shoulder while I gasp for breath.

I'm going to be sick.

This is a nightmare, and I'm going to wake up any moment.

Daniil can't be gone.

I need him.

Niko needs him.

"I'm so fucking sorry, *zolotse.*"

I claw at his jacket, desperate to find any signs of deception, but there's nothing. Just sympathy and worry that makes me numb.

I blink, and the tears I didn't know I was missing spill free.

I'm not aware that he's picked me up until he sets me down on my bed, prying his jacket free from my grasp. His thumb smooths over the back of my knuckles while I bite my lip to the point of pain, holding back screams that want to claw out of my chest.

"Try to get some sleep. The rest can wait until tomorrow." His whisper barely penetrates the fog that I'm stuck in, but my body must understand him because soon after I pull Daniil's pillow to my chest, I fall asleep.

***

As I wake up, it feels like someone has cut me open, hollowed out my insides, and stuffed me full of cotton. I feel the pounding in my skull, but it's distant, almost more like a memory than an actual feeling. It feels like my eyes are glued shut. I burrow my head into the pillow as I take a deep breath, wanting nothing more than to force myself to fall back asleep.

Sleep brought a merciful numbness, but now that it's gone, the cotton is fading away.

I'm not ready to feel the full force of the hurt again.

I'm not ready to face anything.

Sunlight streams through the window, mocking me, and I squeeze my eyes closed even harder.

The reasonable fragments of my brain tell me that I need to get up. That I need to take care of Nikolai and figure out how to tell him what's happened. That I need to check in with Mila.

Oh, god. Has anyone told her yet? What if they haven't?

I can't do it. She already spends all her time ignoring me, but this? This will break her. As it is, I don't know how I'm going to help Niko through this. Adding her grief on top of both of ours will destroy me.

Where the hell am I supposed to go from here?

Giggling echoes through the door, and it's enough to push me into sitting up, grimacing when I realize I'm still dressed in yesterday's clothes. At least if Niko's laughing, he's probably entertaining himself long enough for me to take a shower and change. I doubt it'll make me feel any better, but at least I'll feel more like an actual human being.

When I step out of the shower, I wrap myself in my comfiest sweats, letting my wet hair drip down my back. I step out into the hall, freezing when I smell food cooking.

Who the hell is in my kitchen?

I rub my hands over my arms, trying to convince myself that it's fine, and the bogeyman isn't waiting around the corner, biding their time until I wander into their trap.

A deep male voice rumbles, and I practically sprint toward it. The only person I trust around Niko right now is Andrei. I don't want anyone else near my son.

I turn the corner, nearly tripping over my own feet when I skid to a stop.

It isn't a bogeyman at all. It really is Andrei, his back to me as he flips pancakes on the stove. The adrenaline coursing through my veins washes away like sand. I sigh, relieved while the hollow emptiness leaves me feeling exhausted all over again.

At least I know that he'd never do anything to hurt Niko.

Niko turns toward me with a wide smile, a piece of half-chewed food stuck to his cheek with the sticky sheen of half-dried syrup. "Morning, Mama!" he blurts, and I cringe at how full his mouth is. He's standing on his step stool by the counter, apparently unwilling to carry his food to the table before he digs in.

"Finish chewing before you try to talk, kid," Andrei says without turning around.

Niko's still in his pajamas and Andrei looks like he hasn't slept a wink, but they look comfortable. Brushing it aside, I pull Niko against me, pressing a kiss to the top of his hair, needing him way more than he needs me right now.

"Morning, baby." He looks happy, and I'm not sure how much longer it'll last, so I'm going to savor it while I can. He twists against me, trying to pull free, and I reluctantly let him. "Did Andrei make these for you?" He swallows his food and smiles, nodding enthusiastically. I swallow thickly. "That was nice of him, huh?"

"Uh huh! Thanks, Andrei."

Andrei finally looks over his shoulder at us and flicks off the stove, a stack of pancakes piled on a plate next to him. He wordlessly pushes them in my direction, nodding at Niko.

"No problem. Hey, why don't you go get washed up and play in your room for a while? I need to talk to your mom for a bit." Niko, the little traitor, nods and hops off his stool before darting around me toward his room.

God, it's going to be a nightmare to clean all his sticky hand-prints, but it'll be a welcome distraction.

Once he's gone, leaving me without the flimsy barrier his presence brought me, Andrei's focus is unflinchingly on me, his eyes piercing and looking through to the very fibers of my soul. He's always been able to pin me in place with just a look, and I shift under his gaze now. I'm not sure what he's looking for, but I doubt he's going to find it.

"How're you feeling?" He catches me off guard with the sincerity in his voice. I open my mouth to tell him I'm fine out of reflex before I stop myself.

I'm not fine. I'm so far from fine it'd be funny under different circumstances. For a moment I want to tell him exactly that, but what's the point? It's not like he actually cares. He's just asking to be polite.

Andrei isn't the type of man who's safe to open up to. He's just as likely to weaponize my feelings as he is to ignore them. He's being kind right now, but I can't let myself forget who he is. If he's willing to hold me at gunpoint to get his way, I don't want to know what he'd do if he knew all my inner thoughts and needed something from me.

Instead of answering, I ask the questions that have been screaming in the back of my head since I woke up.

"Has anyone talked to his mom yet? I don't think she'd appreciate hearing the news from me. It would be better to hear it from someone she cares for."

There's a conflicted look on his face before he eventually nods. "Maksim talked to her last night. Before I got here." He clears his throat, turning away as he moves to start cleaning up the dishes. "We both did."

I look at the untouched plate in front of me, nodding to myself. I should have expected that. I know he makes a point of talking to the families of his men after they're killed.

There's a lump in my throat just thinking about it.

I'm glad he didn't come over here. At least I didn't have to deal with his hostility on top of everything else.

"You should eat," Andrei prompts, pushing a glass of water in front of me. I don't know how to tell him I'm not hungry, that I'm not sure when I'll be able to stomach the thought of food, but it sure as hell isn't going to be today, so I take a sip from the glass, trying not to choke around my rickety emotions.

"Does Emiliya know?" I ask when it feels like I can breathe again. I can't bring myself to look at him, staring blankly at the slightly burnt pancakes in front of me instead. She deserves to know. I'm not sure if she has any genuine feelings for Daniil, but she doesn't deserve to find out through the gossip mill.

"Blair—"

"I don't think I can be the one to tell her. I can't put on a polite face with my dead husband's mistress." My throat is thick, the words choked off and quiet.

Andrei moves to stand in front of me, hands braced on the marble counter. "Do you know where his body is? Who should I talk to about funeral arrangements?" I force myself to stop and catch my breath. My heart's pounding, like a dam is breaking inside my chest. "And what am I supposed to tell Niko? He practically worships Daniil, Andrei." He takes my chin in his hand, forcing me to look up at him. "What the hell am I supposed to do?"

He moves slowly, like I'm a wild animal, as he tucks a strand of hair behind my ear. Immediately, his hands fall away sharply as if he's been burned, and he takes a decisive step back.

"Emiliya knows. Maksim told her last night, too." I have to close my eyes against the unexpected wave of betrayal.

Am I the last one to find out?

I choke on a sob, but he continues on, giving me only enough time to absorb his words.

"It was... a mess. There was no way to avoid cops getting involved. Daniil's at the morgue. You and Mila can work together on the funeral arrangements, but he probably had something organized in his will, so you won't have to work from scratch. They'll release his body when they're done with their investigation."

"How long will that take?"

He shrugs. "Depends. They'll probably try to drag it out because of who he worked with, but they can't keep him forever.

And I'll do what I can to grease their wheels and hurry things along."

"Thank you," I whisper, twisting my wedding ring around my finger.

"You only have to worry about taking care of you and Niko, alright? You'll tell him what happened. And, yeah, it's gonna suck. A lot. But you'll get through it." A muscle in his jaw ticks before he starts washing the dishes, turning the tap to boiling hot, steam rising around him. "You're strong, and you'll both be alright. It just might take a while."

Even though his back is to me, I shake my head. I don't believe that, and I doubt he does, either. If I had to guess, he's just saying anything he can think of to stop me from falling apart at the seams.

He did more than enough trying to look after me last night. I won't saddle him with more responsibility. I'll wait until I'm alone again to have my break-down. I can't afford to sit around and feel sorry for myself. In this world, my grief will become a weakness that will make me, and by extension Niko, vulnerable.

"Thank you for looking after Niko this morning." I gather my plate, regretfully scraping it into the trash. I appreciate that he tried, but the effort was wasted. "I'm sure you have plenty of things to do, and I appreciate you taking the time to make breakfast for us." I stand next to him, hoping he'll step out of the way so I can take over, but he's like a brick wall as he glares at my empty plate.

"Stop being stubborn and let me help you," he grunts, taking the plate away from me as he steps away from the sink. Without another word, he opens the microwave and pulls out another plate of pancakes, shoving it toward me. "Sit down and eat."

My shoulders slump, and the look in his eyes has some of my newfound fight fleeing without protest.

"I can take care of myself."

"I know." He nods. "But it won't hurt to have some help, will it?"

I don't want his help. I don't want anyone's help. I don't want to risk learning to rely on anyone, because then I'll be in an even worse position when they leave me high and dry.

But I'm not going to win this fight. Not today, anyway. So, I take the food and sit down, forcing myself to eat even if it tastes like ash.

Chapter 7

Blair

"I hate you!" Niko cries as he stomps away, storming back toward his room. Frustration wars with weariness as I watch him, silently begging the universe to grant me the fortitude to make it through today.

It took the cops two weeks to release the body for burial. Two weeks of Niko asking me when his dad's coming home. Two weeks of breaking both of our hearts when I told him he won't. Two long weeks of sitting next to Mila while she sobbed, trying to get her to give me any sort of preference on funeral arrangements.

Andrei was right about one thing: Daniil did have a lot of his wishes planned out in his will— The plot, the casket, hell, he even picked out a tombstone—but he didn't state if he wanted a large funeral, or a more intimate affair. He didn't say if he wanted a wake. There are so many things he didn't say, things I'll spend the rest of my life wondering.

I miss having him here with every breath, but I don't think I can miss him as much as Niko does. His favorite thing was to be Daniil's shadow, and not having his favorite person around has plunged both of us into the middle of the ocean in a storm without a lifeboat in sight.

He's normally a relatively well-behaved child, but he misses his dad, and no matter how many conversations we have about it, Niko doesn't know how to express grief. So he's refusing to put on his shoes while he screams at me.

We have to be at the church for the wake I don't know if Daniil wanted in twenty minutes, and we've been having his argument for the last fifteen.

"Niko, please," I plead, far beyond the point of having any pride. "We both have to be there, it would look—"

I stop.

Daniil would say that it would look bad if we aren't there on time, but he doesn't get to worry about appearances anymore. He's already at the church. Whether or not we're on time doesn't matter to him anymore. I look up at the ceiling, squeezing my eyes shut so I don't ruin my mascara.

Honestly, does it matter if I'm there at all? Daniil would probably want me there if he had a say, but everyone else? They only care if Niko's there. Andrei might give half a shit, and maybe Maksim wants me there to ensure I'm sufficiently miserable, but I'm barely an afterthought to everyone else.

But I know I'll never forgive myself if I don't go. I need to find some sort of closure, and if the only way I'm going to get it is to be surrounded by a bunch of vindictive assholes, then so be it. I'm going to say goodbye.

They don't get to stop me.

I just have to get Niko to cooperate, and then I can dive headfirst onto that emotional landmine.

"I know you don't want to go, but I don't ever want you to regret not going."

"I want to stay with Baba Mila!" Niko shouts, tears streaming down his already tear-stained face.

He could have slapped me in the face and it would have hurt less. I swallow and try to find the last bits of patience I have left.

He doesn't mean that.

"She'll be at the church," I say gently. "You can hang out with her until it's time to leave." I'm sure Mila will appreciate that as much as Niko. I'm pretty sure the only reason she let me into her house while we were planning the funeral was because I brought Niko along.

As he turns as stomps away, I sigh, letting myself bask in the temporary reprieve from our fight before the doorbell chimes through the house.

God, what now?

I take a deep breath and let it out slowly. "I'm going to answer the door, and then we're going to put on our shoes," I call after him, studiously working to ignore the tension winding my shoulders into a knot.

I don't want to see whoever's at the door. Anyone who matters is going to be at the wake, and I don't have the emotional capacity to deal with anyone else today.

As soon as I get to the church, I'll have to put on the pretty mask that's expected of me. I'll have to be sad, but not *too* sad. I'll have to toe the line of being respectful and quiet, nothing but a pretty little doll who lingers on the fringes of everyone's attention and doesn't get in the way. I don't have to worry about upsetting Daniil if I say the wrong thing or make the wrong face, but I still don't want to go out of my way to upset anyone more than I already will just by being there.

I can't afford to let anything happen before I find a way to keep Niko and I safe.

When I open the door, I freeze on instinct when I see Andrei. He's wearing a somber suit, his hands shoved into his pockets as he leans against the door jamb.

"What are you doing here?" Immediately, I bite my tongue, regretting how harshly that came out. His jaw flexes, and I add this to the list of things I've managed to fuck up today. "I'm sorry, I just... wasn't expecting to see you here. I figured I'd see you at the church."

"I wanted to check in on you guys. Maybe give you a ride, if you want." He shrugs. "Make sure you and the kid are alright before you get thrown into the deep end." I pull the door open a little wider and, reluctantly, gesture for him to come in.

"That's kind of you." I smile, but it feels more like a grimace. He takes a quick look around, almost like he's looking for something.

"Where's the rugrat?"

"Probably in his room." I shrug. "He's refusing to put on shoes."

"What?"

I gesture down the hall, my cheeks heating with embarrassment. Which is stupid. No parent can control the little things their children throw fits over. But even though it's a little thing, the fact that he's refusing to listen to me stings. "He doesn't want to put on shoes. He doesn't want to come to the church with me, and apparently, he thinks if he doesn't put on his shoes, I'll go away, and he can spend all his time with Mila."

"Wait, what?" Andrei's brows furrow, his confusion matching my level of frustration.

"He wants to spend all his time with Mila because I upset him, so he doesn't want to put on his shoes." My voice has taken on a hysterical edge, and the way he's looking at me is too much. Too much concern, too much pity. I close my eyes and take a deep breath. "I'm sorry. We're fine. Today has just been... a lot."

He glances down the hall, then back at me, like he's worried any sudden moves will set me off.

"Would it be okay if I talk to him?"

I sit down on the bottom step and nod. What harm could it do?

"Be gentle with him, okay?" His brows pull together, looking offended. Regret pierces my chest, and I look at the floor. "He's upset. He likes you, but he's probably going to lash out if you push him." Andrei's never been anything but kind with Niko, and I don't think he'll go out of his way to make him feel any worse, but I need to set expectations.

"He's not... acting like himself."

"Yeah, I get that," he mumbles to himself before walking down the hall, leaving me alone, feeling like a massive idiot.

I need help to get a toddler to wear *shoes,* for god's sake, and as soon as someone who can help shows up, I make them out to be some sort of monster.

Andrei isn't a monster. Not to Niko, anyway. He'd never do anything to hurt him. And he's never actually hurt me, just...

threatened my life. But that doesn't mean he deserves to be pushed away at every turn. Especially not when he's here to help, for fuck's sake.

I smooth my hands over the skirt of my dress. Maybe if I look like I have everything together, I'll start to feel that way, too. I double check that my heels are lined up next to the door, right next to Niko's shoes, where he can't pretend he doesn't see them, and follow after the two of them.

I appreciate Andrei's offer, but I can't expect him to fix this for me.

"I miss him," Niko says quietly, and my steps stutter to a stop in the hall, feeling like my breath is stuck in my lungs. "Mama said he's not coming back, but she's lying." He sniffs. I clench my hands together, aching to comfort him.

"Why do you say that?" Andrei's voice is sympathetic but unyielding. "Has your mama ever lied to you before?"

A beat of quiet passes while I try not to drown in my own grief and doubts.

"No. But he promised, and Papa doesn't break his promises." I lean against the wall, letting my head fall softly against it.

"Niko, buddy... He didn't. He fought tooth and nail to come back to you, you've gotta believe me."

"Then where is he? Why isn't he here?" Niko's voice wobbles, and even though he's asked me that question a hundred times, I don't envy Andrei having to answer it again.

None of the parenting books covered this.

"Your mama didn't lie, and your papa didn't break his promise," Andrei eventually answers. "Sometimes things happen that are out of anyone's control, and this was one of them."

There's a shuffle, and Niko's hiccupped cries become muffled. "I miss him, too. And so does your mama."

"Then she should make him come home. He listens to her."

Andrei sighs, and all my failures hit me square in the chest. "If there was any way that she could, she would. Both of them would do anything if it'd bring him back to you, but..." He clears his throat. "But he's gone. And none of us can change that." Niko's sobs get louder, and I slink back to the entryway to give them some privacy.

Andrei's right. I'd do anything to bring Daniil back, if only to make it easier on Niko. That boy needs his father. He always has, and he always will. He was born into this cruel, careless world, and I don't know how I'm supposed to guide him through it alone. I don't know how to make sure he's prepared for everything that's going to be expected of him. For everything that he'll have to do.

All I know is that I can't do this alone. Not for the first time, I want to grab something and break it, just to have control over something.

When Niko was born, Daniil promised me he would look after him and help guide him. Now? Now, I'm just as lost as Niko.

I check my appearance in the hall mirror, swiping under my eyes to clean my ruined mascara as I wait. I don't care if we're late anymore. Hell, we probably will be, but who gives a shit? I'd rather Niko get ready on his own time.

Eventually they join me and Niko wordlessly puts on his shoes. I buckle him into his car seat and give Andrei a grateful smile. The ride to the church is silent. No radio. No talking. Just a quiet drive that makes my stomach roll with nausea.

Sooner than I'm prepared for, Andrei's parking the car, and the church is looming over us, stark against the gray fall sky. My hands are shaking as I reach for the door handle, but before I open it, Andrei lays a hand on my shoulder.

"I'll be here the whole time. I'm not going to let anyone mess with you, alright?" His hand is warm and comforting, a steady weight after weeks of feeling like I'm being tossed around in the wind.

I nod, though I'm not sure I believe him. Andrei's loyalty isn't to me, and the effort is nice, but I'm not going to delude myself. There's virtually no chance that I'll make it through today unscathed.

As I open my mouth to reply, Niko gasps and presses his face against the window. "Baba Mila!" he shrieks, shifting in his seat as his hands fiddle with the buckles, trying to free himself. A quick glance confirms that Mila's spotted us. She's storming toward the car, no doubt determined to make sure Niko spends the day glued to her side.

I want to fight her over it, but at least they're finding comfort in each other.

As soon as I have him out of his car seat, he's out and sprinting toward her, leaving me standing alone with Andrei. She watches me like a hawk until Niko's in her arms.

The cool breeze stings my cheeks, and I take a moment just to feel it before Andrei rests his hand against the base of my spine. He isn't pushing me forwards or holding me back. Just... making sure I know that he's there.

"You're going to be alright," he says quietly, but firmly. Almost as if it's an order.

I shake my head, unable to look at him. It doesn't feel like I will. It feels like I'm going to be forced to endure until something comes along to eventually break me beyond repair.

"You will. You're too strong not to be." He presses against my back, urging me toward the waiting pit of vipers dressed in their best suits.

***

I skirt along the edges of the room, and for the most part, I'm being ignored. It's a welcome reprieve from the worst-case scenario I was dreading.

I look at the atrium, picking at my cuticles. For the first time since we got here, there's no one else there.

If I'm going to have a moment with Daniil, I need to do it alone. Try as I might, I'm sure I'm going to end up crying. And the weight of other people's expectations is too much to deal with. I need privacy if I'm going to fall apart.

Part of me doesn't want to say goodbye at all. But I need to. I owe it to Daniil, even if I don't know how to start. And even though he can't express it, I don't want to disappoint him. It's the least I can do.

Gathering myself, I head toward the atrium.

I'm so focused on putting one foot in front of the other that I nearly run face-first into someone. I look up, the apology on the tip of my tongue dying when I meet Maksim's ruthless glare. I take an involuntary step backward, trying to put as much distance between us as possible without offending him.

"Hello, Blair."

I stay as still as I can, refusing to let him see the shiver that wants to creep down my spine whenever he turns his focus to me. He tilts his head, eyes narrowing like he can see it anyway.

"Maksim." My smile is as pleasant as it is forced. "Thank you for coming. I'm sure Daniil would have appreciated it." He shakes his head, and I feel the knot in my shoulders winding so tight I worry it'll snap. I take a deep breath and force them to relax.

"What are you doing here?" he asks tersely.

I can't keep the surprise off my face, but I school it as quickly as I can. "What do you mean? Why shouldn't I be here?"

"The traditional wedding vows are 'until death do us part,' yes?" I nod, even as my stomach drops like a brick. Surely he's not going to do this here. He won't make a scene or hurt me yet, right? He'll wait until I'm away from Niko. He won't make him watch.

I want to look around, but it'd be suicidal to take my eyes off the biggest predator in the room.

Where the hell is Andrei? Didn't he say he'd fend everyone off? Or was that yet another pretty lie?

"Well, my dear, death has come and gone. Daniil no longer holds any obligation to you, and, by extension, neither do I."

A rush of heat fills my face as I bite the inside of my cheek to keep from giving into the instinct to scream obscenities at him.

I am sick and tired of having to live under the umbrella of worry over what Maksim cares about. He's nothing but an overgrown bully, and the fact that he's pushing back against my presence at my own husband's wake is depraved, even for him.

"Perhaps not, but I would appreciate it immensely if you would allow me a few minutes to say goodbye." I take a step to the side, but he mirrors the movement, his body blocking the doorway.

Slowly, he shakes his head. My eyes burn as I look down, twisting my wedding ring around my finger. The movement doesn't escape his notice. He smiles, face full of a cloying false pity.

I am all too aware that he could decide I no longer serve his interests and have me killed at any time he wants, but, god, I'm not sure I can keep going when his cruelty is going to ruin any tender part of my life that remains.

"You should go home. You've done enough, don't you think?"

A firm hand lands on my shoulder, pinning me in place. I brace myself to be pulled away.

"Let her through, Maksim. What harm could she possibly cause?" I look up, and Andrei's standing next to me, standing toe-to-toe with his pakhan.

Maksim scoffs, a derisive sound that has me looking back at my feet.

"You're forgetting your place, boy." There's a lethal edge to his voice, but Andrei doesn't even blink.

He maneuvers us so he's standing in front of me. "If you don't want Nikolai to resent you, Pakhan, it might be wise to treat his mother fairly." Maksim's eyes cut across the room, and I follow his gaze. Niko sits next to Mila, watching us under his lashes even as he traces the lines on the back of her hand, nodding along to whatever she's saying.

"He's still young, but he's clever enough to see what you're doing and remember it. A small gesture now may well go far."

Andrei looks down at me, his expression as impenetrable as always. "I'll stay with her, if it would make you more comfortable." The near silence of the already somber room starts to soak in past the nerves as I take a bracing breath.

It's too much to hope that this little standoff has gone unnoticed. I'm sure they're all foaming at the mouth over this, practically champing at the bit to gossip.

"Fine," Maksim eventually bites out. "But if you think we won't be having a conversation about this little" —he makes a vague gesture— "performance, then you're even more stupid than I thought." Maksim doesn't wait for an answer. He simply steps aside, leaving me clinging to the back of Andrei's jacket like it'll keep me from being caught up in his storm.

Andrei's voice is gentle, losing all the ice and indifference it had a moment ago when he says, "I'm sorry. I shouldn't have allowed that to happen."

"Are you going to be in trouble?" I whisper, even as he ushers me toward the atrium, acting as a door to keep anyone else from coming in after us.

"Maybe." He shrugs. "But I'll deal with that when the time comes. This is more important." I open my mouth to thank him, but he shakes his head, gesturing for me to go further into the room.

My breath catches as I look at the polished wood coffin, gleaming under the lights. The clicking of my heels echoes against the tall walls and stained glass, making the room feel even bigger. I blow out a slow breath and immediately choke on it when I see how pale Daniil looks, how he's so unlike the warm, lively man that I knew. As I reach out to brush back a stray hair, I flinch when my fingers graze against his freezing cold skin.

His suit is perfect, not a single wrinkle or speck of dust. His tie is straight, tied exactly the way he liked, the knot tight at the base of his throat. Daniil looks perfectly put together, just like he did when he left the house for the last time. If it wasn't for how still he is, I'd almost think he was sleeping.

God, I wish he was sleeping.

"I'm beyond pissed at you. I hope you know that," I whisper. The drone of quiet conversation has picked up from the lobby, leaving a comfortable background noise that keeps my words from feeling like a shout in the otherwise silent room. "You promised me you were keeping yourself safe, so what happened?"

I swallow the ache in my chest, laying my hand on top of his as I gently smooth over the back of his bare ring finger. I fought about it with Mila every day, but she put her foot down. She said he wouldn't be buried with his ring and threatened to keep me from attending the funeral at all if I insisted.

Unfortunately for her, I don't really give a shit about what Mila wants. I slip my hand into my purse, pulling Daniil's wedding band out. I give it a kiss and tuck it into the front pocket of his suit. If she won't let him wear it, then I'll make sure he can have it with him.

She doesn't get to pretend I meant nothing to him.

"I wish I could hate you for lying to me. Instead, I'm stuck loving you, and you're not even here."

Andrei's voice as he speaks quietly pulls my focus back to him. He's crouched in front of Niko, a hand on his shoulder while he tries to squirm away. Andrei looks over his shoulder, and when I catch his eye, I nod. Without a word, he lets Niko go, watching as he darts to my side.

I appreciate that he let me have my moment, but I want to make sure that Niko can have his, too.

There is confusion on his face when he looks at me, and I smile to cover up the way my heart hurts, looking down at this boy who is a mirror image of his dad. He stands on his tiptoes, trying to see inside the coffin, looking frustrated.

"Would you like me to pick you up?" I ask him.

He huffs, but nods. I prop him on my hip, wanting to ask him why he isn't with Mila, but not wanting to do anything to interrupt him. The confusion on his face doesn't clear as he looks at Daniil. If anything, he just looks even more frustrated.

"Why isn't he moving?"

"He's..." Shit, when is this going to get easier? "It's like he's sleeping, baby. He's sleeping, but he can't wake up."

"Why not?"

"Because he's not here anymore. If he could, he would, but..." I trail off, shaking my head even as Niko nods.

"That's what Andrei said."

"Well, Andrei's pretty smart, huh?"

He's quiet for a long moment before he leans forward, and I adjust my hold around him while he puts his hand on Daniil's.

Eventually he settles back against me, a thoughtful look on his face. "Is it okay if I still love him?"

"Of course it is. He still loves you, and that's not going to change." My voice is fierce, and Nikolai rests his head against my shoulder. "I still love him. And I love you, too." He nods, wrapping his arms around my neck and squeezing tight.

Our quiet peace is broken by a commotion in the other room, and shortly afterward, Andrei steps up to my side. His grim expression tells me that our time is running out, but I'm not sure how I'll be able to walk away.

I press a kiss to Daniil's forehead. "I love you. I promise I'll take care of Niko for as long as I can." I carefully wipe away any lipstick and force myself to smile. "Do you want to say goodbye?" I ask my son.

Niko shakes his head against my neck, his tears soaking into the collar of my dress.

CHAPTER 8

Andrei

The endless refrain of the *Jurassic Park* theme is an inappropriate soundtrack to the fear in Blair's eyes, but that's what it's been for the past month. Every time I knock on her door, she answers it the same way. Opening the door just a crack and peering at me with those big green eyes like she's scared I'm going to hurt her.

Eventually, she always lets me in, then sends Niko off to watch his favorite movie while I check in with her.

I've never seen her look as bad as she does today. Her normally shiny blonde hair is limp and frizzy, and she sways as she sits at the island, like she can't even keep herself up. She blinks slowly at me, and I have to move to the other side to keep myself from scooping her into my arms and carrying her straight to bed.

"Are you getting any sleep?"

"Of course." She smiles a beat too quickly, just as she always does. I tilt my head, trying to force her to make eye contact, but it's useless. She could teach a master class on avoiding someone while still making polite conversation.

For some people, I'd consider it a talent, but coming from her? It makes me feel like the lowest scum.

I didn't kill Daniil, but I can't help but feel like this is my fault anyway. If I hadn't had the bright idea of using her as an informant, she wouldn't have been exposed to any of this. She could have lived her whole life pretending people like Daniil and I didn't exist.

She wouldn't have all this pain and grief.

"I'll stop by later and bring you guys some dinner, alright?" She's lost too much weight. Niko looks like he's eating just fine, but it's like she can't be bothered to get a proper meal for herself.

"Oh, you don't have to do that. We're fine."

"I know you are." I can't keep the softness out of my tone. I doubt she even notices it. "But you deserve a night off, you know?" She shakes her head, fiddling with the chain around her neck.

Shortly after the funeral she took off her rings and slipped them on a necklace that she mostly leaves tucked under the collars of her shirts. I want to ask about it, but my phone pings inside my pocket. I don't have to look to know it's another summons from Maksim.

"I'll see you tonight," I tell her, heading toward the front door before she can protest. I wait on the patio until I hear the click of the deadbolt behind me.

I've seen more of Maksim's office since the funeral than I have in the past five years. He used to trust me enough to let me do my job with little supervision. But lately he's been keeping his eye on me to the point that it feels like I'm being slowly smothered.

It's his version of a tantrum. I didn't let him make a show at the wake, so I have to suffer the consequences. If this is the cost to keep him from hurting Blair, then I'll pay it every time.

When I walk through the doors, Maksim's adviser, Nikita Dyomin, follows me to the office. He's a slimy prick, but as long as he's here, he can act as a buffer against Maksim's rage. It's been spreading like a fire, and the more it grows, the more I find that I don't care about putting it out. If he wants to ruin everything he's worked for because something didn't go his way, then so be it.

"You called, Pakhan?"

"Sit."

I'm not a fucking dog, I don't say as I take a seat.

I've never been one to rock the boat or speak out of turn. Like my dad used to say, you learn more with your ears than you do with your mouth. It also has the bonus of being the best way to avoid Maksim's attention.

If I refuse to speak out of turn, it's that much harder for him to turn his wrath onto me.

He wastes no time diving into the details of tonight's arms deal with The Outfit—from the location to the price, to the number of guns he's expecting to be delivered at the end of the night.

On the surface, it seems like any other gun run, and I squint, trying to figure out why I'm being roped into it. I haven't been asked to do this sort of work since my early twenties. At thirty-six, I've paid my dues, and while I'm normally not opposed to helping out when asked, something about the timing is putting me on edge.

"Meet with Dmitri at six. And don't fuck it up, boy."

I nod, but my mind is stuck on one detail.

"Why is this going down so far south of the city?" I ask, sounding bored. I don't like it. Not just because this fucks up my plan to check on Blair tonight, but because he's telling me to go so far out of the way for something that normally takes place closer to home.

"Does it matter?" Maksim's eyes water in a way that betrays how much he relies on alcohol to get through the day as Nikita leans further back into his seat, knowing eyes watching me with an uncomfortable intensity.

"Guess not." I shrug.

"Then shut up and do what's asked of you, yeah? I swear, you've become nothing but a thorn in my side." He wipes a hand over his face, looking far more agitated than he does weary. Nikita's silent, dropping his eyes to his lap.

This sort of thing should be Pavel's job.

Maksim's made it clear for a couple years that he wants to retire, and he's been doing more and more to groom Pavel to take over for him. A deal with an outside organization is the perfect opportunity to thrust him further into that role, so why isn't he taking advantage?

Unless Pavel's working another job. But Maksim's always wanted to focus on one big job at a time. I doubt this is an exception.

Which means he wants to make sure I'm not around for a couple hours.

"*Prosti,* Pakhan. I'll get it done. Is there anything else you need?"

There better not be. If I want to be on time to meet with Dmitri, I need to get out of here and get my shit together. He shakes his head, and I take great effort to seem relaxed as I rise from my seat and head toward the door.

I've just stepped into the hall when he calls out, "Make sure you do your damn job, Andrei."

I always do, but for once, the job he's laid out for me isn't my priority. By the time I pull away from his front gate, I have some semblance of a plan. I check the rearview mirror to make sure there's no one following and pull out my phone.

"Yeah?" Alexei's distracted voice answers.

"Are you working tonight?"

"No. I'm spending time with my sister." He pauses for a moment while I nod to myself. "And if you make me cancel on her, she'll kill us both."

Doubtful. Alexei's older sister, Nadya, is a firecracker with a protective streak a mile wide. Wherever he is, she isn't far behind. But that could work in my favor. If there's anyone I know that can keep Blair from blowing up before the night's through, it's her.

"I need to bring someone to your place tonight, and if anything happens to them, you won't have to worry about your sister."

"And why's that?"

"Because I'll kill you myself."

***

"Would you *please* put down my son?" Blair yells as she hurries after me, her face flushed with anger as I press the call button to Alexei's condo.

"If I did, you'd grab him, steal my car, and run." She's stubborn, and stealing her kid was the only thing I knew that would get her to follow me.

For once, she doesn't argue. "Well, could you at least stop holding him like a football?" I step onto the elevator, shaking my head. Niko giggles as he looks around from where he's tucked under my arm.

Could I carry him differently? Sure. Is this the one way that's least likely to make Blair kick me in a bid to get me to let go? Yep.

The doors slide shut, and she glares at me in the reflection.

"You know, if you told me *why* you were dragging us half-way across the city, maybe I'd have been more agreeable."

"You wouldn't have been. You argue with everything I say."

"No, I don't."

"Thank you for proving my point."

Niko twists to get a better look when the doors open, and I adjust my grip before I step off. "Now, are you coming, or do I have to carry you, too?" For a moment she looks like she's planning on putting up a fight, but she crosses her arms and follows after me.

She still looks tired, but there's more life to her now than there was this afternoon.

If kidnapping her son is all it takes to give her back some sort of spark, then Nikolai and I are about to become best friends.

During the trek down the hall, she's quiet. By the time I knock on the door, she's lost the fight with herself. Pulling self-consciously on her sweater, her silence is deafening.

"Andrei," Alexei drawls as he opens the door, his voice a controlled monotone while his eyes blaze with poorly concealed anger. He looks between Blair and me, jaw tight. Still, he looks more relaxed than he usually is when I see him. His dark blond hair looks like he's been pulling at it, and he's wearing *jeans* with his button-down shirt.

I don't know if I've ever seen him in jeans before.

He's an inch or two shorter than me, and not quite as broad. Then again, he doesn't have to be when he spends most of his time tucked away in an office at his clubs. Though the way Blair moves a half step behind me makes me think his piss poor attitude more than makes up for it.

"I see you've brought guests with you. How wonderful." His face doesn't budge an inch, his glare boring a hole into Blair's skull. I roll my eyes as I put Niko down. He skitters behind me, suddenly shy as he clings to Blair's leggings.

"You've met Blair, right?"

"Briefly," he bites out.

"I'm glad to hear it. Now invite them in."

Alexei's a dick, I'll never deny that, but he's also one of the few men I can trust to watch them while I can't, if only to help clear the debt he owes me.

"Nadya," he calls over his shoulder, making no move to let them in. "We have guests."

A beat passes before Nadya wanders over to him, a hand towel thrown over her shoulder and a streak of flour in her dark hair. Alexei moves just enough to gesture toward us. "Andrei's friends are going to join us. Have you met Blair before?"

When she shakes her head, he makes brief introductions before finally stepping aside. Only then does Nadya notice Niko from where he peeks around my legs, Blair's hand resting on the top of his head.

She shoves Alexei out of the way and kneels, smiling warmly at him. "Hi there. I'm Nadya, what's your name?"

He looks up, and Blair gives him an encouraging smile. "Nikolai, but Mama calls me Niko."

"Well, Niko, it's nice to meet you. Would you like to help me with dinner? I'm making pirozhki." He nods, and when she stands, he moves to follow her, still not letting go of Blair's pants. After a moment of hesitation, Blair moves with them.

"I'll pick you guys up in a few hours."

She looks over her shoulder and nods, not meeting my eyes. When the trio turns the corner, Alexei shoves me out into the hall, closing the door behind him with an angry scoff.

"I know you're doing your best to get on Maksim's shit list, but you're not going to drag me into this. Why the fuck did you bring her here?"

I debate how much to tell him. I trust him to protect them, but what if I'm wrong? He could just as easily call Pavel as soon as I'm gone and toss her straight to the wolves.

Then again, he knows I'd go after him twice as hard. And for all his faults, Alexei won't do anything to risk something happening to him or his sister.

"Maksim's sending me out of town on some bullshit errand."

"And what? You think he's going to go after *her*?"

"Not him, no. But Pavel? Maybe."

He thinks for a moment, tilting his head from side to side.

"So why not send her to her mother-in-law's? Or have her hide at yours? Don't drag Nadya and I into it."

"Mila would have sold her out even when Daniil was alive. What do you think will happen if Blair isn't at home?"

Publicly standing up to Maksim at the wake was the right thing for me to do for Blair, but it also made it clear that I care about her. If she isn't where someone expects her to be, the next logical thing for her to do is lie low at my place.

"After the mess you made at Virgo, why should I do anything for you, huh?"

I don't bother to hide my eye roll. "It was closed for five days, Alexei. Get over it."

"Five very expensive days," he hisses between clenched teeth. "I lost income, I have to pay for repairs, and now I have to woo back the girls and customers that got scared off. That's not even accounting for the bribes I had to pay to make the officials forget that the place even exists. Five days is fucking expensive, *mudak*."

I want to throttle him.

"I need you to do this for me. I have no other way to guarantee her safety."

A beat passes.

"Fine. But find a long-term solution, because if the higher-ups want her dead, they'll keep finding ways to send you away until they get what they want, and I'm not going to harbor her here."

I hate to admit it, but he's right. This is just a stop-gap. But it buys me time that I desperately need.

"I'll watch them tonight." He sighs, rubbing a hand against his jaw. "But this isn't going to happen again, Andrei."

CHAPTER 9

Blair

Andrei showing up for dinner was expected. Dragging Niko and I out of the house and depositing us at Alexei Trenin's doorstep was not.

I wasn't planning on going out today. The most exciting thing I'd accounted for was Andrei stopping by and badgering me about eating while I did my best to pretend he wasn't there, which doesn't require me or Niko to be dressed up.

In fact, if we were hanging out at home all day, it would be perfectly acceptable for Niko to still be in his pajamas. And if I was lounging around in worn leggings and an old hoodie? That'd be expected, too.

So when he parked outside of the high-rise apartment building, my anxiety combined with insecurity in a toxic mixture that I'm half convinced everyone around me can see written plainly on my face.

It didn't help that I couldn't stop blushing as Andrei glowered while he carried Niko around like it was nothing, or that I can't stop thinking about how his stubborn demands stirred feelings I shouldn't be having for someone like him. I refuse to think too hard about any of that right now.

The fact that it's my first time meeting Nadya is only making everything worse.

She tucks a strand of shoulder-length hair behind her ear while I try to get over myself. It's not like either she or her brother are particularly dressed up. In fact, she's wearing loose jeans and a worn-out sweater. Unlike Niko, I don't look too far out of place, but from the way he's focused on mimicking the careful way Nadya pinches shut a lump of filling and dough, I doubt he feels like it.

His work isn't nearly as neat, but he looks satisfied as he presents the messy lump of dough to her, beaming from ear to ear. Shaking my head, I turn back to the pile of vegetables in front of me. Nadya tried to tell me that I'm a guest and shouldn't have to do anything, but that's not exactly true.

We were forced on them. I appreciate that she's trying to put a pretty bow on it, but it is what it is.

After I insisted, she let me cut vegetables for a salad, a small distraction I'm very grateful to have.

"So, not that I mind the extra company, but"—she grins, a teasing glint in her eye as Niko tries again to pinch shut a ball of dough—"why *did* Andrei bring you guys here?" She doesn't sound resentful, just curious, and that keeps me from feeling even worse.

I wish I knew. Andrei couldn't be bothered to answer any of my questions on the way over. He just showed up, grabbed Niko, piled us into his car, and dumped us here.

"Your guess is as good as mine." I shrug. Sure, he's stopped by more often than not lately, but I figured he was making sure I didn't take the first opportunity to run.

"Seriously? And here I was, hoping for some juicy gossip." Nadya bumps her hip against mine.

"Sorry to disappoint." I grin weakly. "Maybe he thinks I've spent too much time cooped up at home, and this is his way of letting me know."

She laughs, head thrown back and looking so at home that I feel cramped, despite the large, open kitchen.

"Man, I was hoping that you were fun so I could actually have someone cool to hang out with."

"Hey, I'm cooler than you are." I flinch at Alexei's voice, but he's smiling at Nadya with steady affection. "Maybe if you could figure out how to make friends without having *my* friends hand deliver them, you'd be able to see that."

"Oh, you have friends? That's news to me." He flips her off, looking chagrined when Nadya glares at him while pointing at Niko. "So, Mr. Popular, when's the last time you hung out with someone you weren't related to?"

He narrows his eyes at her while I toss the salad. "And when's the last time you talked to *anyone* that wasn't me?" She sticks her tongue out at him, and it feels like this is a conversation they've had a dozen times before.

"Alexei, look!" Niko interrupts, completely oblivious as he presents a butchered mess of dough that starts to fall apart in his hands the moment he picks it up. His proud look doubles when the corners of Alexei's lips quirk up, rubbing the top of his head.

"Good job, Nikolai. Do you want to try to throw it in the oven and see how it turns out?" He helps Niko put the hand pie on a baking sheet and stands to leave the kitchen, wiping his hands on a dish towel.

"I have to make a few calls. Let me know when the food's done."

Nadya rolls her eyes, but nods.

"God forbid you have fun for once in your life."

As soon as he leaves the room, Niko's off, following him. I reach out to stop him, but Nadya lays a hand on my arm. "Let him be. If anything, Niko will keep him from getting so busy he forgets we're here. I mean, my brother's great and all, but he's a fucking buzzkill."

I'm still reluctant to let Niko out of my sight, especially since I don't trust Alexei as far as I can throw him, but if I don't give Niko a little space, it'll only be a matter of time before he starts to lash out at me. More than he already has, that is.

"I'll take your word for it," I say, smiling with a brightness I don't feel.

***

Niko's arms can barely reach his plate, and his face is scrunched up in concentration as he tries in vain to cut his hand pie. It's half burnt where he pinched it too thin, but he insisted on eating the ones he made.

His obvious pride makes me smile, even as he struggles.

"Would you like some help?" I ask him.

"No, thank you," he replies, focused on his task while I add a salad to his plate. His fork slips, but he doesn't take any time to pout. Instead, he picks it right back up and tries again.

"At least there's people here to eat something other than vegetables." Nadya grins, shooting a playful glare at Alexei's plate, piled high with leafy greens. He's pointedly ignored everything else, but this is the first time she's pointed it out.

"Not all of us can have the metabolism of a twelve-year-old boy." He points his fork at her long, model-esque body, a playful spark in his eyes. "I don't want to spend all my time at the gym. I have more important shit to do."

"Language, Alexei," she scolds, leaning back in her chair.

His eyes cut to Niko with a cringe.

"Shit. I mean, uh, shoot. Fuck, I'm sorry." The chagrined look on his face is enough to startle a laugh out of me. Alexei's too intimidating and serious to pull off remorse, but I might as well enjoy his attempt.

"It's fine. He knows not to repeat grown-up words. Right, Niko?"

Niko nods, his grip faltering again, fork clattering against the plate.

"Shoot," he mutters under his breath.

"You know, Nikolai, it's fine if you need some help," Alexei tells him soberly.

"I can do it, though."

"I bet you can, but maybe I could get you something to sit on, and that'd give you some more leverage." Niko looks at him suspiciously, but eventually relents with a huff. Alexei stands, and when he leaves the room, it takes all of half a second before Niko's out of his seat and following after him.

Nadya's focus shifts back to me when they round the corner, and I shift uncomfortably, keeping my eyes glued to my plate. "I know Alexei comes off as a hard-ass, but he can be alright. Sometimes, anyway."

I'll have to take her word for it. The only parts of Alexei I've ever known are him glaring at me like I've personally gone out of my way to piss him off.

"He's right about a couple of things, too. Mostly that I could use more friends." She shrugs, looking hesitant. "Actually, his newest club is opening on Saturday. Is there any chance I could talk you into coming with me?" She looks so hopeful, and I try to discreetly wipe my suddenly clammy hands on my thighs.

"I'd love to, I just... I'm not sure it'd be a great idea, you know?" I give a half-hearted smile, hoping that it doesn't come across as a grimace. Based on the disappointment on her face, it doesn't work.

The night Alexei opened his last club turned into one of the most miserable nights of my life, and even though I'd typically love to hang out and cut loose with someone like Nadya, I'm not eager for a repeat.

Finding out my husband was cheating on me, getting caught up in a shooting, and subsequently watching Daniil make sure his mistress was safe while I was all alone was enough fun. I can't picture it going any better without his protection.

And even though none of what happened that night was my fault, Alexei's glares and general air of disdain give me the feeling he would prefer not to see me at another one of his grand openings. Or anywhere, really, but especially not another big event.

Before she can formulate a response, Alexei comes back, a pillow in hand and Niko hot on his heels. He places it on the chair and helps him back into his seat. Niko beams at him before he redoubles his effort to attack his meal.

Thankfully, Nadya lets the subject go and the conversation shifts to less emotionally fraught topics. Nadya and Alexei banter back and forth, laughing easily and making sure to include Niko.

When Nadya chucks a dinner roll at Alexei's head, he catches it, and I find myself smiling at their antics.

It's nice. It's the most fun I've had in ages.

It's been longer than I want to admit since I've just had fun. Even before Daniil died, everything with him had turned into a performance. He expected me to look a certain way whenever we went out. Stay quiet. Smile demurely. Put on a mask of ignorance and pretend I didn't know what anyone was talking about.

It was exhausting, and I decide to accept this reprieve, no matter how brief it might end up being.

When Alexei once again excuses himself to make a few calls in his office, Nadya and Nikolai both put up a nominal fight, but Niko's too tired to really push back, and Nadya seems resigned.

"I'll do the dishes," I volunteer, standing to gather the dinnerware before we even hear his office door shut behind him.

"Don't worry about it," Nadya says, quickly getting up and trying to take the plates away from me. "You're a guest. I can't let you clean up our mess."

"I was an intruder on your dinner. It's the least I can do," I say through a tight smile.

She rolls her eyes and takes the stack of plates away a little more forcefully than necessary and puts them down on the table. "It's not like you had a choice in it, but either way, if you want to do me a favor, you'll leave them for Alexei to deal with. This is his place, and unlike you, he didn't offer to help me cook."

On instinct I want to argue, but her eyes spark with mischief. "If he has any problems with it, he'll take it up with me. And if I'm being honest, I've been looking for a reason to start a fight with him." She brings her hands together in a plea. "*Please* let me have this."

At a loss for words, and against my better judgment, I find myself nodding.

"Thank you!" She pumps a fist in the air, startling another laugh out of me.

She practically trips over herself in her rush to leave everything on the table and herd Niko and I toward the living room, ignorant to the way I cringe when Niko, with messy hands and an even messier face, climbs onto the black leather sofa, leaving smears of grease on everything he touches.

The whole room is full of clean lines and sharp angles, but at least Niko is coordinated enough that I don't have to worry about him tripping over air.

Still, I eye the glass coffee table warily as I sit down next to him gingerly, pulling him close to try to minimize the damage he can cause, feeling silly when Nadya flops heavily into an armchair, leaning forward with her hand on her knees. The way she watches us almost makes me feel like an animal in a zoo, but it's probably fair play.

I don't know what I'd do with us if the situation was reversed.

Still, I have to force myself not to shift under her scrutinizing gaze.

After a few moments she nods to herself, apparently coming to a decision. "How about a movie?"

Niko looks at me, face lighting up with excitement, so I nod, grateful for the reprieve as she sorts through the options, asking for his input whenever she passes over something interesting.

She gives me a look while they're negotiating, and when I shake my head desperately while Niko puts up a case to watch *Jurassic Park*, she smiles before talking him out of it. With a conspiratorial grin, she hovers over her selection.

"Ooh, this is a good one. Niko, let's watch this. You'll love it."

"Does it have dinosaurs?" He eyes her skeptically.

"No," she concedes. "But that doesn't mean you can't give it a try, does it?"

He shakes his head and leans into my side. "Okay. That one."

Which is how he ends up asleep half an hour later while *Singin' in the Rain* plays quietly in the background. I run my hand through his hair, the lights from the television reflecting on his face while he drools on my leg.

This might not have been the night I'd planned, but it wasn't bad. Dinner with relative strangers, easy conversation, and Niko falling asleep without a meltdown. Probably more because of exhaustion than anything else, but I'll take the wins I can get. If he lets me, I'll have to find a way to thank Andrei for this.

"Hey," Nadya whispers, nodding in Niko's direction. "Is he asleep?" I nod, smiling kindly at her. She's curled up in the chair, wrapping her arms around her legs as she shifts to face me. "I'm sorry about earlier. I just got excited, but you don't have to hang out with me."

"It's not that. It's, uh." I swallow. I hate talking about it, but she probably already knows, right? "You remember when Riot opened?"

In hindsight, with all the important Bratva men gathered in one place, it was inevitable that someone would take advantage of it. But at the time, things with the Italians had been relatively calm, so when The Outfit decided to sneak someone in and open fire, no one had been prepared.

"Of course," she sighs. "That's why it's taken Alexei so long to open another club. He's been worried about a repeat. The amount of security that he's hiring is ridiculous."

I doubt anything will happen, considering the amount of heat that the last scuffle brought along with it, but it's good to know he's taking steps to prevent it.

"Well, before all the, you know"—I wave my hand— "gunfire and bloodshed happened, Alexei already wanted to kick me and Daniil out. I don't think he'd want me causing a scene again."

"What do you mean?"

"It was the first time Daniil went out with Emiliya." I smile, watching the way Niko's eyelashes flutter against his cheeks. "I was under the impression we were going there together, probably because he brought me with him. Instead I got to watch his infidelity first-hand. And so did the rest of the Bratva."

"Oh, shit, I forgot about that."

I shake my head. "I would've thought the shooting afterward would have overshadowed it" —I shrug— "but apparently your brother disagrees."

My drama was definitely the subject of all the gossip afterward. We weren't the biggest thing to happen that night, but Alexei must find it easier to focus his anger on me than on a bunch of people who are protected by powerful men.

I get it, even if I don't like it.

It was also the night I realized no one was going to help me while bullets whizzed past. In the chaos, Daniil grabbed Emiliya and fled while I tried to make my way through the crowd toward the closest exit. I ended up stumbling into Andrei, who was a godsend. He got me out of there and made sure I got home, even if he seemed pissed about it.

"How're you guys doing without him?"

That's all she asks. She doesn't try to qualify it or add an asterisk or a footnote. Doesn't try to act like my husband was nothing to me. Just asks how we're doing.

I appreciate that even more than the gentle distraction of conversation.

"Niko's struggling," I answer honestly. "He misses his dad. And it's hard for him to accept that he isn't coming home. This is the first time he's gone to sleep without tears since Daniil died, so, maybe that's progress." I hope it's progress, anyway. I don't know how he's had the energy to fight with me every night, because by the time he finally gives up, I'm dead on my feet, dreading having to do it all over again the next day.

"And how are *you* doing?" She looks at me seriously, and I freeze.

Truth is, I don't know. I've been so focused on taking care of Niko that I haven't had the time to think about it. Besides, it doesn't really matter.

My husband's dead, and I'm too scared to ask Andrei why. Now my days are probably numbered, and I need to make sure that my son is going to be alright when I'm gone. Who cares if I'm constantly fluctuating between desperate fear, burning anger, an all-consuming grief—and in my weak moments, a shameful relief?

No one. No one cares.

"I'm fine," I eventually answer with a practiced smile.

A line forms between her brows. "You sure about that?" She tilts her head to the side, eyes narrowed like she can see past all the barriers I'm desperately working to construct.

"Seriously, I'm fine. Or I will be."

Probably.

Hopefully.

"Alright," she acquiesces. "But if you want to talk to someone, I'm around. And not to brag, but unlike some people around here I know how to tie my own shoes." She nods at Niko, and I can't help but laugh. "So, I like to think I'm pretty good at having adult conversations."

"Are you saying that you're above discussing the subtle nuance of different shapes and flavors of fruit snacks?"

"I would *never,*" she gasps, pressing a hand against her chest in mock offense. I laugh, quickly quieting down when Niko stirs, pressing his face further into my stomach.

"I might have to take you up on that. Here, let me give you my number."

She pulls out her phone, diligently putting in my number before she sends me a text, grinning when my phone dings from my pocket.

"We'll have to plan a time to hang out. But not at a club opening, alright?" I tell her.

She huffs out a laugh, nodding. "Yeah, that wasn't the most tactful suggestion, was it?"

"You didn't know. But some other time?"

"Totally. We'll figure something out."

I hope that Nadya is as genuine as she seems to be. I could use a friend.

CHAPTER 10

Andrei

If I wasn't already convinced that Maksim is doing every-thing in his power to make me miserable, this would have done it. As I leave Alexei's place, my phone blows up with texts telling me to pick up Dmitri, insisting that I drive him all the way to the fucking deal.

I don't like having people in my car. I like spending time in an enclosed space with loudmouthed, cocky idiots even less.

At least I don't have to wait. When I get to his apartment complex, Dmitri's outside and waiting, like an eager child on their first day of school. He slams the car door behind him, and I'm torn between cringing and chewing him out. Before I get a chance to decide, he's already talking.

I want to hit my head against the steering wheel.

"Hey, you're Voronov, right? I'm Dmitri Kamensky." He doesn't wait for a response, shifting the seat to make room for his legs while he drums his fingers against the center console, looking around like he expects me to have piles of weapons and cash in the back seat.

I don't. There's just a car seat.

I've driven around with Daniil and Niko enough times that it became a pain in the ass to keep taking it out, so it's been a permanent installation since Niko's grown big enough to use it.

Dmitri pauses when he sees it, but his enthusiasm doesn't dim in the slightest.

He looks exactly like what he is: a young kid who's getting his first real job. Messy hair, cheap suit, and a muted panic in his eyes that he's hiding behind a cocky grin. Fuck, I doubt he's even old enough to drink, and Maksim's trusting him with something as important as an arms deal?

I don't try to fill the silence, pulling from the curb and starting the long drive toward the meeting point.

We've only gone five miles when he reaches over to turn on the radio. I slap his hand away, and he flinches, hissing as he pulls it toward his chest.

"Fuck, man. That's still tender." I look at him, only now spotting the tattoo on the back of his hand under the passing streetlights.

"Yeah? Is it fresh?"

"Yeah, it's only a little over a week old. Looks sick, right?"

He turns it toward me, showing off a tattoo of a spider that takes up most of the back of his hand. It's realistic enough that if it was on my hand, I'd probably end up smacking it every time I caught a glimpse of it out of the corner of my eye.

I'm not sure if he's just that proud of it, or if he's trying to impress me, so I nod. I'm no stranger to ink, but I don't really care about anyone else's.

But I'm also not trying to be an asshole. It's not Dmitri's fault that I'm having a shitty day.

"Sure, kid. Is this your first time on a job like this?"

He laughs, going right back to drumming his fingers incessantly, this time against the dash. "Is it that obvious?" I grind my teeth together so I don't shove his hands down his throat. "I've been keeping my head down, but it must be working for me if I'm getting to work with someone like you."

"What do you mean 'someone like me'?"

He grins, looking even younger, and any thoughts I had about telling him he is just part of my punishment for pissing Maksim off fly out the window.

"What, you fishing for compliments?"

"That's not worth justifying with a response."

He laughs, the sound echoing through the car.

Fuck, maybe I should have let him turn on the radio. *I just need to get through the next couple hours*, I tell myself. *Then I can check in on Blair.*

"Man, come on. You know you've got a reputation, right? Working with someone like you is cool. And not to sound like some inexperienced kid or whatever, but it's more than I thought I was going to get. Not this soon, anyway."

I try to remember what it was like to be in his place. The problem is I don't know if I was ever that bright-eyed and excited about this sort of work. I was raised in it. I grew up with the expectation that this would be my life. It's all I've ever known.

Apparently, that isn't the case for this kid.

"Do you know what you're getting into tonight?"

Or is Maksim throwing you blindly into the deep end?

If everything goes according to plan, it'll be straightforward, but if Dmitri does something stupid and decides to run his mouth? There's a real chance he's not going home at all.

Dmitri shrugs, looking out the window with his grin still fully intact. "Not really, but how hard can it be?"

I grunt.

Blyad, how fresh is this kid?

"How'd you get into this line of work?"

He's quiet for a moment, and I wonder if I've finally managed to find his mute button.

"I tried to hold up some tailor's shop." He shrugs. "It wasn't anything serious, you know? I just needed some quick cash to hold me over until I got my next paycheck. And that's how I met Mikhail."

"Let me guess, he talked you down and promised you more consistent money?"

Mikhail's an old prick who's been working for Maksim since before I was born and runs his crew like a small army. And like any army, he has no qualms about recruiting young, desperate kids for cannon fodder.

"Pretty much."

"Any regrets?" Even if he's fine dealing with an asshole like Mikhail on a regular basis, the violence can be a lot for anyone who doesn't go in with their eyes wide open.

"Not really. I can handle the work as long as I get paid. I..." He looks at me, a calculating look in his eyes. "Listen, you're chill, right?"

"If you're asking if I'm going to go around telling everyone what you say, then sure. I'm *chill*."

"Okay," he sighs. "It's just, I've got a little sister, right? Our parents died in a car crash last year. I need to have the money to prove to the state I can provide her with a stable home before I can get her out of foster care." There's a quiet resolve in his words, and I get it. If I was in his shoes, I'd put up with Mikhail's bullshit, too.

"She's turning ten next month. I don't want her getting raised by strangers."

Fuck, no wonder Maksim was so willing to put him on this job. He doesn't have anyone waiting for him. Just some kid who probably has no way of knowing if something has happened to her big brother if he disappears.

My hands flex against the steering wheel.

"In that case, let me give you some advice. Learn to keep your mouth shut. Not just tonight, but any time you're around someone carrying a gun."

"Right. Don't want to piss them off," he mutters, shoulders curling forward.

"Not just that. You'd be surprised what people have to say when you let them fill the silence. No matter what anyone tells you, knowledge is an underrated power. When you know the right things, it doesn't take much pressure to put someone on their back foot. Take the guy we're meeting tonight, Luca Sotero. Have you heard of him before?"

"In passing."

I smirk. "He's a hotheaded little shit, but he works with us. You know why?"

"Because his boss told him to?"

"No. His boss doesn't know about the little arrangement he has with us."

A beat passes. "Seriously? Does he have a death wish?"

"No. But he's racked up a hell of a debt. Turns out he has a thing for gambling." Dmitri laughs, shaking his head. "He got in a bit of trouble back in Atlantic City, and it started chasing him home. One of our guys caught wind of the whole thing, and Maksim offered to take care of the debt. Now he owns Luca, and we get a pretty deal on weapons. At least until his boss finds out."

"But the blowback won't be on us. All the risk is on Luca."

I nod. If the kid's clever enough, he'll find a way to go far. "Exactly. One guy kept his head down and passed along smart info, so we have a cushy deal and all the power."

"Huh."

"The only catch is that Luca doesn't like it. Sure, he's backed into a corner and can't do anything about it, but he's going to be primed to lash out when we get there. He wants an excuse to draw blood. Don't give him one. Let his anger burn itself out, and we'll get home before sunrise."

The rest of the drive passes quietly. Whether it's because Dmitri's taking what I said into consideration or if he's just thinking, I'm not sure. But I'm not going to argue with the relative peace his silence offers as I pull into the familiar scrap yard, nodding at the man standing near the entrance as I pass.

Driving slowly toward the back of the lot, I nudge Dmitri's side.

"Keep your head on a swivel. He can't bring much in the way of backup without his higher ups noticing, not all the way out here. But we don't have any either. Check your gun before you get out of the car. He'll have the truck and a second man with him. You're driving the truck back, and I'll be on your tail the whole time, but pay attention to who's around you anyway. You hear me?"

He nods, already checking his gun under the sparse lights as I stop, putting the car in park. Sure enough, Luca's leaning against the side of a box truck, looking like a wet cat in a suit and tie, arms firmly crossed across his chest.

"Andrei, what a surprise. You're late," he snaps before I've even shut my door. I roll my eyes, making an exaggerated show of checking my watch.

"We're three minutes early. You have what we came for, or not?"

He points at the truck with a nod. "What're you doing here, anyway? I haven't seen your ugly mug in ages. I was starting to think this sort of thing was beneath you."

I keep an eye on Dmitri as he circles toward the back, opening the truck with a blank face while he waits for Luca to get off his ass and follow us.

"Or, wait. Don't tell me. You're doing grunt work because you pissed someone off."

I don't answer, climbing into the back to open one of the crates.

"So, what'd you do?" Luca calls, laughing at his own conviction. "You fuck the wrong man's wife? Or does Maksim just not trust a quiet motherfucker like you?"

I check over one of the submachine guns, satisfied to find exactly what I was expecting. Replacing the lid on the crate,

I move to check one of the ones in the back. I don't think he's going to try to fuck me over, but it's bad business to trust anyone. Especially not a man with nothing to lose.

By the time Luca finally joins me in the truck, he's still running his mouth, like if he talks long enough, he'll get a reaction that will justify picking a fight.

Unfortunately for him, his attempts to piss me off are almost identical to the ribbing I get from everyone else. It's as effective as a mosquito.

I nod at Dmitri when I climb out the truck, and head to the trunk of my car.

"Here's the usual," I say, tossing a briefcase at Luca's feet. He sneers but picks it up. I'm sure he's itching to open it up and count the contents, but he doesn't get that luxury. He'll have to wait until we're long gone and hope we didn't short him.

Some guys might, but I won't. Not when we're already robbing him blind.

As long as his family is in one piece, he doesn't have room to complain.

CHAPTER 11

Andrei

Traffic is light, but it does very little to help me relax. I'm not worried about cops tonight. Dmitri is driving like a perfect citizen, and all the patrols in the area are paid generously to look the other way when we're making deliveries. Instead, I'm thinking back to what Alexei said.

I need to find a long-term solution to keep Blair safe. I can't dump her at his place whenever I'm not there to watch her. It was pure luck that he was even home tonight.

I can't let her stay at my place, but I can't let her stay at hers, either. Not just because of tonight. I don't want to gamble that Semyon's orders to kill her died with him. He was a helpful pawn for Pavel, but he isn't the only one who would jump at the opportunity.

When she became an informant for me, she unwittingly learned intimate details of Maksim's drug-running operations. Not just out west, but how he moves his contraband throughout the country. If she were so inclined and could find a cop who isn't on his payroll, she could put him behind bars—and probably keep him there until his eventual trial.

It'd be enough to take down our whole operation, and we wouldn't be able to recover for years.

Would she? I fucking doubt it. If anything, her time working with law enforcement just left her jaded and untrusting of the whole damn system, and that was before she had a kid to think about.

But does Maksim care about that? No. And if he's gotten it into his head that he wants to see her dead, my options are pretty fucking limited.

In fact, by the time we get to the warehouse, I've only come up with one idea.

Mikhail tips his chin in acknowledgment when we pull up, ready to unload the merchandise. "Everything go alright?" he asks, eyes glinting with malice.

"Yes, sir." Dmitri lifts the door on the truck, turning his head to hide the small, proud smile on his face.

I'm dismissed almost as soon as I'm acknowledged, wasting no time as I make my way back to my car.

If Maksim's already trying to get me away from her, I need to act fast.

Blair won't like my plan. She'll cry and try to find a way out of it, but she'll fold. With time, maybe I could come up with a different plan, but I'm a selfish bastard, and I don't want to. She can hate me and glare at me, threaten me with physical harm all she wants, but she'll do as I say. At least in this.

I don't realize how tightly I'm clenching my jaw until I walk into Alexei's condo and see her on the couch, talking quietly with Nadya with Niko curled up in her lap. As soon as she turns her soft smile toward me, all my worry and stress melts away.

Yeah, she's going to fucking hate me even more than she already does for what I'm going to do to her. I can't even find it in me to be upset about it. As long as it keeps her and Niko safe, she'll say yes, and that's all I need for now. I'll deal with the rest of it when it comes.

***

I shift Niko's weight onto my hip, and Blair's eyes are soft as she takes him from my arms. She's smiling gently, absently rubbing his back as she carries him. Something about the sight feels intimate, like I'm an intruder watching something I shouldn't be privy to.

When she lays him in his bed, she's careful to tuck the blankets around his shoulders. Kissing his forehead, she turns off the light, softly closing the door as she meets me in the hall. I wait, unwavering, while she eyes me warily.

"We need to talk." I nod toward the stairs, and she follows me without a word, a dismal air following her like a cloak.

Guilt is a heavy weight on my chest, both for everything I've already done to her, and for everything I'm about to do.

But she needs this as much as I do.

I take a seat at the dining table, waiting for her to follow my lead, but she remains standing in the doorway, hands shoved into the pocket of her hoodie as if it can hide the way she's twisting her hands together.

"Blair," I prompt, and she blinks slowly, as if startled out of a fugue before slipping into the chair next to me. Her expression is closed off, distress is pouring off her in waves.

"How long do you think Maksim's going to let me live?" Her voice is blank, eyes unflinching as she watches me under her lashes. "Or is that why you're here? Did he ask you to take care of me?"

I freeze, unable to answer.

In horror, I watch as she nods to herself, apparently taking my silence as confirmation. "Right. Did you volunteer?"

"Blair."

"Will you still look after Niko?" It's only with that question that her voice begins to shake. Still, she holds her shoulders back, chin raised as her lips twist into a grimace, brows drawing together. "I'm sure Mila will want to raise him, but he'll still need someone to guide him, and Daniil trusted you."

"Blair," I bite. "I'm not here to kill you, *zolotse*. If I have a say in it, no one will."

"Oh."

My jaw works while I take a deep breath. "Why the hell would you think I'd volunteer?" The word tastes dirty.

"When we met, you kidnapped me and threatened to kill me. And when you let me go, you continued to threaten my life. For months. It didn't exactly make me feel warm and fuzzy inside." She shrugs.

I want to tell her it was supposed to be Daniil's job to lure her into our clutches and kidnap her, that he only changed his mind and told me to do it when he first saw her, but that won't make her feel any better.

"Fear is a powerful motivator. I needed you. If I'd walked up to you and asked you to work with me, would you have? Or would you have turned around and run in the other direction?"

She doesn't respond, but that's an answer in and of itself.

"I know it doesn't seem like it, but I never would have hurt you, no matter what I said."

She shakes her head, still not answering me while I pinch the bridge of my nose. This isn't how I imagined this conversation going.

"Regardless," I continue, "you're right that someone wants you dead. Either Maksim or Pavel, I don't know which." She goes stiff as a board at his name, like it'll summon him. "I have a plan that'll keep you safe. It'll keep you around so you won't have to worry about me or Mila looking after Niko because you'll be there to do it yourself."

"What do you need me to do?" she asks instantly, just like I knew she would. Her endless devotion to her son is incredible.

"You're going to have to marry me."

She stares at me for a moment before she smiles, letting out a breathless laugh. In any other scenario, I'd revel in that sound. Instead, I keep my face blank, not looking away from her, letting my stiff posture emphasize exactly how serious I am.

Her smile lingers, but once she looks at me, it drops like a sack of bricks.

"No." She shakes her head, the color bleeding from her face. It hits me like a knife to the chest, but I refuse to flinch.

"Yes."

"Andrei, what the fuck are you talking about?"

A better man would take her at face value and back off. I can get her and Niko new identities. I can get them far away from here, far enough that Maksim won't be able to track them down.

Then she wouldn't hate me for making her do this.

I'd also never get to see her again. I've been torturing myself by being around her for years, but I don't know how I'd cope with the pain of letting her go. Or even if I could.

If she's halfway across the planet, I won't be able to check up on her as much as I need to. I'll have no choice but to let her go and let her live her life without my interference.

If she's close to me, I can make sure she's safe. I look past her at a smear of something dark blue on the wall near the end of the stairs, forcing my hands to still so they don't curl into fists.

"I have a respected position in Maksim's Bratva. Your marriage to Daniil kept anyone from coming after you, right?" She nods slowly, tilting her head back to look up at the ceiling. "Marrying me would do the same thing."

Her shoulders shake lightly, and when she opens them, her emerald green eyes shine with barely restrained tears. She blinks them back, but one carves a wet trail down her cheek regardless.

It takes every ounce of my control to not wipe it away.

"I know it's probably the last thing you want, but this is the only thing that I know will work."

Blair looks down at her hands, and I swallow thickly.

What am I going to do if she refuses? Even if she wasn't widowed less than two months ago, she deserves to be with someone who makes her happy. Not someone like me, who has to strong-arm her into marriage to save her life.

"Daniil would hate this, you know?" Her voice is tight as she closes her eyes.

"He'd kick my ass," I agree. Her eyes are glossy when she glances at me, and my breath catches in my throat. "He'd try to, anyway. His muscles were just there to make him look pretty."

Another tear slips free, a dark stain blooming unceremoniously on her hoodie.

Silence fills the room, suffocating me until she gives a barely perceptible nod. Relief like I've never known makes my shoulders sag.

"Yeah? You'll marry me?"

She sniffs, and it pours a bucket of ice-cold water on the flicker of hope in my chest.

"Yeah, I'll marry you."

"Thank you." I take one of her hands into my own, no longer able to resist the urge to touch her, to comfort her.

There are still a million things to discuss, but this is enough for now. I'm not going to push it and ruin the small victory she's handed me.

"Now what?"

"Now, you get some sleep. I'll come by in the morning, and we can go to the courthouse." I want her to be mine as soon as I can. "Do you think Mila would be willing to watch Niko tomorrow?"

She nods, shoulders slumped.

"She'll be ecstatic to have another day with him." I frown, her dejected tone giving me pause. Daniil and I never really talked about his mother. He called her meddlesome and overbearing, but I have no clue how that might translate to her relationship

with Blair. I figured they'd be taking comfort in each other's company, but maybe not.

"Then we'll stop at her place and drop him off."

She puts on a valiant effort of smiling, but it's weak as she jokes, "What, afraid you'll burn if we have a church wedding?"

"Hey, I made it through your wedding just fine. Remember?" I smile back, immediately wanting to kick myself. The last thing she needs is to be reminded of her first wedding. Fuck, *I* don't even want to remember it.

She looked so fucking beautiful as she walked herself down the aisle, her hair shining like gold under the reflections of the stained glass. Her smile was delicate and radiant, and I wanted to steal her away and kiss her until she could think of nothing but me.

"It's better to do this sooner rather than later. If you want to plan something grand further down the line, that's fine, but for right now"—I shrug—"you'll have to settle for something small." I run a thumb over the back of her knuckles.

If things were different, I'd give her whatever she wants. If she wanted to get married in a massive church, I'd do it. If she wanted to get married on the beach in Fiji, I'd make it happen. If she decides that's something she wants, I'll arrange it in a heartbeat.

It'll just have to wait until the dust has settled and I know she's safe.

She nods, taking my words at face value, even while I want to kick my own ass.

"What happens after that?"

"Focus on step one for now. We'll worry about the rest of it as it comes."

CHAPTER 12

Blair

"I'll be back at the usual time to pick him up." I smile. Mila doesn't acknowledge me and simply holds Niko closer to her chest, like I'm going to try and snatch him away from her.

Her eyes skip over me entirely as she smiles at Andrei like he hung the moon.

"Thank you for bringing him," she says, looking awestruck. I twist my hands together, trying not to cringe. She doesn't move until Andrei, shifting from foot to foot, mutters an awkward goodbye, then she turns away and closes the door behind her.

I tug on the hem of my off-white dress on the way back to the car. It's been buried in the back of my closet for years, and I wish I'd let it stay there. I wasn't sure what I was supposed to wear for a spontaneous courthouse wedding, so I settled on something that was dressy but still casual. Then Andrei showed up.

Instead of his normal faded jeans and leather jacket, he's wearing a suit and tie. Even his hair, which is normally casually tousled in a way that shouldn't look as good as it does, has been tamed.

Am I underdressed?

Maybe I should have done more to dress up, but it took more effort than I have in me right now to put on a little makeup and twist my hair into a braid. And none of it hides the fact that I spent half the night crying and the other half tossing and turning, but I did my best.

Besides, it doesn't matter what I look like. It's not like Andrei actually *cares*.

Part of me wants to ask what he expects of this arrangement, but I'm a coward. It's easier to assume that this will be a marriage in name only.

He'll probably have to make a show of having me by his side at some point, and maybe he'll stop by to check on us a little more often than he already does, but that's as far as I expect him to go. At least until he gets over his guilt and whatever flawed logic is pushing him to marry me. Once that's out of the way, I'm sure he'll go through his life pretending I don't exist at all.

Last night he said he never would have hurt me, but that doesn't mean he *likes* me.

Daniil once told me it was Andrei's idea to use me to help tidy up their drug smuggling operations, but I'd bet everything in my bank account that he regretted it immediately. I mean, he can hardly stand to look at me, and when he does, he's usually glowering.

I've tried to be friendly, but my attempts have always fallen flat. Dinner invitations were often declined and attempts to talk to him when he came over were swiftly shut down.

His consistent rejections are the cherry on top of the sundae of my conflicted emotions and thoughts when it comes to An-

drei Voronov. Lingering resentment, constant doubt, and the stupid attraction to him I've never been able to get rid of are a toxic mixture.

It isn't entirely his fault. I know that. I was always worried that I'd find myself on the wrong end of his gun, which makes it hard to be friendly. But I tried.

At least a little bit.

Sometimes.

Everything would have been so much easier if he'd matched the uncomplicated image I had of him when we first met, in the moments before he pulled his gun. Just a tall, handsome stranger with an easy smile and dark, messy hair. For those few blissful seconds, he gave me an illusion. Then the smile fell away, and he pulled the sense of ease out from under my feet.

I'm jolted out of my thoughts when he pulls into a parking lot next to a boring, drab building that blends in with the rest of the equally lackluster businesses around us.

He clears his throat. "C'mon, I don't want to be late for our appointment."

"Don't we need a witness or something?" I ask, even though it's a pointless attempt at stalling. No matter how many times I've turned it over in my head, I can't find a way out of this.

Andrei's right, marrying him will keep me alive. I don't have a choice.

"Not in Illinois."

My heart stutters in my chest with panic, looking around for something that will get me out of this. Some way that means I won't have to be tied to another man who doesn't want to be with me for any reason other than his own sense of duty.

In the back of my mind, there's a younger, more idealistic version of myself that wants to weep at the injustice of it all. I like to think that I'm a practical, grounded person, but it's hard to let go of the romantic ideas I clung to as a child.

I get out of the car and look at Andrei. His hands are shoved into his pockets, a deep frown creasing his brow. The past five years have run me ragged, but they've been nothing but kind to him. The faint lines around the corners of his eyes are a little deeper, but his shoulders are just as broad. When he turns his head, the sun catches the stray gray hairs just starting to peek out along his temples.

His suit looks like it was made just for him, showing off his powerful, muscular frame. Even his tie brings out the cold color of his eyes. I brush my thumb over a wrinkle in my dress, doing my best to force it into submission.

When I let my mind wander, I still linger over hesitant fantasies of what would have happened if he ever looked twice at me. I've never allowed those thoughts to take root, not even in my imagination.

They're too far from reality to waste energy on them. It'd be just as worthwhile to wonder what would happen if I stumbled upon a unicorn.

My cheeks heat when he catches me looking at him.

It's not fair, I think for the hundredth time.

Andrei deserves to be happy, too. He hates me, and he shouldn't have to tie himself to me. Even if it's just on paper.

With that, my mind goes on autopilot, not kicking on again until we're standing in front of the judge, repeating everything he says.

Before I know what's happening, Andrei slips two rings onto my finger. I look at them, a brilliant pink stone sparkling back at me under the fluorescent lights, complemented by a simpler band right below it.

An engagement ring and a wedding ring in one fell swoop.

"You may now kiss the bride," the judge says, and a flash of dread hits me, freezing my whole body.

I should have pushed Andrei harder last night and insisted we hammer out some of the finer details about this arrangement. Because I'm sure *he* doesn't want to kiss *me*, and I don't know if I can stomach the humiliation of having him explain that to some judge I've never met before. Even if we'll probably never see him again, I don't—

All thoughts come to a sudden stop when Andrei grips my waist, pulling me against him while he tugs gently on the end of my braid until I'm looking up at him. In fact, my mind goes wonderfully, blissfully blank as his lips cover mine, warm and unyielding.

My cheeks heat and I feel like I'm caught in a freefall. All I can do is brace myself against him while his lips make the butterflies in my stomach take off, fluttering under my skin.

My hands find his chest, my whole body swaying into his to keep my balance as my knees go weak. I don't know what I thought kissing Andrei would be like, but I wasn't expecting it to set my blood on fire as his tongue prods gently against the seam of my lips, controlling the kiss as easily as he breathes.

Not in my wildest dreams did I think kissing Andrei would feel like this.

When he pulls away, it takes a moment before I can open my eyes, feeling drugged as I look at his pleased smirk, stunned by the thick erection pressing against me while my stomach swoops.

"Oh," I breathe. He chuckles, the sound rumbling against my chest. It takes another moment before I'm able to find my footing again, pulling back as I try to ignore the way he's looking at me.

"That wasn't so bad, was it?" he murmurs.

I can't tell if he's asking me, or himself. My hands are still shaking when I press my fingers against my lips. They're sparking with electricity, buzzing in his absence.

The judge clears his throat, slamming me back down to earth. "Congratulations, you two."

What the hell just happened?

I take a step back, but Andrei's arm is still wrapped around my waist, keeping me against him. He nods and shifts his grip to my hand long enough for us to sign the papers before he pulls me toward the exit.

I squeak out a quick thanks before the door slams shut. If the judge responds, I don't get a chance to hear it.

Now what?

A couple signed forms, a few words, a couple rings, a hot as hell kiss, and we're married? The butterflies vanish as my stomach knots with anxiety. Now do we go back to how things were? Living in each other's orbit, both of us pretending the other doesn't exist?

That kiss was unexpected, sure, but it was just a blip. A single abnormality that won't be repeated.

Right?

Right.

I settle a little at the thought.

The ride home is just as quiet as the ride there. Before I can find a way to fill the silence, I'm standing on the porch of my house.

"When do you think we'll see you again?" I ask, even though I don't want to. I don't expect anything to change. He'll leave, and maybe he'll stop by in a few days to make sure we're doing alright, but that's as far as this arrangement will go.

Andrei squints at me like I'm a puzzle he can't figure out.

"We'll have to make an appearance at some point, right?" I ask hesitantly.

This whole marriage is pointless if no one knows about it, but I'm not exactly champing at the bit to find out what his plans are, either. I have to find a way to reconcile everything that's happened, and the added weight of other people's judgment will only make it harder.

Instead of answering, he turns on his heel and walks back toward his car.

I guess that's my answer.

My hands shake as I unlock the door, but before I'm able to step inside, Andrei's back at my side, a duffle bag thrown over his shoulder.

"Sorry, I forgot this."

I hesitate, but he nods his head toward the door. I don't get a chance to move before he saunters straight in and drops the bag at his feet, fixing me with an intense look.

"What are you doing?"

"I'm moving in."

He's what?

"You're what?"

"I'm not letting my wife sleep under a different roof, and you're not moving out of the only home Niko's ever known. So, I'm moving in."

His gaze doesn't waver, and I stammer uselessly, grasping desperately for the right words. I understand everything he said, but the order he put the words in doesn't make any sense.

"But you have your own place."

He grips my chin between his thumb and forefinger, forcing me to look him in the eye.

"I need you to listen to me, Blair. You're my *wife.*"

He almost sounds... pleased?

That can't be right. I have to be making it up. It's the stress of the past couple months catching up with me, that's all.

"We're going to be living in the same house. If you aren't ready to share a bed with me, that's fine. I'll sleep in the guest room until you are. But I'm going to be here. With you." His jaw flexes, and I try to pull away, but he doesn't let me. His eyes search mine, but for what, I'm not sure. I don't know if he finds it or not, but he lets me go, picks up his bag, and storms up the stairs. Presumably toward the guest room.

What the hell just happened?

Chapter 13

Blair

"Do you still have that blue dress?" Andrei's voice is right behind me, startling me as I drop the puzzle piece in my hand, jumping half out of my skin and knocking my knee against the coffee table. "The one you wore when Riot opened?"

I look at him with wild eyes while I try to rub away the sting, but if he notices, he doesn't let on.

We got married on Tuesday, and this is the most he's said to me in the four days since then. He's always around the house, but he hasn't acted like he wants to be anything other than a distant roommate who happens to get along with my son.

Niko hasn't wanted anything to do with me since the funeral, and the way he trails after Andrei, asking him every question that pops into his head, is both adorable and isolating. Andrei's patience is heartwarming, but I feel like an outsider in my own home.

"No," I answer after my heart rate settles. "I threw it out when I got home that night."

He nods, running a hand through his hair. "Do you have anything like it?"

"What, something to wear to a club?"

He nods again.

"Why?" I ask slowly, a tendril of unease unfurling in my belly.

He watches me like one would a wild animal, walking around the couch and picking up the puzzle pieces that fell to the floor.

"We need to let everyone know that we got married." Protests claw at the tip of my tongue, and I bite my lip to keep them back. "Alexei's new club is opening tonight. Everyone will be there." He shrugs. "It's the perfect opportunity."

I wipe my sweaty palms on my thighs, heart in my throat.

The night Daniil took me to Riot was the first time he brought me to a nightclub, and after the humiliation I felt, it was the last time, too. That night felt like he was throwing me to the wolves and telling them I was fair game. They don't need another chance to take a bite of me.

"Blair, I know you don't want to, but we're not going to get a better opportunity than this. Alexei's hired more security than he'll know what to do with. Things with The Outfit are stable. And I'm not going to leave your side."

That makes me pause.

"You won't?"

"No. Not unless you ask me to." He takes the piece from my hand, gently prying it away and laying on the table with the rest of the puzzle. "And Nadya will be there, so you don't have to stick with me if you don't want to."

"She actually asked me to go with her tonight," I confess.

One corner of his lips quirks up, a ghost of a smile.

"We only have to be there for an hour, tops. And you can spend most of the time with her."

An hour, I think, blowing out a slow breath. I can manage an hour, right? I've done worse things for longer.

"I'll go look through my closet. I probably have something."

Reluctantly, I pull my hand away from his, and his relief is stark in the way his shoulders sag.

***

The mass of writhing bodies moves with the pulsing beat of the music as I lean against an exposed brick wall, counting my breaths and forcing myself to focus on Andrei's presence beside me.

I can't relax. I'm constantly looking around, keeping my eyes peeled for threats.

I thought I saw Pavel when we walked in, and it doesn't matter how much I want to loosen up, I'm not willing to risk running into him with a trip to the bar.

It's been twenty minutes, and true to his word, Andrei's been stuck to me like glue, using his menacing glare to keep anyone from approaching us.

This probably isn't the way he expected us to debut as a couple. In fact, I'm starting to think we shouldn't have bothered coming at all. If Andrei wanted to make a splash, he would've been better off sending a mass text.

If the glower on Andrei's face is any indication, he thinks so, too.

He takes my hand into his, and the warmth of his touch is like a bolt of lightning down my spine.

"C'mon, let's go get a drink." I open my mouth to refuse but stop when I see the gentle way he's looking at me. He tucks me against his side and presses his lips to the top of my head, and I can't find it in me to resist. "Relax, Blair. I've got you." His arm is a warm band around my waist as he pulls me toward the bar, cutting through the crowd with ease.

They part around him like water, giving me a glimpse of Alexei smiling warmly at the small group of people gathered around him. Tonight might be a bust for Andrei and I, but it's nothing short of a rousing success for Alexei. The club is flooded with people enjoying the stunning atmosphere he's curated for them.

The main area is decked out in stunning reds and oranges, dark walls with warm lights highlighting the decor. No detail has been overlooked, and the care that's been put into the appearance alone is a testament to how much work he's done to make everything perfect.

His smile dims slightly when he sees Andrei's arm wrapped around me, his eyes narrowing. I want to duck out of his view, but before I can, Andrei lifts his chin in acknowledgment. Alexei returns the gesture before turning back to his audience.

Andrei turns to me as he makes space for us at the bar, bringing me in front of him, my back plastered against his chest. "What would you like?" he asks, breath hot against my ear.

"Water would be great," I smile tightly.

"Blair." His eyes are hard as he looks down at me, the top of my head just meeting his shoulder. I've never noticed how tall he is before. He towers over me, even when I'm in heels.

How haven't I noticed that before? I swallow, forcing myself to meet his stare head on.

"Yes?" I answer.

His hands barricade me against the bar, his thumb tapping impatiently against the shiny surface.

"You're so tense you look like you're going to snap in half." The deep timbre of his voice is so close it's effortless to hear him, even over the din of the crowd. "Pick something you like, or I'm going to pick the most obnoxiously colored thing I can find."

I frown in confusion, brows drawing together.

"Why would you pick based on color?"

"Because embarrassment can be an excellent motivator."

"I might be out of practice, but I'm pretty sure the colorful drinks tend to get you drunk the fastest."

His eyes drift to the side for a moment. "I'm not trying to get you drunk, just trying to help you relax."

"Comforting," I mumble, twisting the rings on my finger. The weight of them is still unfamiliar, different enough from what I'm used to that I can't forget that they're there. The stone in my new ring is roughly the same size as what Daniil got me, but it's denser, catching me off guard every time I move my hand.

At the thought of Daniil's rings, I reach for the chain tucked into the collar of my dress, making sure they're still there.

I eventually shrug, resigned. "I don't have a preference." He nods and pulls back, allowing me breathing room as he leans forward, commanding the bartender's attention.

I wrap my arms around my waist, feeling cold without him there. Before he turns back, a pair of thin arms wrap around my shoulders, pulling me backward. I gasp, instinct making me struggle before I register Nadya's voice chirping in my ear.

"Blair! I thought you weren't coming tonight!" Her eyes are bright, her cheeks flushed as she greets me with a wide smile. "I'm so glad you're here, though. The rest of these people suck. What changed your mind?"

I have to force myself to smile at her, feeling like a fraud in the face of her genuine enthusiasm. I point at Andrei's back. "He talked me into it." She looks at him and nods, gasping when she looks back at me.

"Woah, where'd you get *that?*" She grabs my hand, pulling it closer while she inspects my ring. "You weren't wearing this the other night, were you? It's gorgeous."

She's right. It *is* gorgeous, especially under the dramatic lights that line the bar. The padparadscha sapphire glints a slightly different shade of orange and pink whenever the angle changes. The smaller diamonds on either side of it sparkle as she twists my hand around to really study it. At first glance, it's not the most ostentatious ring, but it's stunning when you take the time to look at it.

Whenever I take the time to sit still and think, I end up staring at it, unable to believe it's mine, that Andrei picked it.

"It's new, actually," I find myself telling her. "We, uh..." I glance at Andrei, blindly fishing for what to say.

"We got married," Andrei announces, turning around to hand me a bright red drink. Nadya's eyes dart between us, mouth gaping while I shrug.

"Yeah, what he said."

I take a healthy sip of my drink, surprised by the cloying taste of maraschino cherries and vodka.

I don't realize how quiet the crowd immediately around us has gotten until Alexei steps closer. "What was that?" His eyes blaze with a quiet fury that sends shivers down my spine. Without thinking, I take a step backward, colliding with Andrei who puts a possessive hand on my hip.

"We got married. We didn't want to wait, so we had a small ceremony the other day." He presses a kiss against my hair as if we're the very portrait of happy newlyweds, not the barely functional, mismatched pair that we really are. I force myself to smile up at him, trying to appear more relaxed than I am.

Nadya recovers first, pasting a smile on her face and pulling me into a tight hug.

"Congrats!" Her voice has an air of false cheer to it that makes my stomach drop.

"Thanks," I mutter quietly.

Chancing a glance at Alexei, I swallow thickly. He's glaring daggers at the two of us, and I want to crawl home and bury my head in the sand so I don't have to deal with his seething anger.

"Andrei, a word?" he bites out, jaw tight and fists practically vibrating like he's clinging to the last threads of his temper. Andrei looks down at me, raising a brow in question.

Irrationally, I want to cling to him so that I'm not alone among the piranhas, but that would just bring more of Alexei's fury down on me.

I nod, trying to give an encouraging smile. "You two go talk. Nadya and I can go dance for a while. Right?"

She grins, already gripping my arm, ready to drag me toward the dance floor. "We won't go far," she promises him.

"Fine," he replies after a beat too long. "But make sure you stay where I can see you, alright?" I nod, but Nadya's already pulling me toward the center of the room. She's laughing, and I laugh along with her, ignoring the edge of hysteria building inside me.

I take another sip of my drink as the song changes, letting myself trust that Andrei's keeping an eye on me and letting myself enjoy the moment. Nadya tugs me against her as we dance, grinning while we're enveloped by the crowd.

I can't remember the last time I allowed myself to just relax and have fun. Probably not since before I met Andrei.

Nadya pulls me close, face against mine so she can be heard. "So, you got married, huh?"

I nod, chewing on the inside of my lip. "It was a last-minute sort of thing." I can feel how hot my cheeks are, and I shake my head to push the sensation away.

"I didn't know you were..." She narrows her eyes, no doubt searching for a tactful way to say *sleeping with your dead husband's best friend*. I put her out of her misery before she can embarrass us both.

"We weren't," I rush. "Like I said, this was a surprise. For both of us." I feel like I'm shouting, but she shakes her head like she can't hear me. Rather than belt out the whole damn story for everyone in the room, I point in the direction of the bathroom, hoping it'll be quieter.

Looping her arm through mine, she heads in that direction. And thankfully as soon as we're away from the dance floor, it's immediately easier to hear myself think. She twirls her head toward me, fixing me with a serious look.

"It's a brand-new thing? Totally unexpected?" she asks, and I nod. "Well, from what I've heard, you picked a good one. As far as Bratva men go, anyway. And he's not bad to look at, either." She grins while my cheeks turn pink.

There's no point refuting that. I've always thought that Andrei was attractive. With his broad shoulders, commanding presence, and gray eyes that are so gorgeous they're almost hard to look at, I'd typically consider myself lucky as hell to be with someone like him. If this were a real marriage, and we actually loved each other, I'd want to show him off at every opportunity.

But it's not real, and we're not in love, so I just smile at her.

"He isn't hard on the eyes, I'll give you that," I admit.

"Oh, come on." She gives me a knowing grin. "He's hot as hell. And now he's taken. So, give me something to work with while I'm mourning. How'd he propose? What was the ceremony like? Is he as good in bed as I imagine?"

I can't look her in the eye, and I definitely can't tell her that I don't know.

"Or is this his version of a joke so he can piss off Alexei?" My stomach drops. "Because if that's what Andrei wants, I'm willing to bet everyone out there's talking about his announcement

and not Alexei's big night. So, I'd say mission accomplished."
She's still grinning, and I can't tell if she's joking or not.

I hadn't even considered that.

But Andrei isn't the type of man to go out of his way to
fuck with someone. He wouldn't go to the length of actually
marrying me just to upset Alexei.

"I don't think he intended to upset Alexei." I shrug. "I think
that's just a happy coincidence." She chuckles, leaning a hip
against the sink as she fixes her makeup.

When she speaks again, her voice is quieter than before,
mindful of the fact that the room is still full. "So, he isn't just
fucking around with you? I don't have to kick his ass?"

The image of Nadya facing off against six-foot-something
Andrei with all his muscular bulk makes me laugh as I shake my
head.

"Good, because I might be able to handle myself, but he'd
snap me like a twig. I mean, I think his forearm is as thick as my
thigh."

Soon, we're laughing, the conversation quickly moving on to
safer topics as we exit the bathroom. I don't like that I've misled
her, but something in my chest feels a little lighter at sharing
some part of what happened with her.

I just don't know if I trust her enough to tell her the full story
of how conflicted I feel.

How I don't know how to deal with being around him all the
time. How seeing Andrei at the breakfast table in the morning
makes him look different than the man I thought I knew. How
I'm sure Andrei's only doing this because he feels like he has to.
How I can't stop thinking about the way he kissed me.

How my new husband can barely stand to be in the same room as me.

Nadya's telling me a story about Alexei and one of his other clubs when I blindly walk into a wall of muscle. I glance up to apologize, but my smile dies on my face as my mouth goes bone-dry.

Pavel's deadly glare kills my mood faster than I thought possible. Involuntarily, I try to take a step back, but Nadya's arm is firm where it's linked with mine. I've tried so hard to get over my fear of him, but my body refuses to get on board, no matter what I do.

"Blair, what a surprise." His voice is the same bored monotone that it always is, but I flinch at it all the same. More than anything, I want to run back into the restroom and get away from him, but I'm not foolish enough to think that a sign on a door would keep him from hurting me if he wants to.

"Hey, Pavel," Nadya chimes, proving that she's far braver than me. "What're you doing hanging around outside the ladies' room?" Her smile is serene, but there's a frustrated glint in her eyes. His empty gaze flicks in her direction, and behind him I spot Andrei storming toward us, Alexei hot on his heels. Seeing him allows me to take a breath, but I still ache to turn on my heel and run.

Pavel's eyes turn back to me, something dark brewing while he looks me up and down.

Not a moment later, Andrei's there, putting himself between us while Alexei pulls Nadya to his side and away from mine. It isn't until she's no longer there that I realize how much I was relying on her to keep me steady. I clasp onto the back of Andrei's jacket.

"Ah, here's the man of the hour. Congratulations, Alexei. Tonight has been a rousing success. And Andrei." He grins slowly, looking every bit the predator I know he is. "I hear that congratulations are in order for you as well." He tilts his head to the side while Andrei moves another step in front of me.

I'm not too proud to refuse him as a human shield. It's not nearly as likely that Pavel would hurt him. Not in such a crowded place, anyway. But I don't want Andrei to do anything that would put his standing within the Bratva at risk, either.

"What is it about Blair that made you so eager to marry her?" Pavel asks, voice full of malice. "She must have a magical cunt." Andrei lets loose a growl that vibrates through his chest, rumbling where I cling to him. "How much would it cost for an hour? Or, hell, maybe twenty minutes would do."

My face blanches.

Nadya moves in the corner of my eye, struggling while Alexei holds her, moving them both further away from us. I can't see Pavel from behind Andrei, but I can only imagine the condescending grin on his face as Andrei's shoulders draw tight, his hand flexing like he's itching to grab the gun I watched him slip into the holster at the small of his back before we left.

"I'd ask that you not speak so crudely about my *wife*," he snarls, low and menacing.

"Yes, your wife. For now, anyway. It seems it doesn't take her long to jump from one man to the next."

I roll my lips together to hold back my reaction, his words hitting me square in the chest.

"How long until you can expect her to be another man's bed?"

I want to scream at Pavel that it's *his* fault I had to jump into another relationship, but I can't. I close my eyes, taking a deep breath through my nose.

"What my wife does is none of your business, Pavel. However, you've made what you do mine. When's the last time you stopped by the warehouse near the train yard?" Andrei doesn't move, but the energy around us does.

I lean around him, watching as the vein in Pavel's throbs.

"Why would you ask that?"

"You know why."

A tense beat passes, and I duck back behind Andrei again, shamelessly hiding.

"You don't have any proof."

Andrei lifts a single shoulder, tilting his head to one side. "Are you so sure of that?" It sounds like a challenge, and Pavel must hear it plain as day. "If you want to have this conversation, there are better venues. We don't need to make a scene on Alexei's big night." Andrei's voice is as harsh as I've ever heard it. I look around, only now noticing that the people around us have slowed, lingering while they watch.

Apparently, Pavel notices it, too. "I'll be in touch," he grunts before turning on his heel and storming away. Once he's engulfed by the crowd, Andrei turns around, running his hands down my arms as he looks me over like he's making sure I'm in one piece.

"You alright?" His voice is softer than it was when he was talking to Pavel, soothing my raw nerves like a cool breeze. As I nod, he lets out a breath. "Good."

He looks to his right and I follow, seeing Nadya and Alexei having a quiet argument. I want to say goodbye to her and apologize to Alexei for all the trouble we've caused him, but I'm terrified of hanging around and chancing Pavel cornering me alone.

"Can we go home?" I ask, slipping my hand into Andrei's and twining our fingers together.

He presses his forehead to mine as he nods, squeezing my hand.

Chapter 14

Blair

My head falls back against the seat as I watch Andrei drive, admiring the confident way he navigates around the unfamiliar area. Streetlights flash overhead, illuminating his strong profile every few seconds, each one giving me a glimpse of things I've never allowed myself to notice before.

Flash. I watch his long lashes as he blinks.

Flash. He's let his stubble grow out since the funeral.

Flash. I wonder what it would feel like if I kissed him again.

"I can feel you staring, *zolotse.*"

I scrunch my face as he looks at me for a moment before turning his attention back to the road.

"What does that mean?" It isn't the first time he's called me that. I don't think it's an insult, but I'd like to know for sure before I get used to it.

He sits up straighter, his brows drawn together. "You don't speak Russian?" He sounds baffled, and it's almost enough to make me laugh. I shake my head, refusing to feel shame over it.

"Why not?"

"No real reason." I shrug. The lie tastes bitter, but there's no reason to pick at an old wound.

After I met Andrei and Daniil, I tried to use a language learning app to teach myself Russian. I'd even asked Daniil to help me practice early on in our relationship, but he refused, saying it was better if I didn't know.

At first, I thought he was trying to protect me from overhearing anything that would get me in trouble if things ended up going sideways. Now, I know he just wanted to have some part of his life that I was permanently shut out of.

What was the point of learning when Daniil, the only person I would have spoken it with, was so against it? I gave up almost as soon as I started.

Andrei pulls to a stop at a red light, turning his full focus onto me, like I'm a puzzle that he can't figure out.

"Does Niko speak Russian?"

"Of course he does. Daniil and Mila have been teaching him since he was born. Hell, Mila almost exclusively speaks to him in Russian." Probably because it's a great way to exclude me, but, hey, I'll give her the benefit of the doubt and say she's doing it because she's a big fan of immersive learning.

"Do you want to learn?"

"It'd be nice." I shrug. "I'd like to help Niko learn, but the fact that I don't know how to speak Russian isn't keeping me up at night, either."

His jaw flexes as the light changes, and he eases back into traffic. The drone of tires on the road and the soft purr of the engine wash over us, filling the space with a comfortable white noise that allows me to relax as I watch him. For as stressed out as I was on the way to the club, now the journey is soothing as Andrei navigates toward familiar streets.

When we got in the car, he ditched his jacket and rolled the sleeves of his shirt up to his elbows, something I'm grateful for as I watch the muscles in his forearms flex while he drives. Each movement is strong and confident as he turns the wheel, the veins in his hands captivating my attention.

What would those hands feel like against me? Would he be soft and gentle? Or would he be strong and domineering? Is Andrei the kind of man that takes what he wants, not giving me even a moment to second-guess myself, and only let me feel what he wants me to? Or would he be content to lie back and let me set the pace, let me decide how he gets to touch me?

I bite the inside of my cheek as I shift in my seat.

I need to wait until I'm alone to ask myself those sorts of questions.

"I could teach you, if you'd like," he offers, tearing me out of my daydream. He doesn't even blink, but it feels like he just shifted the foundation I'm standing on.

I can't afford to let myself fall for him, but when he offers something like that, without a *but* or an *if*, I can picture a world where, like a total idiot, I throw away my dignity and let myself fall. Just a little bit.

He isn't even interested, I tell myself. *Don't set yourself up for heartbreak like that.*

I swallow thickly, clasping my hands together in my lap. "If you have time, I'd appreciate that."

"We'll find time." He smiles, making my stomach flip like I'm at the top of a roller coaster, waiting for the descent into oblivion.

I mutter a quiet thanks, unable to meet his gaze.

As the car pulls to a stop in front of the house, I can't help but wonder if Andrei's comfortable here. He's taken up residence in one of the guest rooms, just as he promised, but there has to be something I can do to make it feel more like a home for him.

Maybe I should clear out a room for him to use as an office, something so he doesn't have to feel cramped in one spot.

As Andrei dismisses Mila, thanking her again for coming over at the last minute, I slip into Niko's room and check on him. He's tucked into his bed, safe and sound. His breaths come out in easy, sleepy puffs.

I expect to feel a momentary flicker of guilt over leaving him, but if it's there, it has no teeth in place of the gratitude I feel for what Andrei did at the club.

He defended me. Even though it might have consequences for him later, he didn't hesitate. He just put himself between Pavel and I, like it wasn't even a choice. Like it was an instinct.

I can't remember the last time anyone did something like that for me. I swallow the lump in my throat.

God, I hope Andrei doesn't get in trouble for it.

When I step into the hall, I'm only mildly surprised to see him leaning against the wall across from me. I close the door behind me and move to step around him, even less surprised when he follows me toward my room.

"I'm sorry that I let Pavel get close to you," he says, voice husky, hands shoved deep into his pockets. He looks contrite, his face absent of the scowl I thought was a permanent fixture. He's always been such a stalwart figure, never betraying what he's really feeling, that the sight catches me off guard.

"It's my fault. I was the one who wandered off, remember?"

Andrei wraps his arms around me suddenly, pulling me against him, so close that I can hear his heart beating in his chest. I relax against his hold, trying to keep the rapid racing of my own heart under control.

"None of this is your fault." He presses his lips against the top of my head. "Don't be so hard on yourself."

I hide my smile in his chest.

"You know, I really did have a good time tonight."

He laughs lightly, sliding his hands down until they rest on my hips. "For some reason, I'm not sure I believe you."

"You don't have to believe me for it to be true," I chuckle. "It went better than I thought it would." The fuzzy feeling in my chest is making me dizzy, but the firmness of his hands keeps me grounded. I pull back and look at him, mesmerized by the different shades of silver and gray in his eyes glinting in the low light. "And thank you. For standing up for me."

His face relaxes, a smile playing at the corners of his mouth. It's a sight so intoxicating I couldn't look away even if I wanted to. "Anytime."

His grip is loose enough that I could pull away from him if I wanted to, but I don't. I don't want to be any further from him than I am.

His warm breaths intermingle with mine, making me realize just how quiet it is, how dimly lit the hallway is. My skin feels like it's buzzing. Before I can second-guess myself, I stand my toes and press my lips against his, my blood rushing in my ears.

His grip tightens, holding me even closer against him as his lips move against mine, his tongue gently prodding against my mouth, testing without being tentative. I lean into him, letting him take my weight.

The way he holds me against him, tight enough that I know I wouldn't be able to pull away even if I tried, has the heat between my thighs rising faster than I know what to do with. When I shift, I can't miss the outline of his growing erection as he pulls me closer, not an inch of space between us.

Oh.

He pulls back just far enough to ask, "Can we go to your bedroom?"

I nod in a daze, his nose brushing against my cheek and setting off sparks under my skin. I pull away with great reluctance, taking his hands in mine as I lead him down the hall.

The heat in the way he looks at me makes me feel like I'm standing on the edge of *something*.

Something big and scary that I don't want to give up. Refusing to shy away from it, I open the door, stepping through and pulling him with me, his hand scorching in mine.

As soon as the door shuts behind him, his lips are back on mine, kissing me in a way that feels like he's the master of every sensation coursing through my veins, directing every nerve until I'm feeling exactly what he wants me to.

Andrei unzips my dress, and with just a tug it falls, pooling around my ankles. He steps back, looking at me as if trying to memorize every inch of my body, while I try not to shift away from his hungry gaze. I shiver under the force of it while his hands skim along the edges of my bra, goosebumps breaking out across my skin.

"Beautiful." His tone is almost awed.

"You're not so bad yourself," I say, hands undoing the buttons of his shirt, pretending the way he's watching me doesn't make my insides squirm.

Each button reveals more and more skin, granting me access to the tattoos I didn't know he had, winding designs that flow into each other. They cover his chest and shoulders, a work of art that does nothing to distract me from his tight muscles.

And fuck me, I want to trace them with my tongue.

As his hand trails along my stomach, I instinctively flinch away, cursing internally when he freezes. His hand pauses in its perusal and when I reluctantly meet his eyes, they're sharp and unrelenting. He looks at me reverently, like he's ready to worship every part of me.

His pupils are fully dilated, swallowing the silver of his irises to a thin ring. Still, he manages to make it feel like he's reading me like an open book, every single insecurity exposed to his hungry gaze.

For the most part, I've come to terms with the stretch marks that mar my hips and stomach. I've told myself a hundred times before, they're nothing but proof that I managed to create something incredible, just faded silver lines that helped bring me my son.

But what are the odds Andrei will see them that way? I don't want to see any inkling of disappointment—or worse, disgust—on his face, so I drop my eyes and start tugging at his belt before he can say anything.

My head tilts back when he wraps his fingers through the ends of my hair, tugging until he has my attention, compelling me to back at him. "Don't hide from me, *zolotse*." His expression is greedy, and when I take a step back, he follows, his breath warm on my face and his grip unwavering as his fingers dip into the band of my panties.

My nipples pebble in my bra, aching as Andrei's hands find my hips before sliding down to my ass. I let out an embarrassing sound when he grips tightly, lifting me until my legs wrap around his hips, my arms winding around his neck so I don't fall.

He walks toward the bed, lips against mine. "I want to see you. All of you. Every inch of your perfect skin, every shiver, every mark and imperfection." His lips trace along a freckle on my shoulder. "I've waited a long time to see you like this. Don't even *think* about depriving me." Bending forward, he deposits me gently on the bed, completely at odds with his hard tone. "Tell me you understand."

"I understand," I breathe, lightheaded in the face of his confession.

"Good. Then finish undressing." He shrugs his shirt off, letting it fall to the floor and exposing more ink on his shoulders and arms. I scramble to undo my bra, tossing it without care and rushing to do the same with my panties.

For long seconds, I stare at a tattoo of a raven in mid-flight escaping from the rest of the designs on his chest before I blink, focusing on the smattering of chest hair before my eyes eventually settle on the dark hair that trails into the waistband of his pants as he takes off his belt. He hooks his thumbs into his pants, pulling them and his boxer briefs off in one fell swoop.

A thrill runs along my spine when I see just how big he is. Thick, long, and pulsing in his hand as he gives himself a slow stroke.

He's like this because of me. *For* me.

Fuck.

Not giving me time to properly admire him, he drops to his knees and wraps his hands around my thighs, pulling me to the edge of the bed. I shiver, too turned on to feel embarrassed over how wet I am as his hot breath washes over my pussy.

"You're even more gorgeous than I imagined," he says right before impales me with his tongue, pleasure shooting through me at the first touch. My hands tangle in his hair while he attacks my clit, my hips bucking under the assault. When he pulls back enough to laugh breathlessly against the crease of my thigh, I choke on a sob.

"Please don't stop," I whine, trying to urge him back where I want him. I pull on his hair, and he hums a pleased sound against my pussy, the vibrations echoing through me.

"*Fuck.*"

Without warning, he slides two fingers into me, pushing me right over the edge.

"Andrei!" My muscles jerk tight, my world narrowing down to his touch, to the pleased sounds he's making as I come apart. Self-doubt, insecurity, and worry all fall away in the wake of his onslaught. He laps at my release, drawing out each wave until I'm too sensitive and have to pull him away.

He smirks as he sits up, pressing urgent kisses against my stomach.

When he crawls over me, I reach out to run my fingers over his tight chest, desperate to know what his muscles feel like under my hands.

He rearranges my body, and when my hands slide low enough to wrap around the base of his cock, he grips both of my wrists tightly in one hand, pulling them above my head, while leaving a wet trail of precum where he grinds his length against my hip.

Lips against my neck, he groans, "Please tell me you're on birth control. Tell me I can fuck you bare." His voice is thick with want, and even though I just came, I want him inside me more than I want my next breath. He tweaks a nipple, and I swallow a gasp as I nod. "You're fucking perfect," he grunts.

With his free hand, he runs his length up and down my slit, hitting my clit with every pass. With his next swipe, I move my hips, urging him exactly where I want him, but Andrei ignores me with a chuckle.

"What do you want, Blair?"

Without hesitation, I answer, "You."

"You already have me," he rumbles lowly, pressing hot kisses along the column of my throat, down the valley between my breasts. I whine, silently begging him to fuck me, to stop this delicious torture.

"Precious," he whispers against the top of my breast, so quietly I wonder if I heard him correctly. "*Zolotse* means precious, like gold."

Before I can process his words, he slams inside me in a single movement, knocking the air out of my lungs in a silent scream.

I'm so fucking full I have to gasp to get a breath; it feels like he's setting me on fire. On his next thrust, he lets my hands free and grabs my hips. His grip is just shy of bruising as my legs wrap around his hips, holding tight.

I hold onto his shoulders. The scrape of his chest hair against my nipples slowly drives me insane, each touch sending sparks that push me closer and closer to the precipice.

I roll my hips against him as each slow, powerful thrust fills me completely, again and again.

"Fuck," he pants into the crook of my neck, his hand slipping between my legs so his thumb can rub unrelenting circles on my clit. "Come on my cock, Blair. I need to feel you." Like my body was waiting for permission, the wire snaps, and my vision flashes white.

"Blair," he chants as he ruts into me until he stills, moaning as he swells inside me, each pulse filling me with warmth. Collapsing on top of me, he rolls to the side just enough not to crush me. I press a kiss against his strong jaw, limbs feeling like jelly as I catch my breath.

"Holy shit," I pant as he pulls me into his arms, rolling onto his back, his legs still tangled with mine. He runs a hand along my spine, and I shiver.

"You alright?" he asks against my hair, like he didn't just fuck me into the mattress and knock me off my axis in the process.

"Better than alright," I snort, half asleep against his chest. "You?"

"I'm perfect," he answers, voice soft with a smile. I close my eyes, feeling more comfortable than I have in months as I listen to his contented breaths until I fall asleep.

CHAPTER 15

Andrei

Blair and Niko's laughter echoes through the house, their combined happiness a balm over my frustration as I close the door to my new bedroom. In an ideal world, I'd be with them. I'd be able to join them in the kitchen, laugh with them, and bask in the warmth of everything that's changed in such a short amount of time.

If Alexei wasn't a fucking asshole, I'd be able to watch Blair as she moves comfortably through her own space, her eyes flitting to me when she thinks I'm not watching, and relive every moment of last night.

I've spent so long dreaming about having her underneath me, of having the opportunity to worship her body and delighting in hearing her cry out as she comes for me. For years, I've laid awake at night, aching to make her mine as I take her over and over again.

But my dreams had nothing on reality.

Blair has my ring on her finger. I'm living in her house. And I never have to wonder what she looks like when she's screaming with pleasure because the image is permanently burned in my mind, a sight so glorious I'll savor it until my dying breath.

I should be over the fucking moon, but every time I try to indulge in the fruits of my labor, someone's there to blow up my phone and drag me away from my new life.

"You couldn't think of a better way to announce your farce of a marriage? You could've announced you were going away for a honeymoon, or sent out a fucking postcard, but *no*. You had to show up and overshadow my hard work and make the evening about you," Alexei seethes, not giving me a chance to interrupt him.

Honestly, I'm impressed he was able to wait until the next afternoon before he decided to rip my head off.

"I'm sick of Blair's love life being the center of attention at my nightclubs, Andrei."

"She's not thrilled about it either, you know." I fight to keep my voice level, to not let him know what I really think of this little tantrum.

Niko's better behaved than he's being right now.

"Sure," he spits. "It's just a coincidence, right?"

"If you really want to know, I practically had to drag her there last night. And, for the record, it isn't her fault Daniil used Riot's opening to humiliate her," I tell him with an edge to my tone.

That night was a disaster on all fronts, but none of it was Blair's fault. The only reason I even went was for a chance to see Blair all dressed up, and instead I was treated to the torture of watching her curling further and further into herself while she watched Daniil flirting with Emiliya, broadcasting his infidelity to the entire Bratva.

Then some *mudak* from The Outfit decided to make a splash and shoot up the place, and I got to watch Blair's heartbreak firsthand when instead of hurrying to her, Daniil made sure Emiliya got out safely.

Instead of going home with her husband after a night out, she silently cried while I drove her home, and I couldn't do a damn thing to comfort her.

Unfortunately for Alexei, the shooting wasn't enough to overshadow the gossip about the Krutikovs and their soap opera-worthy marriage. And apparently he still hasn't learned to let it go.

"Besides, Pavel's the one who caused a scene last night. The only thing Blair and I did was share our good news with your sister."

I don't want to waste my day calming Alexei down. It was bad enough when, instead of waking up with Blair, I had to sneak out of the house before sunrise to handle a mess of someone else's making. Every time I think I'll get a chance to apologize to her and make up for it, I get pulled away for one thing or another.

"And yet the only thing anyone wants to talk about is the two of you. I've worked for the past two years to ensure last night went off without a hitch, Andrei."

"What are you, a child?" I scoff. "I wasn't aware you were so insecure you needed a pat on the back and to be made the center of attention in order to feel gratified. In that case, good job, Alexei. Everything was great. You did a wonderful job."

His growl would be amusing if I weren't preoccupied with straining to listen to whatever song Niko's singing while he and Blair play in his bedroom.

"That has nothing to do with it and you know it," Alexei bites out.

"Then tell me what your real issue is. If it isn't your ego, then what's your fucking problem with my wife?"

His silence is loud and it's more than I have patience for right now.

"You want to know what I think?" I ask him.

"Not really, but you're going to tell me anyway, aren't you?"

"I think you're still pissed everything went wrong when Riot opened, but you can't take it out on the people you really want to blame. You can't lash out at Maksim for how shitty our relationship with The Outfit was when the shooting happened. You can't tell Pavel what you really think about him being an asshole last night, and you know I won't put up with it if you try to blame me for it. So you're taking it out on Blair because she's an easy target and, until now, no one's said anything when you treat her like shit."

"I didn't treat her like shit," Alexei protests, but there's no heat to it.

I'm not foolish enough to think he's going to apologize to her, but Alexei needs to understand things are going to be different now.

I'm not Daniil. I'm not going to let people treat Blair like she's anything less than she really is. Alexei—and everyone else, for that matter—can start treating her with the respect she deserves, or they can fuck off.

"Next time you two have a big announcement, don't do it at my fucking clubs, alright?"

"About that," I can't help but say just to get a rise out of him. "Can we rent Savage for a late wedding reception?"

Not that I think Blair would even want a reception. I'm willing to bet she'd like to keep news of our nuptials under wraps, but if I want to keep her safe, we don't really have that option. Whether her hesitation is because she regrets marrying me entirely, or because she isn't ready to deal with the judgment of marrying so soon after Daniil's death doesn't matter.

Eventually, when she's more comfortable with our new relationship, we can do something more public.

A vow renewal. Or a honeymoon, like Alexei said.

Until then, I'll settle for the whole Bratva knowing that she's chosen to be with me, no matter how fraught the circumstances may be.

"Fuck off, Andrei," he snarls and hangs up.

Good. I hope he gets so worked up he's still livid come morning. It's the least he deserves.

I look around the guest room to calm myself down. I'm not used to being here yet, but I refuse to make the space my own, no matter how many times Blair insists I'm free to do so. I'm not going to let myself settle in until we're sharing the same bed every night.

The few pieces of clothing I brought with me are still mostly shoved into the single bag I brought with me after the wedding. I'll need to go back to my condo and get the rest of my clothes at some point, but every time I leave the house, the only thing I can think about is coming back as soon as I can.

Coming back to Blair, being welcome in her home, is a greater high than I ever thought possible.

If I'd been thinking, I would have packed up my whole condo and arranged to sell everything inside it after the wedding, but I didn't. My thoughts had been consumed by an almost giddy feeling, knowing she was welcoming me into her life.

After years of being nothing but her kidnapper, her husband's best friend, the man she's spent so much time hating, I finally have a chance to take care of her.

After so long watching her look after Daniil and Niko, I can finally take some of the weight off of her shoulders and help ease her burdens.

I just have to convince her to let me.

It'll happen eventually, but I've spent years lamenting lost opportunities with Blair, and my patience is running thinner than I'd like it to.

My phone dings with yet another text from Maksim demanding I attend to even more bullshit I don't care about, and I bite out a curse, tempted to chuck the damn thing at the wall.

So much for my plan to join Blair and Niko for dinner.

After everything is a little more settled, I'll be free to start incorporating myself into their lives. Last night was everything I could have ever asked for, but I want more.

I want her to do more than just accept me into her life; I want her to crave me the way I do her. I want Blair to understand the depth of my feelings, and I want more than an occasional night in her bed.

I want to spend every day and night by her side. I want her to love me the way I love her.

Maybe tomorrow people will learn to handle their own shit, and I'll be able to savor Blair's laughter the way I want to.

I snatch the jacket off the top of my bag and head toward the sound of her melodic laughter. If I have to leave, at least she's going to know I'm coming back later.

CHAPTER 16

Blair

"Where's Niko?"

I peek over the top of my book at Andrei as he leans against the door jamb, eyes assessing.

"It's Thursday," I shrug. "He's at Mila's." He's quiet for a moment, and I go back to my book, assuming the conversation's over.

"When will he be back?"

"At the normal time."

"Which is when?"

His brows are furrowed in confusion, and if I weren't so annoyed with him, it'd be endearing. "I typically drop him off with her in the morning," I say, sliding my bookmark between the pages. "They like spending time together and it's nice to have a day off from being a parent. I'll go pick him up after dinner."

I kept Niko home last week, wanting to keep him close with so many things changing at home, but I couldn't refuse to take him to Mila's again.

Andrei doesn't reply, but I don't expect him to. Instead, I'm treated to the sound of his footsteps as they fade down the hall.

I shouldn't have expected sleeping together to have changed anything between us, but, apparently, I did. When I woke up the next morning, Andrei was long gone, the sheets where he'd been were cool to the touch, and I was left pretending I wasn't disappointed.

That disappointment slowly turned to anger as the day went on.

It's not that I expected him to wake me up with breakfast in bed or anything, but it would've been nice if he hadn't rushed away at the first opportunity.

He didn't need to make his regret so obvious.

I try to tell myself that he did his good deed in defending me against Pavel, and he got what he wanted out of it. And I try to ignore the little voice in my head that's so eager to point out that when I looked up what *zolotse* meant, it did, in fact, mean exactly what he said: Precious.

It doesn't matter if that doesn't align with something a man who just wanted to get laid would say. Accepting he might have cared about me before that night would mean I have to accept that sleeping with me changed things for him, and I might not be enough for him, either. And I'm not ready for that. Not now, and maybe not ever.

I just have to accept things as they are and hope Andrei doesn't turn his back on me when this arrangement gets inconvenient.

If I felt a flicker of hope things would be different when I fell asleep in his arms, that's on me, not him. It was a foolish mistake, and I don't plan on letting it happen again.

My thoughts stop dead in their tracks when Andrei storms back into the room and drops a gift bag from one of the fancy shops downtown in my lap, knocking my book out of my hands.

"What's this?" I ask hesitantly,

"Open it," he prompts. With shaking hands, I remove the delicate tissue paper to reveal a stunning dress that's nicer than anything I own. I sit it up straighter as I pull it from the bag, holding it up so I can see it fully.

Deep blue silk flows through my hands like water while I examine the details, from the thin halter straps to the plunging neckline. I stop to admire the button detailing at the bottom of the backless design. Everything about it, from the color to the way it's cut, is stunning, and I'm not sure if I want to put it away somewhere so I can look at it when I need a pick-me-up, or sprint upstairs and try it on immediately.

"Andrei, this is beautiful."

"Go get ready. I'm going to take you to dinner."

"You're what?"

He shrugs, looking me straight in the eye. "If I had known you built date nights into your schedule, I would have taken you out last week, too."

Wait, what?

"What're you—"

He turns around to leave, cutting me off before I can figure out what I'm trying to say.

"Just wear the dress, Blair. It'll look nice on you," he calls over his shoulder, leaving me even more confused.

I haven't been on a real date since before Niko was born.

Wait, is this even a real date? Or some sort of work event? I want to think that Andrei would give me a heads up if he was taking me out somewhere where I might run into his colleagues, but it wouldn't be the first time I was wrong about him.

And what did he mean when he said he would've taken me out last week, too? Does Andrei *want* to take me on dates?

How long do I have to get ready? What if we're going somewhere that requires a reservation?

I check my phone for the time. A quarter to six.

I sprint upstairs for the bathroom so I can put on makeup and do my hair in time to comply with the unwarranted deadline I've set for myself.

So I don't make us late. For the dinner I wasn't expecting.

Maybe I'm over-thinking this.

Taking a deep breath, I force my shoulders to relax. Andrei called it a date, but it's probably just another chance to make a public appearance. There's no reason for me to get worked up over nothing.

Half an hour later, I pull on a pair of silver heels that complement the dress I'm still not convinced is real. I might not be a dispatcher anymore, but apparently, I can still work well under pressure. Regardless of what happens tonight, it won't be my appearance that embarrasses me. For once, I don't look like a frumpy mom. Instead, I look like someone who actually belongs at Andrei's side.

The dress hugs my curves like a dream come true. The open back leaves me with no choice but to pray gravity looks kindly on me, and when I look in the mirror I had to stop and convince myself that he actually bought this for me and this isn't some cruel joke.

I haven't been this dressed up since my first wedding, and part of me is excited to go out and have a chance to show off.

Andrei waits for me downstairs, and when he sees me his mouth quirks into a pleased smile. The butterflies in my stomach break free of their cages, tearing apart the locks I've used to bar them shut and fluttering through my chest, tickling my ribs.

He's looking at me like I'm the most beautiful woman in the world, and his silence is a compliment I don't know how to accept.

I want to tease him and tell him to pick his jaw up off the floor, but my confidence is still too shaky.

"So, where are we going?" I squeak out while I pick up my purse. I nearly jump out of my skin when I stand up again and find Andrei right behind me. He doesn't say a word, just places one of his strong hands on the back of my neck and twists me around until we're standing chest to chest.

"You look stunning, *zolotse*," he whispers before he leans down, slotting his mouth over mine for the first time in nearly a week.

The part of me that's worked so hard to be mad at him is silent in the wake of his quiet affection. I lay a hand against his chest as I breathe in the warm, woodsy smell of his cologne.

Maybe it would be easier to hold onto my anger and indigna-tion if I didn't know how good it can be when I let myself give into him. Or maybe I just don't want him to stop.

But he does, and I can't help but whimper at the loss. He smirks and rests his forehead against mine, his minty breath wrapping around me like a physical embrace while his hands caress my hips.

"I don't want to leave," he murmurs against my lips. "But if we don't, I'll end up tearing this dress off you. And I want to show you off first."

My thighs clench.

"Is it still an option later?"

He gives me a wicked smirk as he reaches around me to open the door. "If tonight goes well, you can plan on it."

"Oh, well, in that case," I chuckle, "let's go."

I'm still smiling when he guides me into the passenger seat of his car, his hand on my knee for the whole drive, making it hard to think of anything except for that singular point of contact.

It's like he has a blueprint that tells him exactly how to get under my skin, and I don't know how to get him out.

It'll only end up hurting me, I know that, but I can't figure out how to stop feeling like this. I *like* that he consumes so much space in my thoughts, not giving me room to worry about anything else. I *like* that there are little signs of him around the house everywhere I look.

A pair of shoes next to the front door. A jacket thrown carelessly over the back of a chair. A notepad with his messy handwriting discarded when he's forgotten about it. They're all little things, but they make me think he's planning on sticking around for a while. And that's a dangerous thought to have.

Because when he leaves—and he will, it's inevitable with a man like him—I'll never recover.

He parks the car and circles around the front to open my door, waving off the valet. With my hand in his, he reluctantly tosses his keys to the kid, face looming with unspoken threats that have the valet looking like he's going to piss his pants.

His hand scorches against my back as he guides me into the restaurant.

"Mr. Voronov," the hostess greets with a polite smile before he can announce himself. "Right this way." Wordlessly, she guides us through the dining room, toward a private table softly lit by a trio of votive candles.

He surprises me once more, and like the gentleman I know he isn't, Andrei pulls out my seat for me. I can't keep my smile to myself. As he takes the seat across from me, I seize the opportunity to take him in.

He's wearing a finely tailored suit with a crisp gray shirt that stretches tight across his chest as he settles into his own seat. It's a welcome sight, but I find myself missing the casual outfits he usually wears around the house.

I look at the fine art in gilded frames hanging on walls, then at the delicately folded napkins decorating the table. Maybe his jeans would be frowned upon here.

Well, that's their loss. They don't even know what they're missing.

Still, he manages to look right at home among all the luxurious details.

How often does he come to places like this? It must be pretty regularly if the hostess knows who he is by sight alone.

For all I know, maybe he owns this place. He's never struck me as someone who's bothered with running a legitimate business for the guise of respectability, but maybe he does. Or maybe he just happens to frequent a place that seems perfectly designed to woo a date.

God, I hope he's secretly a business owner.

A moment later, a waiter appears, and Andrei takes the liberty of ordering for us both. I could be offended, but I feel so frazzled I don't think I'd be able to pick something for myself if I tried.

The way he's looking at me makes my cheeks heat, and I self-consciously fiddle with my rings as we wait.

"You know, you really didn't have to take me out," I eventually blurt, if only to deflect from the look in his eyes that I can't begin to describe. I cringe, hating how ungrateful I sound. "Not that I don't appreciate it! I do. I really do, actually, I just…" I bite my lip to force myself to shut up, but Andrei leans back, looking amused. "I guess I'm trying to say thank you. That's all."

"You're cute when you're flustered." He smirks, looking exactly like the smug asshole I should have known was lurking under his polished veneer.

"You kind of suck, you know that?" I mutter, but I'm smiling

He tilts his head from side to side like he's considering it, then shrugs.

"Maybe, but I still got you worked up, didn't I?" He smiles, and it softens the sharp angles of his face. The way the candlelight dances along the shadows of his brows and the scruff on his cheeks momentarily stuns me.

A man as dangerous as him has no business looking so handsome.

I take a sip of water and clear my throat. "This is a nice place."

"It is," he agrees easily, oblivious to the way I'm hardly able to tear my eyes away from his face.

"Seems like the type of place that would typically have reservations booked out months in advance."

"Usually, that'd be the case."

"Then how'd you get us in?"

"I know the owner." He shrugs. "And he owed me a few favors." I dread to think what those favors entail, but I don't ask. I don't want to cross any sort of unspoken line and bring the night to an early end. "And being here with you, especially while you look like that"—he pointedly looks me up and down—"is more than worth cashing in a couple of them."

I'm mercifully spared from having to reply by a waiter delivering our food.

Truth is, I'm not used to getting compliments anymore. And I'm definitely not used to going on dates. Even when Daniil and I weren't dancing around the issue of his infidelity, it got harder and harder to spend quality time together after Nikolai was born.

Andrei's foot knocks against the inside of my ankle, pulling my attention back to him. He reaches out, holding my hand loosely and running his thumb against the delicate skin of my inner wrist.

"Where're you at, *zolotse*?"

I half expect him to look offended that I'm already distracted, but he looks calm and collected, maybe even curious. I take a deep breath and squeeze my hand around his before I answer him as honestly as I can.

"I'm here. With you."

As he chuckles, shaking his head while he smiles at me, it doesn't feel like a lie at all.

CHAPTER 17

Blair

A ndrei kisses me with a tenderness that is completely at odds with the ferocity he's using to pin my body against the door while his thumbs stroke against my temples, smoothing back the stray hairs that have fallen free from my ponytail.

When I decided to ignore everything else and focus on our date, I realized that it is really easy to spend time with Andrei. When he asks questions, he genuinely seems to want to hear my answers. He's engaging and charming and funny. I never would've guessed that he could make me laugh more than I have in ages, all while stoking the fire between us with gentle touches and sly looks.

I couldn't figure out if my face felt warm because I was blushing or because I wanted him.

Until he leaned across the table, looking at me with a starved expression that had nothing to do with our dinner and told me to text Mila to let her know we'd pick up Niko in the morning. Then I decided the why didn't matter.

"I don't want her to worry," he told me. "As soon as we get home, you're going to be busy with my cock stretching those pretty lips until you're choking on me."

Now, Andrei's being gentle, but it's a tease that only has me wanting more. So, I nip at his lip as I tug against his tie, wanting absolutely nothing between us. As soon as the knot's loose, I drop it to the floor, moving to the buttons of his shirt, hoping to pry his control away, but he holds firm.

I'm one moment of weakness from begging him to give me what I want, but he's just as collected as he always is, taking charge and refusing to give an inch.

In a fit of desperation, I grip him through his pants, a silent plea for him to end this slow tease. In a flash, he removes the space between us, licking against my lips before he pulls away. I whimper, because the couple inches between our faces are far from what I want.

"Do you like this dress, *zolotse*?"

Eyes glazed, I nod. I'll answer anything he asks right now, as long as he just *touches me*.

"Do you want me to tear it off you? Because if you keep touching me like that, it'll be nothing but pretty scraps, and I'll have to buy you a new one."

Reluctantly, I pull my hand back, moving it back to his chest and stroking my thumb over the fabric, imagining the designs inked hidden underneath.

His pupils are dilated, and I feel drunk on how powerful his blatant desire makes me. With a strong grip, he moves my hand down to his belt, smirking as I tug at it until I'm able to shove his pants down enough to free his length and stroke it with one hand. When he nods, I sink to my knees. I look up at him from under my lashes, his cock twitching when he meets my eyes.

"Fuck," he breathes, head falling backward as I run my lips against his head, tongue darting out to taste the precum that smears against my thumb on my next stroke. I want his cock in my mouth so badly I ache with the desire burning through me. I press my lips against his length, teasing him with chaste kisses before he growls, hips twitching when I finally put us both out of our misery, parting my lips enough for him to press between them.

God, I need this. Need *him*.

Slowly, he rolls his hips, his cock filling my mouth and bumping against my throat. I swallow to avoid gagging, and it isn't long before he's filling my mouth while my eyes water freely.

Andrei groans a low and throaty sound, while his hands slip through my hair, pulling it free of my hair tie and pulling my head back just enough for me to look up at him.

"Pull up your dress," he orders. "I want to watch you play with yourself while my cock is in your mouth. Show me what you like."

Heat flashes through me, the heavy look in his eyes enough to spark me into obedience. I pull back to catch my breath as I lift the skirt of the dress enough to give myself room to slip one hand between my thighs. He inhales sharply while I slip my panties aside, happily tracing along my pussy, getting my fingers wet before I plunge two of them inside me as I bite back a moan.

With a starved growl, his grip on my hair tightens.

"*With* my cock in your mouth, *zolotse*."

He pulls me toward him, and I don't hesitate to part my lips, sealing them around him and moaning at his clean, musky flavor.

His grip in my hair stings against my scalp when my tongue flicks against the vein that runs along his length.

The edge of pain does nothing to discourage me when I try to control the pace. I savor the burn when I move faster than he wants, moaning as I bob my head up and down. He growls, forcing my head back far enough that I have no choice but to accept his withdrawal, whining when he teases me, only rubbing the tip of his cock against my lips.

He shakes his head. I whine in the back of my throat, tongue darting out to coax him back.

"If you want me in your mouth, you have to learn to behave." Bracing a hand on his thigh, my nails dig into the fabric covering his thighs while my clit pulses against my hand, fingers working in tight circles. "Will you behave?"

I nod as I sigh shakily.

A beat passes as he strokes a thumb over my wet lip.

"Then come for me," he orders as he slams his cock into my mouth. My throat convulses around him, and I blink back tears. "Get yourself nice and wet so when I get you into bed, I can sink every inch into that tight little cunt of yours."

When I pull back, he lets me. I suck hard as I pull off, releasing him with a wet sound as I stroke him in my hand while I look up at him, fluttering my lashes.

Andrei's eyes are feral.

With a spark of daring I didn't know I possessed, I pout my lower lip, fluttering my lashes at him. "I like this dress, Andrei.

How do I know you won't ruin it?" I ask, dragging my tongue from base to tip, swirling it around the head.

"There's only one way to find out," he growls as he urges me to take him back into my mouth. It sounds like a threat, not a reassurance, but I don't want to do anything that'll make him stop. With a hitched breath, I plunge my fingers deeper.

Between the hot, heavy weight of him on my tongue and the way his hands stroke through my hair, shooting heat along my spine, I'm already on edge. Part of me wants to hold out, draw out my own orgasm as long as possible, but when I let my thumb circle my clit, I know I'm not going to last.

My thighs shake while my release hits me, muting every sensation except pleasure. I moan, clawing against Andrei's thigh to brace myself against the onslaught.

"Sexiest thing I've ever seen," Andrei rasps, voice gruff with lust. His expression is awe-struck as he strokes my cheek.

I'm still floating when Andrei pulls me off him, taking his cock in the hand not wrapped in my hair and squeezing around the base. I whine at the loss.

"When I let you go, you'll have two minutes to get upstairs and get out of this dress," he rasps. "Then you're going to spread yourself out on the bed and wait for me. If you're still wearing anything when I get there, I'll tear it off you with my teeth."

His voice is firm, leaving no room for argument, but I can't resist the urge to push him anyway.

"And if I don't?"

"Then I'll have no choice but to take you over my knee," he answers easily, the effect only emphasized by his hungry expression. A bolt of pure lust shoots through me at the mental image.

Holy shit.

"Do you understand me, *zolotse*?"

I nod as much as his grip allows me to.

I squeeze my thighs together, trying to relieve some of the pressure.

If Andrei wants to spank me, he's more than welcome to. Even though I have a feeling he wouldn't be playful and teasing.

No, a spanking from him would be just like every other part of him. Focused and intense. He wouldn't give me an inch unless he wanted to, and the untamed look in his eye says that he isn't feeling very generous.

"Two minutes."

He releases my hair, and I scramble to stand, hesitating for only a moment before I rush to obey him. His eyes silently track my every move as I dart upstairs.

I pause on the top landing, carefully undoing the thin halter straps at my neck and letting the dress fall to pool at my feet, leaving me in only my panties as I turn down the hallway, giving him a full view of the wonders these heels to for my ass.

I know better than to think he'll chase after me. Andrei does things in his own time, and if he's giving me two minutes, there's a reason. But I can still have my own fun in the meantime.

As he chuckles, my bravado fails me, and I end up scrambling to remove my heels and panties and crawl onto the bed. I can hear him moving around downstairs, checking the locks and turning off the lights while my nipples bead with anticipation. I shift eagerly, but there's nothing I can do to rush him.

It feels like I've been lying here for far more than two minutes, and I huff out a frustrated breath.

Well, Andrei never said I had to wait for him, did he?

My hand ghosts down my stomach, causing my skin to break into goosebumps as I trace a path to the bundle of nerves between my legs, pleasure shooting through me with a groan as my fingers move in slow circles, not even bothering to be quiet as I lose myself.

A throat clears, and it's like someone has thrown a bucket of ice water over me.

"Not that I mind the show, but I don't remember saying you could play without me." Andrei leans against the doorway, naked as the day he was born. I can't help but admire his gorgeous, tattooed muscles as he crosses his arms over his chest. Unwittingly, my eyes drop to his cock, standing at attention as he watches me.

"You didn't tell me I couldn't," I counter, spreading my legs wider so I can push a finger into my soaked core. He growls, stalking across the room to take control of my hands, pulling them above my head.

"But I didn't tell you that you could."

He lets go of my hands and grabs my hips instead, flipping me onto my hands and knees faster than I can react. Not giving me a chance to brace myself, his hand lands against the fleshy part of my ass with a sharp *smack* that has me crying out.

Fuck, I'm so wet it's practically dripping down my thighs.

I have half a mind to argue with him, to tell him that he isn't being fair. But his hand strokes over the spot he just hit, soothing away the sting. I arch into the touch, and he lets out a low groan that sets my nerves on fire.

"Do you like a little bit of pain, *zolotse*?" He hums, running his hands up my back as I nod. His fingers bite into my shoulders so hard I wonder if he's going to leave marks. "I'll have to remember that."

That's the only warning I get before he slams himself inside me, stretching me open with a delicious burn. I collapse to my elbows, scrambling to find my balance as he pounds into me hard and fast, not even giving me time to catch my breath between thrusts.

My nipples rub against the sheets underneath me, an incredible friction that has me spiraling higher with each thrust. I roll my hips back against him, meeting Andrei stroke for stroke.

"You're fucking perfect." He wraps an arm around my waist, pulling me against his chest as he uses his knees to spread my legs wider, letting him thrust even deeper inside me. Ecstasy builds, and there's nowhere in the world I'd rather be in this moment than right here.

"The way you squeeze my cock, the sounds you make... You'll drive me to madness."

My breaths are short pants as I wrap my arms back around his neck, twisting my head around to meet him in a messy kiss. His hand moves down to my clit, pushing me over the edge in just a few short strokes. My muscles draw tight as my core flutters around him, squeezing tight like no part of me can bear to have him apart from me.

He breaks the kiss and presses his face against my neck, holding me tight against his chest. His cock pulses as he grunts so lowly I can feel it rumble through my chest.

He pulls away slowly, and I collapse, unable to hold up my own weight while my mind rebels at the thought of him walking away from this again. If he really wants to keep this hot-and-cold routine, I'm not sure I'll be able to keep up.

"There's never been anything as beautiful as you."

I jolt at his words as much as I do at his fingers running along my slit, slick with our combined release. Before I have the chance to take a breath, he slowly thrusts his fingers inside me. My oversensitive nerves protest as I try to move away, but I have no energy left to fight him. All I can do is mewl pathetically as I shake my head.

He chuckles, kissing my shoulder. "Easy, Blair." The mattress shifts as he stands up and I let out a quiet whine, hating myself for it. "I'm not going anywhere," he promises, as if he can hear the insecurities creeping into my mind, eager to fill the space he's leaving behind.

Forcing myself to trust him, I relax for the few minutes before he returns with a wet cloth, cleaning up the mess between my thighs with gentle care and attention.

When he's finished, I roll over and grab his arm, keeping him close. The pathetic, desperate creature in my chest claws at my ribs, demanding I force him to stay with me.

"Will you stay?" The words escape me before I get a chance to bite my tongue.

I hate how pathetic I feel. If he says no, I'll have no choice but to go back to the same routine we had this morning, acting like roommates who tolerate each other enough to fuck occasionally and forget how he made me feel when he held my hand over dinner.

"I want to wake up with you. Just once."

He looks at me in that evaluating way of his, and I feel beyond vulnerable. It's like he's stripped me of every protection I have, and my soul has been laid bare. I both hate and savor the experience of feeling seen, even as I have to resist the urge to squirm away from it and hide.

Slowly, he smiles, and it's like the first rays of sun coming out after a freezing winter.

"I'd stay with you every night if you'd let me." His tone is serious, and my heart skips a beat. It doesn't silence the desperate, anxious creature that's made a home for itself in my chest, but it does help put a muzzle on it.

Wrapping my arms around his neck, I pull him against me in a kiss, basking in the warmth of his skin against mine. "Then stay," I murmur against his lips.

He nods, kissing me as I smile.

Chapter 18

Blair

Andrei's kisses quickly become a gentle reminder throughout the day of how sweet he's capable of being when he wants to be. Sure, he can be terrifying when the moment calls for it, but when he's at home, he's become such a steady presence that I find myself missing him when he's gone.

When I'm falling asleep, occasionally I'll stir to find him playing with my hair, and more than once I've caught him looking at me like I'm the only person in the room, regardless of where we are and who we're with.

He's considerate, patient, unexpectedly funny, and the way he's insisted on taking me out on weekly dates makes my heart flutter.

But part of him always seems to be playing defense, and whenever I notice it, it's hard to look past the fact that all his sweet moments are just that: moments.

Moments that all seem meaningless now as I blink up at him, feeling like he's throwing me into the lion's den. Mila blinks at him like she can't believe the words that just came out of his mouth.

I can't blame her, because neither can I.

"What?" I can't stop myself from hissing.

Andrei shrugs easily.

Traitor.

"It's been long enough. We should all sit down and have dinner together," he says. His hand is on the small of my back as he looks away from me, focusing on Mila. "Can you come over tonight? Or should we find a different day?"

How about never?

"Tonight," Mila answers without hesitation, a triumphant grin on her face. "I can't wait to spend an evening with you and Nikolai. Now, go, I have to start cooking!" She shoos us away while I'm trying to figure out if I want to laugh or cry.

I've been trying so hard to let myself trust Andrei, and this is what he does with it?

Sure, I've asked Mila to come over for dinner before, but that was on *my* terms. It wasn't something that was sprung on me by someone else. I guess it was too much to hope that Andrei would know better.

I'm quiet as we all pile into the car after picking Niko up, but only because that seems like a better alternative than screaming. Luckily Niko's happy enough to fill the silence, making sure to recount every minute of his slumber party with Mila.

Meanwhile, Andrei and I were curled up on the couch watching an old movie, and now he's inviting Mila to dinner. Without checking with me first.

I'm not sure if it'd be better to ice him out or strangle him.

"Andrei, are you my papa now?"

I freeze, Niko's question cutting me to the bone. I turn around in my seat to look at him, but he's focused on the toy dinosaurs in his lap, totally oblivious to the ticking bomb he's thoughtlessly thrown into the middle of this car.

Shit, did I make him think Andrei's here to replace Daniil?

"Of course not," Andrei answers with a small shake of his head, eyes still on the road. "I'm not going to take your papa's place. I'm not trying to, either."

"But you're always around Mama, and you make her smile, just like Papa did."

Does he?

Irrationally, I want to cover Niko's mouth before he says anything else. Andrei doesn't need to hear about how much I supposedly smile around him. He doesn't need to know that I'm starting to get attached to him.

If Niko's noticing it, then I have to do a way better job of covering up how I feel.

"I'm not trying to be your papa, Niko. Only your mama's husband. I just want to make her happy, you know?" He clears his throat as he navigates a turn. "But I *am* hoping that you and I can be friends."

"We *are* friends," he says, like it's a long-established fact. Like the sky being blue. Or gravity simply existing. He nods to himself, turning his head to watch the scenery flying by through the window. "Can we go to the park, Mama?"

"Of course," I hear myself answer, though I'm dizzy with emotional whiplash. If Andrei's going to invite Mila over, he can't follow that up by being sweet and patient with my son. He has to give me a chance to find some middle ground first.

"After lunch?"

Niko's face is bright with excitement as he nods. The smile on his face makes him look so much like Daniil, I have to force myself to face forward. Apparently done with conversation, Niko goes back to playing, holding up his toys and making exaggerated *roars* for the rest of the drive.

***

Mila is due to arrive in twenty minutes. That should be plenty of time to get my oscillating mood under control, right?

On the one hand, I'm furious. If Andrei wanted to tell me to shut up and make myself scarce because he wanted to talk to Mila alone, it would have been kinder for him to just say so to my face. Having Mila come over is just setting me up for misery.

On the other hand, he was perfect with Niko this morning. In my wildest dreams, I never would have pictured that conversation going as well as it did. As mad as I am, I feel part of myself melting when I realize exactly how good he is with Niko. In the big moments and the little ones, he's present and aware of exactly who he's talking to.

I adjust the silverware, making sure that everything is perfect while dinner finishes cooking in the oven. Part of me wanted to make a show of picking up takeout and tossing greasy burgers on everyone's place, but instead I went to the store and got everything I needed to make a wonderful last-minute dinner for someone who's inevitably going to pretend I'm not there anyway.

Because I'm pathetic and still can't help but want to impress Mila.

I have to run upstairs and get dressed, but I need to make sure everything is set up in case Mila gets here early, trying to catch me off guard.

Like she did the last four times she came over.

Doing my best to brush aside my irritation, I make my way upstairs, pausing outside Niko's door long enough to make sure he's alright. Despite seeing her this morning, he's been acting like he's going to be reunited with his long-lost other half, and it's been a challenge to keep him calm and tell him to be patient.

Mila and I might not like each other, but I'll do everything in my power to protect Niko from having to bear witness to our combined bitterness and resentment.

He's sitting on the floor with a book in his lap, running his finger along words he can't read as he makes up the story, and I can't help but smile.

I'll put up with tonight, but I'll also have to make it clear to Andrei that this isn't going to happen again without discussing it with me first.

Maybe I should just seek him out and clear the air now. He's probably tucked away in the spare bedroom that he's using as an office since he started spending most nights sharing my bed. Or maybe I should wait until I've had some time to calm down.

That's probably the smarter move.

I head into the closet to pull on something suitably nice, but not so nice that it screams *I'm trying to impress you! Please give me your approval!* Settling on a conservative sweater and simple skirt, I change quickly, nearly falling backward when I bump headfirst into Andrei's chest, only remaining upright when his hand wraps around me, keeping me in place.

"You alright?"

"Yeah," I answer while I shake my head, trying to reorient myself.

"Well, which is it?" He chuckles. "Yes or no?"

As much as I wanted to find a way to let go of my anger and approach him when I was feeling more like myself, his little laugh is the straw that breaks the camel's back. I can't repress the low boil in my blood or hide the way my hands flex, wanting to lash out at something.

"You know what? No. No, I'm not okay." My chest heaves. "Why the fuck did you invite Mila over without even asking if I was okay with it? Who does that? I mean, for fuck's sake, Andrei, that woman hasn't spoken more than a dozen words to me since the first time I met her! If you want to spend time with her, fucking feel free, but you don't have the right to drag me into it."

The corner of his lip curls upward, and I shove against his chest, trying to put some space between us.

"Stop smiling, you jerk. I'm serious."

"This is why, *zolotse.*"

"Because you wanted to piss me off?" I scoff. "Well, congratulations, you did a great job."

"No," he smiles, voice soft. "Because *she* pisses you off. And you don't deserve it."

"So you invited her over? If you weren't actively trying to annoy me, then that's a little counterproductive." He keeps smiling, and I smack my hands against his solid chest, twisting hard so I can get free of his grasp, but he doesn't give me an inch.

"Do you trust me?" There's a hit of vulnerability in his voice, and I can't stand it. I try to look away from him, but he chases my eyes, pinning me in place when I don't answer.

Do I trust him?

For the most part, Andrei's been amazing. But eventually he'll get bored, or he'll get worn down from having to deal with Maksim's bullshit, and he'll pull away. He'll stop taking me on dates, or he'll spend more time out and about under the guise of working. Or, if he's feeling spiteful, he'll take a card out of Daniil's playbook and have an affair, making a show of how little he cares that it hurts me.

He's here for now, but he won't be forever.

And I'm trying to trust him, but it's hard to let my guard down when I know he'll only be here for a while.

"That's alright," he eventually sighs. "We'll get there."

He lets me go, pressing a kiss to the side of my head as I pull away.

"Finish getting ready. I'll let Mila in when she gets here, okay?"

I stand there, unable to do anything but watch as he leaves the room. He didn't seem surprised. If anything, he seemed disappointed, which is so much worse.

I try to ignore how shitty I feel as I finish getting dressed.

Before I'm ready for it, I'm standing at the top of the stairs, taking a deep breath while Mila chats away with Niko and

Andrei as they greet her in Russian, half wondering if I should even bother going down to join them.

It's just a few hours, I tell myself as I close my eyes. In a few hours, she'll be gone again, and I won't have to feel like a stranger in my own home again.

Niko sounds excited as he blabs away, and I don't understand a single thing he says.

I paste a wooden smile in place as I go to join them, pretending for everyone else's sake that I'm not upset about being excluded from yet another conversation, even as I trail after Niko as he guides Mila toward the dining room, urging her to take the seat next to his. Andrei eyes me curiously, but I ignore him as I serve dinner while I bite my tongue.

God, I'm pitiful.

There used to be a time that I would stand up for myself, but this isn't a battle I'm going to pick anymore.

What's the point? She's never viewed me as a person worthy of her respect, and no amount of pleading or kindness has changed her opinion in the slightest. It didn't change after Daniil and I got married, it didn't change after Niko was born, and I don't expect anything to change now that Daniil's gone.

Mila says something as everyone eats, looking at Andrei in a pointed way that makes me think she's asking a question. I look at my food, wondering how soon I can start pushing her out the door.

I'm only capable of putting up this farce for so long, and eventually something's going to give. Either I'm going to snap, or I'm going to start crying, and neither option will do much for my already battered ego.

"I didn't have anything to do with that," Andrei replies, startling me out of my personal pity party.

Has he been speaking English this whole time? I watch him curiously, but his expression remains unchanged.

With the lack of tact that only a child can possess, Niko launches back into conversation in Russian, only stopping when Andrei clears his throat.

"Speak English, Nikolai. It's rude to exclude someone you care about from the conversation."

"But Baba Mila says—"

"And I said no. Your mother doesn't speak Russian. Until we teach her, don't cut her out."

"That's not..." I start to say, but Andrei cuts me off with a sharp look. I know I'm only arguing out of habit, so I smile, turning my head away to try to conceal it. Mila glances between the three of us, looking uncomfortable.

"Sorry, Mama," Niko mutters to his plate, looking confused.

I pat his hand, smiling. "It's okay, baby. Eat your dinner."

For several long moments, the only sound is his silverware clattering against the plate as he eats while Andrei and Mila glare at each other.

"As I was saying, I don't have anything to do with Niko going to your place every week. That's all Blair. If it were my choice, you wouldn't be alone with him until you learned to treat Blair with respect." I blink while Mila gapes. "I don't understand why she allows it, but she's proven time and time again that she's far more generous than I am. So, if you insist on thanking someone for ensuring you're still a part of his life, thank her. Anyone else would be a waste of breath."

For the first time since we met, Mila looks at me. Actually looks at me. Her jaw is tight, and she looks like she's swallowed a lemon, but at least she isn't looking *through* me.

Only then do Andrei's words click.

"Wait, did you really think I was going to try to keep Niko from you?" The question tastes bitter on my tongue. "You two adore each other. Regardless of how you and I feel, I'm not going to keep you from him."

She doesn't respond, but I never expected her to. I'm grateful for what Andrei's trying to do, and I make a note to tell him as much later, but some feelings are too deeply ingrained to be erased with a single, tense dinner.

The rest of the meal is quiet, only broken up by Niko's tentative questions and attempts at conversation, and he speaks in a mixture of English and Russian. He glances between Andrei and Mila whenever he switches, like he's worried that one of them is going to yell at him every time he does.

When she's getting ready to leave, I'm startled when Mila rests her hand on my arm.

"Thank you for dinner," she mumbles as she passes by. "I'll see Niko again next week?"

For a moment, I'm stunned.

"Of course," I tell her. Over her shoulder, Andrei smirks as he helps Niko tie his shoes so he can walk his grandmother to her car.

CHAPTER 19

Andrei

The more I see how happy small things make Blair, I get angrier and angrier with the majority of the people around her.

Demanding she be respected shouldn't make her so happy. She should expect it. She shouldn't be so pleased whenever I make my appreciation for her known. And she definitely shouldn't light up from within whenever I give her my undivided attention, like she's unused to being cared about.

I've made it my goal to make her so happy that she'll never have to accept anything less than what she deserves again.

After the near disaster that was dinner with Mila, I figured she'd be pissed at me, but the way she slipped into my arms that night, curling close and wrapping herself around me like she didn't want any space between us, erased any lingering doubt over what I did.

I promised her that this week we'd have a more relaxing time together. I wasn't sure if she'd like this, but the grin on her face tells me she's having the time of her life as she checks out every shelf in this little used bookstore.

Blair darts down another aisle, laughing as she pulls me along by my hand. She doesn't have to, but I cling to her hand anyway. If she let go, I'd still be right behind her, carrying the stack of worn paperbacks she's selected.

She crouches in front of another stack of books, running her finger along the cracked spines as she inspects every title lined up in their tidy rows.

When her pile of books grew tall enough that it began to wobble in her hands, I took it from her so she's be free to select as many as she wants.

"I knew you like reading, but I think I underestimated just how much," I say as I take another book from her as she slips it off the shelf. There's a line between her brows whenever she reads the blurb on the back, and I can't help but smile at it.

"Books are reliable," she replies distractedly as she puts the book back on the shelf. "They don't change for me, and I can't do anything to change them. I like knowing that I have no choice but to get immersed and go with the flow, you know?"

I can't say that I do, but I hum anyway, helping her stand.

"Are you looking for anything specific?"

"No. Just... looking for something that speaks to me, I guess." She eyes the pile of books tucked under my arm and huffs. "Or maybe I should call it quits for now." I shift so that she can't see them anymore.

"Don't stop on my account. I've got nowhere else to be."

In truth, I could watch her do this for days. She's so careful when she picks something, and despite what she said, it's like she knows exactly what she wants to read, only picking the books that tick every one of her secret boxes.

She hesitates, looking in the direction of the single cashier toward the front of the store.

"Are you sure? I don't want to take up the whole night with this."

"Take your time. I'm never going to complain about you enjoying yourself." She takes a moment, cheeks pink, before she nods, resuming her idle wandering among the stacks.

She rarely takes time for herself, always looking after Niko or worrying about the many things that are outside of her control. I'll gladly encourage her to forget it all for a bit. Watching the joy on her face while she looks around eases a rope around my chest, allowing me to breathe a little easier.

"If you'd like to do something else next week, just let me know, and we'll do it."

She looks at me out of the corner of her eye for a moment, considering. Then she shakes her head and turns back to the books.

"What?"

"I was just thinking that I haven't been to the museum in a while. But I'd feel bad going without Niko, and going with a toddler is a little bit like a field trip to hell, so I don't want to subject you to it."

I almost laugh. "What do you mean?"

"It's just... When we go, I want to look at the exhibits, you know? Read about the gems in their collection, take my time looking at the dioramas, that sort of thing. Before I moved here with Daniil, going to the museum was one of my favorite things to do in my spare time. And you know how Niko is." She shrugs, looking unbothered. "He gets to the giant T. rex, loses his mind, and immediately wants to run to the dinosaurs. It's the *only* thing he wants to see. Which is fine, but I can only look at the same bones so many times before I get bored."

"Would it be easier if I were there with you guys? That way, when Niko gets bored, I can entertain him while you take your time." She blinks slowly, a smile breaking across her face, and with it any of the restraint I've held in my heart leaves.

Fuck, how did Daniil deny her anything when she smiles like that? It's the most precious thing I've ever seen, and I'll do anything to make sure I see that smile as much as I can for as long as I possibly can.

It's the prettiest thing I've ever seen in my life.

"Are you sure? Because Niko can be a lot. And when there's a promise of dinosaurs around, he's almost unbearable."

"Any time."

I'll do anything to see her and Niko happy. Even if I hadn't promised as much to Daniil, I'd do it for myself. And for them. They deserve it, and I want to be the cause of their happiness. I want them to think of me and smile because they like having me around.

I cradle her careful joy in my chest the whole way home, protecting it like a candle in a windstorm. I let it keep me warm when she reaches out to hold my hand as I drive.

And when I get home and see that the front door is open before I even stop the car, I know that I'll do whatever it takes to keep it safe.

At a glance, the house is dark, but there's a boot print outlined by the splintered wood near the lock. A quick look around doesn't show any strange cars on the street, but it's dark, and I know better than to assume that there isn't anyone watching.

Blair moves to open her door, oblivious that anything is out of place.

"Wait for me," I order, reaching across her to pull my gun out of the glove compartment, checking that it's loaded and flicking off the safety before I'm even out of the car.

"What's going on?" she asks as I open her door and pull her behind me, grabbing her hand and looping it through my belt at the back of my jeans. "Andrei?"

I don't want to worry her, but I don't have any other option right now.

"The door's been kicked in. I need to make sure whoever did it isn't still in the house."

Her stress is immediately apparent, and it makes me more determined to kill whoever's responsible for this.

"I need you to hold on right here"—I tighten my hand around her wrist, jostling her hand until she clenches it closed—"and stay right on me until I say otherwise, okay?"

She nods, looking scared, but I can't worry about that right now. She presses herself firmly against my back as I move cautiously through the house, sweeping each room and shadowed corner until I'm able to assure myself there isn't an immediate threat. Everything looks exactly as it should, but that doesn't change the fact that I can hear Blair's hitched breaths behind me as she tries not to cry.

My jaw aches from how hard I'm grinding my teeth. We make it to her bedroom—*our* bedroom, the one I've thought of as ours since the first time I slept there. Stepping cautiously into the room, I find the first sign that someone's been inside in the form of a note in the center of the bed, cutting mindlessly through the red dotting the edges of my vision.

Stop hiding her.

I don't recognize the blocky handwriting, but only one man would be stupid enough to pull off a stunt like this.

Pavel's more than hammered his point home just by showing up here, and he's done nothing but leave me with very few choices in how I can move forward.

I check the rest of the house before I relax, wrapping my arms around Blair while she shakes against my chest. She was strong as we moved from room to room, but that strength is gone as I try to soothe her, rubbing a hand along her back while I try to form a plan.

I can't let her stay here tonight. Niko's already at Mila's but he can't come back tonight, either.

Beyond fixing the door and undoing whatever the fuck he did to disable the security system, I still need to sweep the place for any gifts that Pavel might have left behind.

I wouldn't put it past the fucker to try to plant bugs or cameras if he thought it'd give him an edge.

My condo isn't a great option, but it'll do for a night.

"C'mon," I say, pulling away just enough to look at her terrified eyes. "Let's pack a bag. We'll stay somewhere else until I can get this place cleaned up and fix the door."

"I hate that fucking door," she sniffles, making me chuckle. "Daniil said we had to get a black one so it'd match the neighborhood, but what good did that do? Someone still came and broke it."

I pause, but only for a moment. If she wants to focus on the damaged door, then that's what we'll do until I'm able to get her settled in at my place.

"What color did you want it to be?"

"Blue. Or yellow, maybe. Something fun."

"I'll go to the store tomorrow and pick out a white one that's ready to be painted. When you're ready, you can pick whatever color you want." She sniffs once and nods, pulling away and heading toward the closet.

She's quiet until we get to my condo, looking around the space while I put her bag in my bedroom. Her arms are wrapped around her torso when I come back, and I guide her to the couch.

There isn't much to look at here, so I don't bother with a tour. Before we got married, my condo was nothing but a place to sleep, eat, and maybe make a phone call or two. It was fine then, but now that I've actually lived in a home, it seems empty.

The fridge looks blank without Niko's paintings stuck to it. The coffee table looks wrong without stacks of books placed haphazardly on it. The whole place looks like a showroom, not a place where someone lives.

I make a mental note to put it on the market before the end of the week.

"Are you alright?"

She shakes her head as she settles onto the couch, knees drawn to her chest. "Why would someone break into our house?"

Because Pavel's a pathetic coward who will do anything to gain a little more power for himself.

Unfortunately for him, fear isn't a currency I recognize. He can't force me to give him the loyalty he craves, no matter what he tries.

"I don't know." I shrug. "But I'll handle it."

"What about Niko?"

"I already texted Mila and let her know we'll pick him up in the morning. He's safe with her."

I hold her until she's calmed down enough to stop shaking. Only then do I regretfully go to the house, making phone calls as soon as I'm in the car. I don't want to leave her alone, but I need to make sure that it's safe for her.

The image of Blair curling up as small as possible when I showed her where I keep a gun in the living room haunts me the whole way.

***

I've searched the house twice from top to bottom, but I still use the stupidly expensive device that I got from Artyom to sweep the room for a third time. If Pavel went to the trouble of fucking with the alarms and breaking in, I don't trust him to leave the house alone. But no matter where I search or what I use to check every corner, I find nothing.

I pull out my phone and call Alexei. I haven't spoken to him much since the day after Savage opened, and I don't want to now, but I can't let this farce with Pavel continue. And though we get on each other's nerves, Alexei doesn't deserve to be left high and dry when I blow us all to hell.

"Whatever you have to say, I don't want to hear it," he answers as I pinch my temples.

"What would you say if I ever had good news?"

"Do you?"

"Of course not, are you fucking kidding me?"

"Figures. You've never had good news in your life." A sigh. "If you're trying to get out of the meeting with Lavrov tomorrow, then forget it. It isn't happening."

Ironically, I'm the one who set up the stupid meeting.

Konstantin Lavrov is a powerful ally in times of need, and while it's foolish for Maksim to push him away, it'd be even worse if I let him get away with it.

Konstantin's wealthy, loyal, and well connected. Most of his connections are redundant to us right now, but with Maksim's paranoia, they might not stay that way for long.

"The meeting's still going to happen, but you can handle him on your own."

"*Blyad*," he swears. "And what happens when it all goes to shit? I take the fall while you ride off into the sunset with Maksim none the wiser?"

"It won't blow up. Besides, if Maksim finds out, he'll be pissed that we're meeting with him at all."

I just need them to act as an alibi later. I know that Konstantin will have my back, but I need Alexei to get on the same page.

"If anyone asks, I was there with you. That's all. And if Maksim does find out, I'll take all the blame."

Though I doubt it'll come to that.

He's quiet for a beat.

"And what're you planning on doing? Why the fuck are you going that you need a cover story?"

I could tell him. Sure, it would likely end up getting me killed, but it'd be nice to get some feedback or have him tell me that I'm not digging my own grave.

Either I'm going insane, or I just miss having someone I can talk to about things like this without having to worry that they'd turn around and stab me in the back later.

Fuck, why did Daniil have to get himself killed before I really needed him?

"Never mind," he eventually grunts. "I probably don't want to know."

"Probably not."

"Why the fuck should I back you up?"

"Because Lavrov will regardless of whether you're on board or not."

"You sound sure of that."

"He owes me a favor, and unlike you, he's doing everything he can to keep it from hanging over his head."

It's always a benefit to know exactly what sort of trouble men like us get into, and an even bigger one to know how to make that trouble disappear. Having a debt to collect is more valuable than gold, and I always make sure to cash in eventually.

It's something that Alexei should figure out sooner rather than later.

***

It's late by the time I get back to my condo, but I've done as much as I can to keep Blair safe tonight. Tomorrow I'll do a little more, but for now, my focus is on the way she's curled up on my sofa, wrapped in an old hoodie that I'm pretty sure was buried in the back of my closet. Her eyes are red and puffy as she watches me rearm the alarms.

Her legs are bare beneath the hoodie, and I follow suit, stripping to my boxer briefs before I pick her up. She doesn't protest, instead wrapping her arms around my neck as I carry her to the bedroom.

Blair stays quiet as I lay her down in my bed, wrapping the comforter around us. She doesn't relax, staying stiff until the lights are off and I'm urging her to rest her head on my chest.

I'm sure her head is full of questions, but I don't push her to voice them. For months—fuck, *years*, really, everything has been out of her control. I want her to be able to take it back.

But until she can, I'll let her control this.

She can be quiet. She can choose when to ask her questions and when to bite her tongue.

Eventually her breaths change from panicked, barely suppressed sobs to something slower and more consistent as she falls asleep. I press my lips against the top of her head, taking a moment to appreciate the weight of finally having her in my arms.

Chapter 20

Andrei

As Blair tugs on the hem of her short dress, I have half a mind to tell her to call Nadya and ask her to stay home. Her legs look fucking incredible, and her tight dress hugs every inch of her torso, caressing her curves like it was made just for her.

I want to tear it off her and enjoy everything underneath it.

I don't want every other man in the club staring at her while I'm not there.

"Are you sure this is a good idea?" She glances at the new front door warily, but she doesn't have anything to worry about. There won't be a repeat of last night.

"It's a great idea," I assure her. She deserves a night out, to let go and have fun with a friend. *Especially* after last night. She hasn't had a chance to let loose in ages, and Nadya won't judge her for it.

"And this isn't too much?" she asks, biting her lip as she gestures to herself. "Or too little, I guess."

"Fuck no." I twist a lock of her hair around my finger. "You look divine. If I had any say in it, I'd toss work out the window, take you right back to bed, and you'd be hoarse from screaming my name." Her cheeks turn an enticing shade of pink, and when I'm done for the night, there's a real chance I'm going to do exactly that.

"Well, if I'd known that was on the table," she murmurs, looking at me through her lashes. My cock twitches in my slacks as I run my hand along the curve of her neck.

"*Zolotse*, if I didn't have to go to this meeting..." Her bottom lip sticks out in a pout, and I can feel my resolve wavering. "When I'm done, we'll pick this up again."

Next time, I tell myself. *Next time I'll throw all plans out the window to spend more time with her.*

I hold her hand, lacing my fingers with hers as she goes back to adjusting her dress. "You'll have fun with Nadya, and I'll pick you up after I'm done." She nods but doesn't meet my gaze. Unease fills me, and I lift her chin, forcing her to look in my direction. Still, she refuses to meet my eyes.

"What's up? I thought you liked Nadya."

She nods, pulling away from my grasp and busying herself with looking at everything but me.

"Then what's wrong?"

I assumed they'd been becoming friends.

They frequently text back and forth, and the few times I've seen them together they seemed to get along. So what the hell isn't she telling me?

If the way she's refusing to meet my eyes is any indication, Blair isn't looking forward to tonight.

If she's having issues with Nadya, then it's enough to tell me that Nadya, contrary to what I thought, isn't better than most of the women in our circle and I'm going to have to pivot on the fly.

Blair might hate it, but she could spend the evening with Mila. Things seemed less strained after dinner last week, so maybe it would be a good thing. Or she could spend an evening being ignored while Niko gets frustrated because he doesn't know what to do.

Either way, it's less painful option than her going out with someone she doesn't want to spend time with. At least if she's with Mila, she'll be able to retreat to another room and have space to breathe.

It won't be the relaxing night I want for her, but she'll still be safe.

I'll just have to be quick.

"You're actually working, right?" she finally asks, tentative as she looks at me. "Not just trying to distract me?"

My heart drops.

Is that what she thinks? That I'm trying to fuck around on her?

"I promise you, *zolotse*, I'm actually working." She nods, but still won't look at me, and I want to dig up Daniil's corpse so I can punch him in the face for planting this doubt in her.

"Blair, look at me." I crouch down, forcing her to meet my eyes. "I have a work thing tonight, but I'd rather be hanging out here with you and Niko. You're the only one I'm interested in going out with. You're my wife, and I'm not going to do anything to jeopardize that. Tell me you understand."

She hesitates for a moment but eventually nods.

It's not the answer I want, but it's a start. I kiss her, willing her to trust me. She doesn't have to believe me yet, but I'll find a way to convince her.

She's still quiet as we make our way to Alexei's, and I stop her before she's able to get out of the car. "Just so we're on the same page, you *do* like Nadya, right? She isn't being weird, or shitty, or anything like that?"

"What? No, she's great. I'm really looking forward to hanging out with her. I've just..." She slumps in her seat.

"Been burned before and aren't looking for a repeat?"

"Yeah. That."

If I thought I could never hate Daniil more than when he asked me to be his best man, I was a fucking idiot. Every time I see how much insecurity his actions caused, I hate him even more.

I wind my fingers through the hair at the base of her skull and lean forward until my forehead rests against hers. "I'll meet you at the club when I'm done. Okay?"

"Okay."

She uses both hands to keep mine in hers while we ride the elevator up to Alexei's apartment. I let myself smile until his door closes behind the girls, and at that same instant he turns his scowl onto me.

"I remember when you were reliable," he bites out, disgust lacing every syllable. My spine straightens, but I don't let him affect my resolve.

"Yeah, well." I shrug. "I take it you've given your security a heads up?"

He scoffs, making a show of buttoning up his suit jacket, projecting an air of authority despite his simmering rage. "Of course. Don't forget, your girl's going with my *sister*. If anything happens to Nadya because of Blair, I'll have your head."

"I'd expect nothing less." Though we both know that he won't do anything to me. It wouldn't take much for me to make his cushy life disappear, and the stiff line of his jaw tells me he knows it.

Alexei enjoys living his life under the radar. Running Maksim's main fronts isn't glamorous, but it keeps eyes off him and, more importantly, off Nadya. It prevents him from having to take on more dangerous jobs that would potentially put her in someone's crosshairs. As much as he doesn't want to go to a meeting with a dangerous man on his own, making an enemy of me is too dangerous for him to fight me.

He won't do anything that could put Nadya in jeopardy. Even if he hates me for it.

"Do me a favor. Don't get shot," I call over my shoulder as I turn on my heel.

Lavrov is clever, but he isn't known for controlling his temper. For that matter, neither is Alexei. If things were different, I'd love to watch them try to navigate a business meeting, but it'll have to wait for another day. If tonight goes the way I expect, then I'm sure there will be plenty of opportunities for those two to square off against each other.

"Don't worry, I'm only planning on getting stabbed. It's easier to clean up, you know?"

I almost laugh as I close the door behind me. "You do that."

***

Being able to break into secure locations is a necessary skill for my line of work. The key lies in being prepared for various levels of difficulty and making an estimated guess of what you're up against.

If you're breaking into an average Joe's place, for example, there's no point in bringing much beyond the standard lock-pick as long as you can get the alarm disabled, but if you're breaking into the condo owned by the son of the head of the Chicago Bratva? You should probably expect some more serious security.

I approach Pavel's door and try the knob on instinct, letting out a deep sigh when it turns freely.

Some people have reputations fearsome enough that they don't need security; to access their space without explicit permission will ensure you beg for a swift death.

Pavel is not one of those people.

Apparently, his delusions of grandeur go much deeper than I anticipated.

Tucking my tools back into my pocket, I step inside and set about searching the condo before Pavel gets home.

When he was messing with the warehouses, that was one thing. He was throwing around weight that he didn't have, but it was inconsequential. I only own them as something I can claim on my taxes.

But Pavel got sloppy when he destroyed the last one. It took more digging than I was expecting, but between me and Lev, we were able to find a camera that caught him down the street before he torched it, a ski mask in hand.

It probably wouldn't have been enough to convince Maksim, but it was enough for me. It gave me something I could hold over his head and force him to back off.

He pissed me off, but I wasn't about to go out of my way to ruin his life for some property damage.

I would've let him live his life in peace if he hadn't fucked with Blair's peace of mind. Now he's left me with no choice but to end this pissing match for good.

Fuck, I should've ended it years ago.

I pull back the cushion of the couch, pulling another knife out, and add it to the stash of weapons I've managed to find. There aren't nearly as many as I'd imagined there would be. I should be weighed down by so many guns and knives that I'm struggling to find somewhere to hide them before Pavel gets home, but I only have a handful.

There was a single handgun in the bedside table, a handful of knives in the main living area, and brass knuckles in the bathroom. Too few weapons scattered too far apart to be of any real use in a fight.

I dump them behind one of the heavy curtains and slip away from the main room to wait for him. I already know he's out partying, and the only thing I'm leaving to chance is whether he comes home alone or not. If he does, great. If he doesn't, it's a minor inconvenience, but I'll handle it.

The arrogance in his lack of security is ridiculous for a multitude of reasons, the main one being that he holds his routines so closely. Which means I can check my watch and have a decent estimate of how long it'll be before he stumbles home, half blind and sloppy drunk.

Right on cue, the front door opens and slams shut, a single set of footsteps shuffling through the living room, muffled as he makes his way onto the rug. I wait a while longer, listening to the sound of him throwing himself down on the hideous leather couch, then drunken snoring.

I wait another five minutes before I return to the living room, rolling my eyes at the way his arm is thrown over his eyes and how he wears the stench of debauchery like a favored coat. Booze, sweat, and cheap perfume fill the room in a nauseating mixture.

I'm willing to bet that if I looked close enough, he's still covered in a sheen of body glitter from whichever stripper had the misfortune of spending an hour with him.

A quick glance at the heavy curtain shows it's undisturbed.

The whole space is a perfect reflection of Pavel. Brutal lines, repugnant red walls, and disgusting art pieces on the wall that look like something he would've had to talk the interior decorator into. The curtains are closed tightly over the windows, blocking out the lights of the city below.

For a moment, the heavy fabric is reminiscent of his father's office, and I wonder if it's intentional or not. Either way, they work in my favor, so I choose not to think about it too much.

I crouch next to him, watching his chest heaving, even in his sleep. It's as if he's climbed a mountain instead of drinking himself into a stupor. I wait several long minutes before they finally even out and then decide *fuck it*.

I roll my neck, remembering the way Blair's eyes were still red when she woke up this morning, and stand for leverage before I punch him in the face, a satisfying crunch immediately following. He jolts awake, gasping wetly as he scrambles into a sitting position, swinging at the empty air in front of him.

Blood flows steadily from his nose as he blinks, and I take a single step back when he swings hard enough that he falls forward, nearly tumbling off the couch in his panic.

I don't normally take pleasure in killing people. It's a dangerous habit to fall into, and I don't want to do anything that will add any risk to the rest of my life. Especially now that Blair's in it.

But I'm sick and tired of Pavel, and the prospect of killing him feels like a reward for all the shit he's put me through.

Right now, I feel like a kid on Christmas morning.

"What the fuck are you doing?" he yells when his watery eyes clear enough to see me standing before him. He sways as he pats himself down for a weapon. "Are you trying to get yourself killed, *suka*?"

"Not today."

His face is red, and his movements are jerky as he steps toward me. I shake out my fist and punch him again, sending him stumbling back onto the couch. I feel the skin on my knuckles split open, but the pain is more than worth the sight of his busted lip and obviously broken nose.

He lunges toward me, stumbling over his feet when I sidestep him.

Hitting him felt good, but I'm not looking for this to become a whole fight. He's drunk enough that it's worth losing the advantage of surprise, but I don't want to give him a chance to let his adrenaline sober him up.

As he falls, he grabs onto my arm, pulling me down to the floor on top of him. Using my weight to pin him in place, I grab blindly at the couch. With a pillow or cushion, this can be done within a matter of minutes.

He snarls, rolling to flip us while I'm distracted. The edge of the coffee table hits my shoulder right on the nerve. I hiss in a breath as he throws me off him, flexing my arm to try to stave off any cramps.

"What's your fucking problem?" Pavel sneers, tearing away from my grasp as he scrambles to his feet. As long as he's moving away from me, I'm fine. The only thing he can do to cause me any issue is walk out the front door, and I'm standing long before he gets the chance.

I'm smirking when he pivots, rushing toward the kitchen, probably in search of a knife. Lucky for me, Pavel's doesn't seem like the type to cook much. When I checked the room, other than a standard set of silverware and a single, matching set of dishes, it was bare of any suitable weapons.

He swears as he pulls open a drawer, finding it empty.

Grabbing the collar of his shirt, I pull him back and twist as I slam him against the wall. His eyes dart around wildly as he tries to slip free, his nostrils flaring. Before he can brace to swing out again, I pin a hand around his throat, squeezing tight. His hands claw against my sleeves as he tries to push me back.

In an ideal world, I'd beat him to death. I'd make sure he feels every moment of his suffering before I finally snapped his neck.

There's a gurgling noise, the capillaries in his eyes bursting as his attempts to fight back grow weaker with each passing moment.

We're about the same size, but Pavel's slow. That doesn't make it a quick or easy process to strangle him, though. It always takes ages, and it's harder than you think. Even when he eventually passes out, I have to keep up the pressure until I'm beyond sure his heart is no longer beating.

I can't afford to gamble on this. Not when the price could be Blair's life.

I count the seconds, waiting a full two minutes after his hands fall away and his legs go limp before I let go. As Pavel crumples to the ground without any support, I'm filled with a sense of disgust.

He has caused so much unnecessary grief for everyone associated with his father that it's a wonder no one's done this for me yet.

A quick glance around the room tells me that everything is still in order. The furniture has moved a little thanks to our tussle, but there isn't any debris to pick up, and his shirt soaked up most of the blood that poured from his nose. Still, I take a moment to wash the remnants off my hands, wanting to rid myself of any part of this.

If I want to, I can move his body and stage it somewhere, put on a whole production to pull Maksim's attention elsewhere when Pavel's finally found, but honestly? Neither of them is worth the effort.

I leave his corpse in a heap in the kitchen, only taking time to wipe my fingerprints off his doorknob as I close it behind me, leaving it unlocked just like he would have.

CHAPTER 21

Blair

Hair sticks to my forehead as I throw my head back, laughing at Nadya shouldering her way through a group of men that can't keep their eyes off her. I wouldn't have guessed that someone as thin as her would be so effective at shoving a grown man out of her way, but she makes it look effortless.

She looks back at me with a smile, her hand firm on my arm as she pulls me toward the bar. She says something, but I can't hear it over the crowd and the roar of the music. I shake my head, already dreading how my ears are going to ring tomorrow. Raising a single shoulder, she points to the shots on the bar, raising a single brow in challenge.

One that I meet readily.

The alcohol burns on the way down, but it's exactly what I need to be able to let go, to make myself be *here*.

We've only had a couple drinks tonight, but they've been enough to help numb the thoughts pounding away at the back of my skull.

Thoughts like the fact that Andrei kept his condo. And still keeps a full closet there. Like it's a place he regularly returns to.

Which tells me he's a man who's not planning on sticking around long-term, despite any assurances he's given me.

But that's not a useful thought right now, so I shake my head to get rid of it and grab onto Nadya's arm, urging her to head back to the dance floor with me.

I can't do anything about Andrei. I can't do anything about how he feels or what he thinks, or even what he does when I'm not around. All I can do right now is try to enjoy myself.

Throwing myself into the rhythm of the pounding music, I share a smile with Nadya as she throws her hands in the air and twirls around, wild and carefree. We dance with reckless abandon, pretending the mass of people around us doesn't exist.

And despite the worry in the back of my head, it's fun. Letting go and ignoring everything else with good company is *exactly* what I needed, and I wish I'd done this sooner.

I'm jolted back to reality when someone moves into our space, shifting like he's trying to get between us. All hints of amusement drop from Nadya's face as she rolls her eyes, reaching around him to grab my hand as she urges me to follow her away from him and toward the VIP lounge.

"Next time we hang out, I'm taking you to a pottery class," she grouses as the bouncer nods his chin at her and lets us through. "Somewhere we can actually talk, and we don't have to worry about random dudes crashing the party."

I can see the wisdom in what she's saying, but still...

"Pottery?"

"Yeah! I've always wanted to try it, and we can make ugly little pots. Who doesn't want useless, ugly trinkets around their house?"

We plop onto a couch, and as soon as we do, I realize just how much I hate the heels I'm wearing. As soon as I get home, I'm getting rid of them. I don't care how pretty they are.

"You know, if we really looked, I bet we could find a pottery class that encourages drinking. Like one of those paint and sip places," I tell her.

As if summoned by the mention of alcohol, a server appears before us with a bottle of champagne.

"Oh my god, you're so right." She grins, nodding eagerly as she pours herself a glass. "We're doing that. Let's get drunk and play with mud." We both laugh, and I feel younger than I have in ages.

I'm only twenty-seven, but some days I feel like I'm ancient. Trying to raise a child on top of everything else that's been going on has run me ragged for years, and most days all I want to do is fall into bed and sleep before it's time to get up and do it all over again.

Over the past month, that's changed.

Dates with Andrei give me something to look forward to, and I didn't know how much I needed that until I had it. And beyond that, he does so many little things that help ease the burden of running the house and taking care of Niko.

He takes out the trash, he makes me laugh, and he's incredible in bed. Not to mention the fact he manages to get Niko to go to bed on time without a fight. I don't know which devil he sold his soul to in order to make it happen, but I'm so fucking grateful for it I could weep.

If he wasn't insisting on taking me out every week, I'd probably be asking *him* on dates.

But I don't have to. He makes time for me, and I'm determined to enjoy it for as long as I can, doing my best to ignore the persistent thought at the back of my mind that he's not planning on sticking around longer than he has to.

"So, what's going on with you?" Nadya asks when we've settled down, startling me out my thoughts. "Things going alright with Andrei?"

"We're great, actually," I find myself saying. "He's been taking me out every week, and he's just..." I can feel my cheeks turning pink. "He's pretty fantastic when he wants to be."

"I told you he was one of the good ones."

"If I recall, you said he was good-looking, too." I take a sip of champagne while she throws her head back with a loud bark of laughter.

"Well, I wasn't wrong, was I?"

I laugh as I shake my head. No, she wasn't wrong. Even more so now that I've gotten to know him, Andrei is the most attractive man I've ever met. And like she guessed, he's a fucking beast in bed. Not that I'm going to tell her that.

I twist the rings on my finger, smiling down at my lap. "He's... he's pretty great, actually." And I don't know what to do with that. If he were distant and barely around, this whole situation would be so much easier. It'd be no problem to hold him at arm's length and live my life. Instead, he's endearing. And sweet.

And I hate to keep reminding myself that he isn't doing it because he likes me, but because he's trying to keep me safe.

"Oh, wait, when we left your brother's place you were saying something about work stuff?" I ask, just to distract her. Based on the way she immediately takes a long sip of her champagne, it works.

"They say you shouldn't work with family, but I'm an idiot, so I didn't listen."

"So, you work with Alexei?"

"Unfortunately. I balance the books for this place." She gestures around at the impressive club. "And I've needed him to give me a few forms for *days*, but if something has numbers on it, my *darling* little brother's just as likely to toss it in the trash as he is to remember he needs it." She rolls her eyes. "He needs to get his shit together after he's done with his meeting, or I'm not going to be able to do my job." She pouts, looking surly as she crosses her arms, and I almost regret bringing it up.

"I mean, seriously, he can't tell the difference between a balance sheet and a cash flow statement, but will he try to organize things to make my life easier? Of course not! Why would he bother with that?" She waves her hands around as she rants, and I smile.

I don't understand half of what she's saying, and from the sound of it, neither does Alexei, but she makes it fun to listen to.

Halfway through a story about what happened last tax season, she trails off, looking annoyed. I can't figure out why until a voice I'd love to never hear again rings across the lounge.

"Nadya! It's so good to see you again," Emiliya croons, sitting primly in the open seat next to me, crossing one toned leg over the other.

Her pretty brown hair is perfectly styled, delicate waves framing her impeccably made-up face. I glance at what she's wearing, and have to resist the urge to squirm. In comparison to her classy, designer dress, my outfit feels garish and too revealing.

Contempt practically drips from her fingertips, but is it any wonder Daniil was attracted to her? I blame him for more things than I'd like to admit, but not for that. She's everything I'm not.

Instinctively, my shoulders fold forward, trying to make myself as unnoticeable as I can.

"And Blair. You're here, too," she intones, sounding annoyed. She tosses her hair over her shoulder as she eyes me disdainfully, managing to make me feel like an outsider, even though she's the intruder in this conversation.

I bite back the annoyance battling the nerves in my gut. I'm not sure where she gets off being so hostile to me. I've done everything I can to be accommodating even though she was fucking my husband, but despite that, she seems determined to loathe me.

"Emiliya," Nadya's flat voice answers, despite her face being the very picture of pleasant surprise. "It's so lovely to see you, but I'm afraid we were just getting ready to leave. Weren't we, Blair?"

I nod, trying to seem unaffected, despite how badly I want to throw my drink in Emiliya's smug face. I hate that she's chasing us away from here, but maybe we can go back to dancing.

"Oh, that's a shame." She grins, flipping her thick hair over one shoulder. She looks me up and down before dismissing me and flicking her eyes back to Nadya. "Is your brother around?"

Nadya squints, her smile dropping entirely.

"He's working. Tonight, and every other night this week." She taps a finger against her chin as if she's thinking. "And I'm pretty sure he can do better than associate himself with a conniving snake like you." She shrugs. "But, hey, if public humiliation is your thing, you could try to talk to him yourself next time you see him."

Without another word she stands, looping her arm through mine and leaving Emiliya sitting there, silently fuming.

I choke on a laugh as Nadya walks away with her chin held high, like Emiliya isn't even worth thinking about.

"Emiliya and Alexei?"

She shakes her head. "I don't think he even knows her, but she's been trying to sink her claws into him for longer than I want to think about," she replies with a shudder. "But that's enough time wasted on that witch. Want to dance some more?"

"Absolutely." I'm not going to let one minor setback ruin my night.

We ease back into the crowd, moving with the beat and taking in the energy of the crowd as we dance. Out of the corner of my eye, I watch the guy who tried to interrupt us earlier grind his way up to another woman who looks even less amused by his antics.

I point in his direction, and we both end up laughing until a possessive grip on my hips pulls me back against a strong chest.

I look back, relaxing into him as the smell of Andrei's cologne wraps around me like a blanket, smiling as he buries his face in my neck. My hands slip over his, but I pause when I find the split, swollen skin of his knuckles. I blink up at him and he looks right back, smiling softly.

I want to ask him what happened, but Nadya scoffs in our direction. "Gross. Get a room."

Andrei huffs out a warm breath that sends shivers down my spine. Even in the hot room, the heat of him against my back is scorching, and suddenly I'd love for nothing more than to be burned.

"Now that you mention it, I'd love to. You going to be alright if I steal my wife for the rest of the night?" His thumbs stroke circles on my hips while Nadya makes a show of rolling her eyes, playing up her disgust.

"Yeah, yeah," she answers, waving her hand dismissively. "Get out of here."

"Do you need a ride?" I ask.

"I'm good. Alexei should be meeting me here soon anyway, so I'm going to hang out in his office and get drunk on the good booze." We laugh as we say goodbye, but Andrei keeps me in place while she retreats down a concealed hallway, disappearing into the shadows before he pulls me toward the exit.

He pauses after he opens the door for me, his hands flirting with the hem of my dress, making me realize how much it's ridden up while we danced.

"I really do like this dress," he murmurs, his lips dancing against the back of my neck. "Tell me, *zolotse*, are you wearing panties?" I nod, my cheeks heating. "When you get in the car, be a good girl and take them off for me."

I hesitate, glancing at the tinted windows and then back at him. They're dark enough that someone would struggle to see inside the car, especially at night, but still. They *could* see if they really wanted to.

He raises a dark brow in an unspoken challenge. I take a deep breath before I slide into the seat, keeping eye contact with him until he shuts the door, a smirk gracing the corners of his lips. As he walks around to his side, nerves make my hands shake.

When his door closes behind him, he simply looks at me. There's no one around the car, and it's dark, but there's still a possibility of being seen.

Am I seriously going to do this?

Under his hungry gaze, I feel a little braver. I arch up and slip my hands under my dress and into the band of my panties, making a show of pulling them off for him. As the pink satin slides down my legs, I shiver. His hands clench into fists. When I drop them into his lap, he growls while I laugh, an unexpected burst of excitement filling my chest.

"Spread your legs," he orders with hooded eyes. I glance out the windshield at a group of men passing by. When I look back, Andrei's eyes are dark, possessive, and hungry. I shudder, powerless to resist him in the wake of his want.

His desire erases any traces of reluctance, and when I spread my legs, my dress slides up my thighs, denying me modesty.

But I don't feel exposed when Andrei looks at me. His eyes burn with desire, the air around us filled with a tension that leaves me breathless.

He glances away for a moment, his eyes focusing on the men. They're standing around talking to each other, not paying us any attention, but something in Andrei's eyes shifts.

Andrei growls, turning on the car and focusing on the road.

The absence of his eyes is a physical weight.

It presses down on my shoulders until Andrei reaches across the center console, his hand tossing it away with a single brush against my bare thigh.

He teases me, smirking when he skims his strong hands over the sensitive skin of my thigh, the wet seam of my pussy, only skimming his hands over my clit long enough to make me gasp. He draws all my attention with small touches, only ever grazing his calloused fingers over where I need him.

He brushes his thumb over my clit, but as soon as my hips start to rock, he pulls away, maddeningly moving his hands to stroke against the soft skin of my thigh.

It's never enough to give me what I want, but his touch doesn't offer me a reprieve, either, slowly driving me to the brink.

Every mile of the drive takes an eternity, winding me tighter and tighter, until I'm dripping all over the leather seat, needing him to the point I'm ready to beg and plead for him to stop torturing me.

As soon as the car is stopped in front of our house, one hand is on the back of my neck and the other on my hip, hauling me out of my seat and into his lap, his mouth pressed against mine like he needs me as much as I need him.

Andrei's hands slip under my dress, gripping my ass as he maneuvers me exactly where he wants me while I cling to his shirt, hips bucking against him. I never had a hope of containing the way I burn for him, especially not when I find the hard ridge of his cock against his thigh.

He kisses me like a man possessed, mouth moving against mine like he wants it more than his next breath. His hands pull against me, encouraging me to move against him as the fabric of his pants ignites a delicious friction against my aching clit. I pull back, gasping against his lips.

"Andrei," I whimper as he winds his fingers through my hair and pulls my head backward, granting him more room to drag his teeth down my throat. "Please, Andrei. I need you."

I cling to the soft material of his T-shirt as his lips, teeth, and tongue abuse my delicate flesh, his hand running along the smooth skin of my thighs under my dress. At the same time that his terrible, talented fingers trace my wet core, his lips follow the line of my collar bone, startling a moan out of me.

"That won't do," he scolds as he thrusts two fingers inside me faster than I can complain. "Those noises are just for me. Not the neighbors, not for those *mudaki* back at the club," he growls while I drop my head against his shoulder, biting my lip while his hand moves, slow but relentless. "I'm a selfish man, Blair. I don't share."

As if possessed, my hands slip to his belt, but he pulls away from my pussy, placing a heavy hand on my wrists as he shakes his head.

He's barely touched me, but I'm already so wet that I think I should be embarrassed by it. He presses a kiss to my shoulder.

"Keep quiet, or I'll have to stop."

I bury my face against his throat, trying to keep back a desperate whine. My hips move against him, trying to urge him to hurry up, but he clamps his other hand on my hip, keeping me still.

"Andrei, please," I whimper.

Like an emotionless stone wall, he chuckles.

"Please what, *zolotse*? Please stop? Please let you scream my name? Please fuck you so hard you can't walk and the whole neighborhood knows exactly who you belong to?" I shake my head, eyes closed tight as his fingers trace my slit, tormenting me. "Then tell me. What is it that you want?"

"I want you to make me come."

He hums, but finally, *finally* thrusts his fingers deep inside me. But he's moving too slow, being too gentle to give me what I really need.

"And if I do that, will you stay quiet? Or will you wake up the whole neighborhood the moment you're dripping around my cock?"

I want to tell him that I can bite my tongue, but the truth is, I can't.

Something about being with Andrei makes me want to shed my inhibitions.

When we're like this, my insecurities don't matter. I'm not afraid he's going to judge me, and I'm definitely not worried that he's going to react poorly when I end up screaming until I'm hoarse, breathlessly begging for more.

"I'll be good," I pant, tracing the line of his throat with my tongue. His fingers move up my spine, a featherlight caress that feels like a kiss until his hand is back in my hair, urging me to hide my face in his shoulder.

My orgasm builds, and I just need a little more. A single touch to my clit, just a little faster, another pull of my hair, and I'll explode.

"Prove it," he says, curling his fingers to brush against my G-spot on his next thrust, even while I groan. His pace increases and I moan against him, my back arching. "Prove you can be good." Like he's answering my prayers, he flicks his thumb against my clit, teasing a third finger against my entrance.

"Andrei!" I sob as the dam breaks, pleasure coursing through me like a tidal wave, throwing me against the rocks. I ride his hand through the aftershocks until my thighs shake. He presses gentle kisses to my hair as I recover, shivering when I blink at him slowly. His expression isn't just hungry, it's *starved*.

He pulls his hand away slowly, evidence of my arousal sticking to my thighs as he pulls down my dress.

"That's my wonderful, beautiful wife," he murmurs, a smile apparent in his tone. "Now we can go inside, and you can scream my name as loud as you want."

Chapter 22

Blair

I blink as I look around the table and realize how *normal* this feels. Andrei nods along, looking far more engaged in what Niko's favorite bug is than he should be. It still astounds me that a man of his stature can give all his attention to my son without a care in the world.

Everywhere through the house, there are reminders that he's here, that he's carving out a place for himself in our home. But still, I can't ignore the image of the full closet in his condo, patiently waiting for Andrei to return home to it.

For the most part, he either spends his days working outside the house, or tucked away in his office. He emerges for dinner, spends the evening with us, and then spends his nights sharing my bed.

But sometimes I run into him doing chores, and it catches me off guard. I'll cook, then find him doing the dishes without prompting. More than once, I've run into him in the laundry room, already folding clothes before I even get a chance to get to it.

His coat hangs next to mine in the front closet. His shoes have been added to the shoe rack. His toothbrush is next to mine in the bathroom.

The way he looks after Niko is calm and gentle, but never overbearing. He defers to me whenever there's an issue, like he's taking care not to step on my shoes, even if it's for something as small as letting Niko stay up ten minutes later than normal.

His coffee is seemingly forgotten as he leans forward, asking Niko whether he prefers bugs that fly or crawl, his expression as serious as it always is.

Swallowing thickly, I shove the feelings building in my chest aside and instead glare at Andrei's phone.

I've told him before that I don't want phones at the table, but it's there more often than not. It's face down, and every time it's rung he's ignored it, but still. It's there. It's been pinging all morning, but he doesn't spare the thing a single glance.

I try to will myself to summon something more than minor annoyance, but I can't find the energy for it.

But if I want to be able to keep my distance, I need to find something. Some glaring flaw, some neon sign that I can't ignore until I remember to hold him at arm's length.

It just seems like everything's falling into place too easily, and I'm tired of waiting for the other shoe to drop.

His phone starts ringing, and he looks at it just long enough to silence it before his attention is back on Niko, nodding along to whatever topic they've moved on to.

I'm poking at my breakfast when Niko gasps suddenly, dropping the thread of conversation as he looks at Andrei with wide eyes. He looks at Andrei as if he holds the answer to every prayer he's ever had.

"Can we go to the park?"

I can't help but smile, but I cover it with my coffee.

On the one hand, it makes me uneasy how easily he's taken to looking at Andrei as an authority figure, but on the other, it's like watching a puppy chasing down the most dangerous man in the room and begging to play.

"*Please*, Andrei?"

Andrei takes another sip of his coffee, silent and unyielding in the face of Niko's big, brown eyes. He glances at me, lifting a shoulder in question. "If your mama says it's okay, then sure."

Niko looks at me, morphing his face into a picture of desperation, like he's been held prisoner and would sell his soul to see the sun again. When it's for easy things like this, I adore his dramatics. They let me know that despite everything that's happened, he's still the same silly boy I love.

"Okay."

He throws his hands into the air in celebration, and even Andrei can't help but chuckle.

An hour later, Niko's head is thrown back with full-bellied laughter as Andrei pushes him on the swings. The sun is warm on my skin, even as the fall air bites at my cheeks as I sit on a bench. The other kids at the park are running around, laughing and screaming as they play in the fallen leaves, climbing the playground equipment.

I wouldn't have expected Andrei to look so content playing with Niko, but he does. He's smiling, shoulders relaxed in a way I've never seen before. I use his distraction to my advantage and pull out my phone to snap a couple of pictures of the two of them.

They look like a father and son enjoying an easy day together.

I don't want to put any pressure on Andrei to make him think he has to fill that role, but maybe there will be a day when he'd like to look back on little moments like these. Or maybe these photos will end up just being something for me to look at and remember.

Either way, I'm smiling as I put my phone back into my purse, stopping when it lights up with a text from Nadya.

Nadya: Did you hear about Pavel?

Me: No. What about him?

Nadya: Andrei didn't tell you???

Nadya: Rumor has it someone found him in his apartment.

Nadya: And according to that same rumor, it looked like someone killed him

I force myself to slow down, reading her words again and again, until the words start to lose meaning.

Someone killed Pavel?

He's dead? What does she *mean*, Pavel's dead?

My hands shake as I put my phone away, ignoring the way it continues to ping with incoming texts.

I look at Andrei while my thoughts scatter in a thousand different directions. He already knows, right? There's no way he doesn't. His phone was blowing up this morning, and he ignored it.

He knows.

Shouldn't he be doing something?

Maksim must be livid. Surely, he's demanding answers and retribution.

Blinking, my gaze focuses on Andrei's bruised knuckles as he pushes the swing, like he doesn't have a care in the world, and my heart stops as realization clicks.

Andrei wouldn't kill Pavel.

He's loyal to Maksim. He wouldn't kill his pakhan's son.

That wouldn't make any sense.

Right?

Niko says something and Andrei laughs in response, loud and full-chested, and it feels like I can take a deep breath for the first time in years. It probably says more about me than it does Pavel, but the relief crashing over me makes me feel weightless.

The monster that's been hiding in the shadows is gone. I don't have to worry about him ever again.

For a moment, I feel like I could cry.

My mind keeps nagging at me, telling me that there's no way Andrei had anything to do with Pavel's death, but my heart rebelliously whispers that maybe he did.

My steps feel light as I walk toward them.

"You okay?" Andrei asks, raising a brow as I wordlessly wrap my arms around his solid torso.

"I'm great." I nod. "Are you able to stay home tonight?"

He eventually nods, and I don't bother trying to smother my grin as he wraps an arm around my shoulder, pulling me tight against him.

"Good."

I want to keep him close right now. I want to show him how much he's starting to mean to me. I want him to know how much I appreciate him, for both the small things and the potentially life-changing things he's done for me.

"Thank you," I murmur, standing on my toes to kiss his cheek. If he asked me to pinpoint exactly what I'm grateful for, there's a chance it would all pour out of me, but he doesn't. The little candle of peace that's found a home inside me remains undisturbed.

We're hand in hand as we walk back to the car while Niko races ahead, jumping on every fallen leaf that crosses his path.

"Would you like to go trick-or-treating with us next week?" I ask him.

He looks at me, looking so startled that I start to second-guess myself.

"You don't have to." I try not to let my disappointment show, but I shrug and slip my hand free. "I just thought I'd ask." At least I can blame the cold for my red cheeks.

Maybe I'm asking too much.

Within moments, he seizes my hand in his again, holding it even tighter. "I figured you already knew I was going to tag along." His voice is soothing. "I don't want the two of you wandering around alone after dark."

That's actually... really sweet. And unexpected.

Our neighborhood is safe, and now that I don't have to worry about Pavel, I feel even safer. But his concern thaws out my heart just a little bit more.

If I'm not careful, I'm not going to have any barriers left to protect myself.

"Should I wear a costume?" he asks as a line forms between his brows. Without thinking, I reach up and smooth my thumb over it, pulling my hand back as soon as I realize what I've done.

"What would you even go as?" I laugh, trying to brush off my embarrassment. He shrugs, watching Niko carefully as he chases a squirrel up a tree. "You don't have to wear anything special. I just want you there."

With us, I think, but don't say. The setting sun catches his face in profile, and I bite my lip, focusing on the path in front of us so I don't do anything else stupid. Like drag him to a stop and kiss him until I forget why I can't afford to fall in love with him.

"I'll be there, *zolotse*. I wouldn't miss it for the world." His smile tells me that he means it.

***

A soft foam tail smacks Andrei in the shins as Niko spins in a circle, showing off his costume. He's practically jumping up and down with excitement, a plastic bucket shaped like a jack-o'-lantern bouncing in his hands. The stuffed mouth of the T. rex costume flops backward, showing off his messy hair and pink cheeks.

I smile as I put on my coat. He's hidden his costume in his room for weeks, pulling it out every time Andrei's working and asking me to help him try it on. Now the grand reveal is here, and Andrei looks like he's holding back laughter.

Niko looks ridiculous, but he couldn't be swayed after he picked out this costume. He wanted to be a bright green and yellow dinosaur, and he's only going to be this young and care-free for a little while. If looking silly makes him happy, then that's exactly what he's going to be.

Andrei acts suitably impressed, making Nikolai beam from ear to ear, squirming impatiently while Andrei helps him with his coat. As soon as his arms are through the sleeves, Niko's turning around and pulling on my hands.

"C'mon, Mama!" he whines, grinning as soon as we're out the front door. As we make our way through the neighborhood, he slips his hand into Andrei's, barely containing his excitement as we move from house to house.

Part of me wants to fight against how comfortable Niko feels with Andrei, how easily he's accepted him. I beat back the urge when I see how surprised Andrei is, like he can't believe Niko wants to make sure he's close by.

Instead, I smile as I watch them, nodding along when Niko points out the over-the-top decorations that litter the yards, knocking on door after door and holding out his bucket for candy at each one.

His enthusiasm never fades, even when his energy starts to lag. He's having the time of his life, but if he doesn't get some sleep soon, he's going to turn into a tiny tyrant in a dino suit.

"Alright, kid," Andrei announces after we leave a house that has a giant spider propped against some overgrown shrubs. "One last house, and then we're heading home."

I blink, momentarily stunned. I'm so used to having to be the bad guy that I don't know what to do. Niko looks at me sleepily, not quite pleading, but not really trusting Andrei's word, either. I nod at him, but he doesn't fight. Instead, he marches up the last driveway with determination.

Keeping a close eye on him, I linger at the bottom of the stairs to the porch, gesturing for Andrei to do the same. The warmth in my chest from last week still lingers, and I lay my head on his shoulder as I lean into him.

Niko stretches up to ring the doorbell, looking back at us uncertainly before the door opens. He faces forward, belting out a cheery, "Trick or treat!" Andrei wraps an arm around my shoulders, pressing a kiss against the top of my head while we wait.

When Niko skips back to us, his arms are heaving under the weight of his candy bucket. Clearly the neighbors can't resist giving him all their candy.

Either that, or they've taken a single look at Andrei hovering in the background, using his presence to act as the most menacing parent you've ever seen, and decided they'll do whatever it takes to get him to leave. But I'm going to choose to think that it's just because of Niko.

To be fair, he does look really cute.

And it isn't like Andrei is trying to scare everyone in the neighborhood—he's just being protective, glaring at any man who looks like they might even think about stepping in our direction.

"Ready to go home?" I ask, offering my hand out for Niko's candy bucket. He nods, handing it over without a fight as he rubs a fist over his eyes.

"Will you carry me?"

"Sure." I smile, already reaching for him when he shakes his head and steps away.

"Not you, Mama. Andrei." I look at Andrei, and he has that same startled look on his face. For the first time, he looks uncertain. Niko's never asked him for anything I was willing to do before. He's only sought him out as a matter of convenience, and the weight of that trust can feel crushing when you aren't prepared for it.

I nod and, taking a deep breath, Andrei scoops Niko into his arms. "Sure, kid. No problem." Niko wraps his arms around Andrei's neck and settles right in, resting his head on his shoulder without a single care or worry.

Andrei's jaw is clenched tight while he looks around. I can't help but grin at how overwhelmed he looks. Niko rubs his face against his jacket, already half asleep when I take mercy on him and reach out to hold his hand and begin the slow trek home.

When Andrei turns his head, blinking rapidly, I pretend that it's because of the cold wind and lift our joined hands so I can kiss the back of his.

CHAPTER 23

Andrei

I'm still in a daze the next morning.

When Niko hugged me before falling asleep in my arms, it was both the greatest thing I've ever felt and the most terrifying. I spent the walk home trying to hide my conflicted emotions from Blair while she just smiled at me, a small glow lighting her up from within.

Niko's an amazing kid. He's curious, clever, responsible for his age, and knows how to listen. When he wants to, he's quick to show off his temper, and if he learns to control it, it'll be an asset as he gets older. He's a reflection of the best parts of his father and so much of his mother.

If he's guided by the right hands and learns how to be patient, he has the potential to go far in this life.

He was born with the expectation that he would follow in Daniil's footsteps, but if he wants to do something else when the time comes, I'll fight tooth and nail to make sure he gets the chance. Especially if this supposed brotherhood doesn't find a way to shape itself into something that deserves him.

I duck into the living room, continuing my search for Blair. She's supposed to be going to some pottery class with Nadya soon, but I can't find her anywhere. She's not in our room, not in the yard, and not in the living room, either.

She wouldn't leave without saying anything.

As a last resort I check Niko's room, hoping that he knows where she is. Peeking in, I find her sitting on the floor next to his bed, holding a hand to his forehead. His face is simultaneously flushed and paler than I've ever seen him.

"Everything alright?"

She sighs as Niko buries his face in his pillow. "He isn't feeling well, and it feels like he has a fever." Her voice is soft. It doesn't hide the way her shoulders are slumped in concern, but I can also see a little disappointment in her face, too. She was looking forward to her pottery class with Nadya. "I'm going to get you some medicine, then I'll be right back, okay?" she tells her son.

Niko makes a quiet sound that sounds like an okay, and I follow her out of the room.

"Can you watch him for a little bit? I have to call Nadya and cancel, but I'll be right back."

"I can stay with him," I say before I can think it through.

Blair's been excited about spending some time out of the house, and I can probably manage to watch a sick kid for a few hours.

There's a frown on her brow while she considers it.

"Are you sure? He's not going to be much fun," she eventually says, eyeing me warily. I school my face so she can't see how much that hurts. "He's probably going to complain and fight you whenever you try to help him."

Just like his mother.

"I can handle it. Say goodbye, then go and have some fun. We'll still be here when you get back."

Reluctantly, she nods, and I trail after her while she grabs a bottle of medicine.

"You'll call if anything happens?" She digs through a drawer, producing a thermometer which she also thrusts in my direction.

"Of course, *zolotse*. But we'll be fine."

I feel like we've been making progress, but it isn't as fast as I'd like it to be.

Blair's like a stray cat. I can't rush her. I go out of my way to make her feel safe, do everything I can to assure her that I'm here for her, but one wrong move and we'll be right back at square one.

I don't want to risk doing anything that'll scare her off. Asking her to trust me with Niko is a big ask, but if we're ever going to get to a point where she feels safe enough to love me the way I love her, it's a hurdle that she's going to have to overcome.

We'll get to the finish line eventually.

I'll wait for as long as I have to. And even though the words have been on the tip of my tongue for years, I'll keep waiting until she's ready.

She stays long enough to make sure I give Niko the right amount of medicine and gives me the number for his pediatrician, just in case, before she finally relents and leaves. I pretend not to notice the concerned way she eyes both of us when she does.

Only after she's gone does the worry set in. What the hell was I thinking, volunteering to watch over Niko on my own? Blair clearly wasn't comfortable with it, and I bet he won't be, either. Especially not after the way he put up a fight while taking his medicine.

I take a deep breath, trying to disguise my worry. Kids are like sharks. He'll smell my fear and take advantage of it.

I go back to his room, nearly choking on my worries. He's quietly crying into his pillow, cutting to my core more effectively than anyone ever has before.

"You alright, buddy?" I ask, running a hand over his forehead. "Does something hurt?" He nods pathetically, turning his watery eyes to me. "Need-to-go-to-a-hospital hurt, or need-a-hug hurt?"

Instead of answering, he reaches out for me so I can scoop him into my arms, and I run a hand up and down his back.

"Does that help?"

He shakes his head, wiping snot on my shirt.

"Do you want to watch a movie?"

Hopefully a distraction will help him relax enough that he can fall asleep.

"Yeah."

We sit side by side on the couch, watching a movie with cartoon dinosaurs until his tears finally dry. He yawns, resting his head on my arm, alternating between pushing a finger against the veins in the back of my hand and playing with my fingers.

Thank fuck he's managed to calm down. I don't know whether to thank the meds or the distraction, but if Blair came home and he was still crying, I don't know how I would explain the situation without making it seem like I can't handle this.

Niko means the world to her, and I need her to know that I'm capable of looking after him. Of looking after them both.

My phone pings in my pocket, and I check it, just in case it's Blair. I scowl when I see another text from Maksim and shove it back into my pocket while I pull Niko closer, not bothering to read it.

I should have predicted that Maksim would start lashing out at everyone and anyone after Pavel died, but I honestly hadn't considered him in my decision. Every day he greets me with mountains of shit to clean up, but that's a problem I can deal with in a few hours.

The bodies can cool, blood can stain, and egos can stay bruised. They'll still be there at the end of the night. I'm not going to abandon the little family I've claimed as my own just so he can maintain his rampage unimpeded.

After Blair's home and I know that she and Niko will be alright, I'll deal with his wrath. Until then, I don't give a single shit about what he wants from me.

Only a half hour into the movie, Niko goes quiet. I glance at him, half expecting him to be asleep, but he's fighting it. He's still, staring straight ahead and blinking slowly. Nudging him, he looks at me, his flushed cheeks and tired eyes making him look miserable.

"Do you want to go to bed?"

He shakes his head and crawls halfway into my lap, using my thigh as a pillow while he makes himself comfortable.

Maybe it's not as comfortable as he'd be in his bed, but this works too.

"What's your favorite color?" he asks as I pull the throw blanket off the back of the couch and wrap it around his shivering form.

"Why? Who wants to know?"

He makes a face before turning back to the television. "Me. I like blue," he offers.

"Blue's good. I like green."

"What's your favorite dinosaur?"

"I don't think I have one."

"Mine's a brontosaurus. They're tall, like you." I chuckle while he shifts around, making himself comfortable. "I want to be tall."

"Give it time, kiddo. You'll get there," I say, adjusting the blanket around his shoulders. He pays me no attention as he watches the movie.

"Do you love my mama?" he asks as casually as anything, while I turn to stone.

"Why're you asking that?"

"Because you're married to Mama like Papa was. And Papa loved Mama, right?"

"Of course he did."

"So you love Mama, too?"

Fuck. This is a conversation I wanted to have with Blair first, but Niko's too clever for his own good. Without meaning to, he's pinned me into a corner. I don't want to lie to him, but I don't want to confuse him, either.

"Yeah. I love her. Just don't tell her that, alright? I want her to hear it from me."

He nods, fiddling with the edge of the blanket.

"And you love me?"

"Of course I love you. You're pretty hard not to love, you know?"

He nods with a yawn.

"That's what Mama says."

"Well, she knows what she's talking about. You should probably listen to her."

With that, he lets the conversation drop. I wait for him to fall still, an exhausted mass wrapped in his PJ's, before I lift him up and carry him to his room, still bundled in the blanket. He's shivering, but when I touch his forehead, he's burning up. If I'm lucky, he won't remember what we talked about in the morning.

Niko stirs when I tuck him into his bed, clinging to me when I try to leave the room.

"Do you want me to stay?" I ask rather than pry myself loose.

"Yes, please."

So, I sit next to his bed and hold his hand while he snores, wondering again how I managed to trick him and Blair into this. A year ago, she never would have trusted me enough to watch Niko, not even for a few hours, and especially not while he was sick.

She used to eye me warily every time I came over, which wasn't uncommon since Daniil was an asshole. It always made me feel like an asshole, too, and I'd make excuses to keep my visits further and further apart as the years went by.

Now? I'm not quite sure how to process everything. I'm not sure how to navigate her allowing me to sleep in her bed, or the way she curls around my pillow when I wake up before her, or the way she studies me when she thinks I'm not looking.

Niko's lashes flutter against his cheeks as he sleeps, lost in his fevered dreams. He's accepted me into his life as easily as breathing, and I'll never be able to tell him how much that means to me.

I stay exactly like that for hours, holding Niko's hand until Blair cracks open his door, light from the hall filtering in around her silhouette.

"Hey," she whispers, poking her head in. "You guys doing okay?"

"Yeah. He was fine."

"Thank you," she breathes, sounding relieved. "You have no idea how much I appreciate you helping out." She leans down and kisses me, renewing my determination to make her fall in love with me.

"Any time, *zolotse*."

CHAPTER 24

Andrei

Blair is skilled in a number of ways.

She can see through bullshit better than anyone I've ever met. She always called out Daniil on his, and I can always see it when someone around us is running their mouth just from the way she purses her lips.

She's also unfailingly loyal to those she cares about. Even though she hasn't known Nadya long, I don't think there's anything that would get her to turn her back on her. She was the same way with Daniil, even though he never deserved it. And now she's extending that favor to me, both in what she does and doesn't ask me.

Daniil made a point of not letting her know any particular details of his work, and I can see the way she's biting her tongue with me, like she isn't sure if questions would be welcome or not.

But that doesn't change the obvious shift in the way she's acted toward me since Pavel died.

Even if I wanted to keep it a secret from her, dangerous men and their women are just as inclined to gossip as anyone else. And the death of the pakhan's son? That's too juicy to pass up.

From the way she's warmed up to me, I have a feeling Blair knows I had something to do with it. She doesn't ask, but she also doesn't seem offended by it. If anything, it's the opposite.

The one skill that Blair lacks?

She has no poker face.

My phone rings on the table next to me, but I steadfastly ignore it while she practically stabs at her dinner, hand clenched on her knife hard enough that I'm starting to get a little nervous. I silence the call again, but even Niko is giving me side-eye.

I know she doesn't want phones at the table. She wants to have some part of our day where there's no demands from anyone else, and we're focused on each other. Not the rest of the world.

I get it, and this is my concession. I won't answer it. I won't even look at it, but I need to be available in case World War III breaks out during dinner time. For a moment, silence reigns across the room and her shoulders relax a hair.

"So, Blair—"

It rings again. Her eyes cut like daggers, pinning me in place.

"Just answer it," she snaps while Niko pokes at his broccoli.

"You're in trouble," he sing-songs while I pick up my phone and kiss the top of her head as I pass. He got over his cold in a few days, and now he's acting as right as rain. And he might very well be right, but I'm sure I can find a way back into her good graces.

Stepping out of the room, I answer without looking at the caller ID as I head back to my office.

"Da?"

The word is hardly out of my mouth before Maksim's barking at me. Just as quickly, I regret not turning the fucking phone off, repercussions be damned.

"Where the fuck are you? I need you in my office. Now." I pinch the bridge of my nose, but before I can respond he hangs up, like I'm a trained dog that would never even *think* to disobey an order.

It's anyone's guess whether he wants me there because he wants to berate me for some imagined slight, or if he did something colossally stupid that he expects me to handle.

The only time I've been able to spend with Blair and Niko is the little time I've managed to steal away from his bullshit, and it's starting to wear to my nerves.

At least I know that Maksim's attention is focused elsewhere, and they aren't in his crosshairs for a while.

No one's found out my connection to Pavel's death, and I'm taking full advantage of it. Even if someone does suspect it, Maksim's becoming more unstable with each passing day, and no one's in a place to do anything about it.

That said, I miss the days when my workouts consisted of a run and weightlifting. Moving bodies around is getting tiring, and it's even worse when I know the names of more and more of the bodies.

Maksim's paranoia has gotten so bad that no man can consider himself safe in his presence. Not that they ever could, but even his right-hand man, Nikita, has started to look uncomfortable when they're in the same room together.

And as far as I'm aware, they've been as thick as thieves since the very beginning.

If we're all very, *very* lucky, Maksim's violence will end up getting him killed sooner rather than later. And if *I'm* lucky, I won't have to be the one to do it.

Unfortunately, I know better than to rely on luck, but until my hand is forced, I'll happily stand aside and offer the opportunity to someone else.

I wouldn't want to get greedy, after all.

With a kiss against her hair, I let Blair know I'll be out late and head over to Maksim's place, telling myself to be patient. His security rushes me through the gates, and I can't help but notice there are fewer men than there were the last time I was here.

The whole mansion is quiet, and I'm on high alert as I seek out his office, finding Maksim at his desk, feet propped on the corner as he takes a long drink from a crystal tumbler. In the center of the room lies a corpse, face beaten beyond recognition, surrounded by a still puddle of blood.

"Are you going to stare at it, or are you planning on *doing* something, you useless *mudak?*" Maksim slurs drunkenly, the dark liquid splashing over the rim of his glass as he gestures crudely toward the body.

The whole room reeks of blood and booze, and his slur tells me that this is far from his first drink of the evening. His hair is wild, the wrinkles on his face pronounced with exhaustion.

I doubt he feels any grief over his son's passing. That would require him to feel any warmth for anyone other than himself, something that's simply beyond a man like him.

No, he's only worried that someone might be gunning for his crown, and if they are, he has no clear successor to cement his legacy.

The only thing he has are the thin reeds of power that connect a group of violent, money-hungry men and the over-the-top furnishings he's surrounded himself with. The control that he's managed to forge for himself is coming apart at the seams.

Instead of answering him, I grab the roll of industrial plastic from the hall closet and crouch next to the corpse to get to work.

I pat down the body to check for ID or a phone, mildly grateful when I don't find any, then I start manipulating the limbs so I can force the limp limbs into a position that's easy enough to carry and dispose of.

I freeze when I flip the left arm over the chest.

The intricate spider tattooed on the back of his hand stares back at me. Looking back at the face, I don't recognize a single feature, but I can't forget that tattoo.

Dmitri was loud-mouthed and obnoxious, and now his face has been beaten to the point that it's unrecognizable. Instead, it's a mess of mangled flesh and exposed, shattered bone.

He was just a kid, looking for enough money to take care of his sister, and now he's nothing.

Just another victim of Maksim's untempered rage.

If Maksim keeps killing the people who've sworn their loyalty to him in his own home, there will be no legacy left for him to leave behind. There will only be blood and ashes. We'll end up killing each other before anyone else gets a chance.

"Where the fuck have you been?" Maksim's derision is clear, but the slur mutes the effect, not that he notices. The glass in his hand shakes as he throws the rest of his drink back in a single go. "You haven't been answering your fucking phone."

The hell I haven't.

I only make myself unavailable for one hour a day while we're having dinner. If he can't manage without me for a single hour, that's his problem, not mine.

I bite my tongue, knowing better than to try to justify anything to him. He doesn't want an explanation. He only wants to lash out, and he'll take any excuse he can find.

"Dinner with the wife." I shrug, rolling up the body. Maksim's lip curls, but before he gets a chance to berate me, I continue, not wanting to listen to him any longer than I have to. "Anything else I can do for you, Pakhan?"

Not for the first time, I'm grateful that Semyon inherited our father's temper instead of me. I know how to keep mine in check, but if Maksim decides to run his drunken mouth about Blair, I can't be sure I'll be able to stick to my resolve and let someone else handle him.

Doing anything to him now, when his few remaining guards know I'm here, would be nothing short of suicidal.

"Sotero," he offers.

"Luca Sotero?" I ask, raising a brow in question.

"*Da*. You met with that little shit a while back, right?"

"Sure."

I want to point out that if he had questions about the night I met with Luca, he could have just as easily asked Dmitri before he killed him, but I think better of it. For all I know, he did, and Dmitri didn't have the answers he wanted.

He stands, swaying on his feet. "What do you know about him?" He leans heavily on his desk, watery eyes locking onto me like an anchor.

"Not much. He's a capo, loyal to his guys." I shrug. "Best I can tell, outside of his gambling problem he doesn't cause issues, and always has his boss's money at the end of the month." It isn't anything that Maksim doesn't already know, and if he wants more, then I'm not the person to ask. I don't make a habit of digging into other outfits.

Unlike Maksim, I'm not interested in starting a war.

"I need you to find *something* on that motherfucker," he bellows, voice echoing in the enclosed space. He nods at Dmitri, his eyes suddenly slipping from me like he's no longer capable of keeping them in one spot. "This little shit didn't know anything." Stepping around the corner of his desk, he stumbles over his own feet, taking any heat away from the threat.

What a pathetic sight.

"Sure. Give me a couple days, boss." The vein in his forehead throbs a persistent beat, and I stand, hauling Dmitri's body over my shoulder. Fuck, he's still warm. "Am I good to finish up here first, or should I call someone else in?"

Maksim blinks at me slowly and nods before he stumbles out of the room slamming the office door shut behind him. I wait until the sound of his uneven footsteps fade before I head downstairs and dump Dmitri's body in the trunk of my car, giving myself a second to breathe.

He didn't deserve to go out like this.

I close the trunk lid and head back inside, rolling up the blood-stained rug while I pull out my phone and dial Alexei's number.

"Please tell me you have dirt on Luca Sotero," I say as soon as he answers.

"Don't tell me. He got sick of playing along and fucked up the last job." He laughs, but it's hollow at best. We both know that if Sotero had fucked up, I wouldn't be asking about it so long after the fact. I wouldn't be asking at all unless Maksim was involved.

"I need something, man. I'll owe you one."

He gives me a considering silence before he concedes and agrees to send me whatever information he's got.

***

It takes hours before I'm finally able to go home, and I'm left feeling unsettled. I wander around the lower floor, making sure all the windows and doors are locked, then spend a few minutes checking and rechecking that the alarms are set before I even think about going to bed.

It's redundant. Blair would have checked them before she went upstairs for the night. I know that, but I need to reassure myself that everything's exactly as it should be.

Pavel's gone. He was the most immediate threat, and Maksim's too caught up in his drunken stupor to know where to point fingers. There's no reason for me to think anyone else will go after either Blair or Niko for any reason other than because they're important to me.

And for the most part, I've done an alright job of keeping my head down and not pissing anyone off.

Nothing's out of place, but the knot in my chest refuses to loosen. Upstairs, I stop by Niko's room, breathing a little easier when I find him fast asleep, spread across his bed like a starfish. Closing the door softly, I head toward our room.

A small thread of hesitation curls around me when I see the light on under the door. I doubt Blair would have stayed up because she's still mad about my phone going off at dinner, but as I check my watch and see that it's a little after one in the morning, unease winds tighter in my chest.

She has no business being up this late.

"What're you still doing up?" I ask hesitantly as I open the door to see Blair sitting against the headboard, book in hand. The soft glow of the lamp makes her look angelic. She looks up at me with a soft smile, the green of her eyes almost startling in their intensity.

Not still mad, then. I breathe out a sigh of relief.

"I couldn't sleep." She shrugs, her entire demeanor soft and sleepy. She's wearing one of my old T-shirts, her hair tumbling around her shoulders in loose, messy waves.

Fuck, I love her.

"I'll be able to sleep now that you're home."

I grin, stripping out of my suit as I head toward the bed. "Is that so?"

"I always sleep better when you're here."

I grin as I crawl in next to her, cupping a hand around the back of her neck. "I'm very happy to hear that, *zolotse*," I murmur against her lips. She pulls me into her arms, and warmth floods my chest as I rest my forehead against hers.

"I missed you," she whispers, lips brushing against mine in a ghost of a kiss.

She nips at my bottom lip, and I grin at the tease, my free hand caressing the smooth skin of her bare thigh. I trail upward as she splays a hand across my chest, smirking when I find nothing but miles of soft skin under her shirt. When I reach her breast, I squeeze it and brush my thumb over her nipple, chuckling when her back arches, pushing her further into my hands.

Blair whimpers, letting out a shaky breath that makes my cock throb. I want to hear the sound again while I'm inside her sweet cunt.

"I missed you, too."

I kiss down the column of her neck, rucking up her shirt until it's gathered under her breasts, nipping at her collar bone where the shirt's slipped off her shoulder as I settle my hips between her thighs. She shudders as I roll my hips against her, licking the seam of her lips.

On her worst days, she's fucking stunning, but nothing brings me to my knees like the sight of her in our bed, spread out for me.

Like this, I want nothing more than to drive deeply into her and seek out the heaven that lies between her thighs, but I don't want to rush. Not tonight. Not when she's looking at me like I'm the key to her salvation. Not when I need her, need to know that she's safe and happy here with me.

The sight of her breasts makes my mouth water. They're a perfect handful, nipples beaded tight, begging for my touch.

And who am I to deny her?

I work my lips down her neck, her chest, and flick my tongue over her nipple, gently pinching it between my teeth. She gasps, hips bucking into my stomach. "You're so fucking beautiful, you know that?" Her nails dig into my shoulders as I pop the other into my mouth, sucking deep while she smears her wetness against my abs.

I'm already throbbing, and she hasn't even touched me. Fuck, I've hardly touched her.

I slide down her body, lifting her thighs over my shoulders as I kiss every available inch of her.

"Can you be a good girl and stay quiet again?" I ask, nipping at the soft flesh of her inner thigh, smirking as she shivers. "If you can't, I'll have to leave you here and take care of myself in the shower." My cock aches, miserable at just the thought when Blair's right here, ready and wanting.

She shakes her head furiously, pulling my hair as she tries to force me closer to her pussy, wetness shining in the lamplight.

In truth, I want to hear every breathy sigh, ragged moan, and choked groan.

She's terrible at being quiet when we're together, but I love it. Every sound tells me exactly how much she's enjoying herself, how much she wants to be with me.

But there's something irresistible about watching the desperate plea on her face as she tries to restrain herself, the way she gives in with her whole body that I can't pass up.

Her chest is flushed pink, eyes wild. Her nipples are tight nubs, red from my attention. I nudge my nose against the crease of her thigh, inhaling her sweet scent. I want to devour her, to forget everything except how delicious she is.

"Well?" Her teeth sink into the cushion of her bottom lip, hesitating, but she eventually nods. "Good girl."

It's the only permission I need before I spear her with my tongue, alternatively licking up the length of her to tease her clit and plunging it as deep as I can inside her, drinking up her wetness like the sweetest manna. She shudders, her muscles clenching, trying to pull me deeper.

I smirk as she bites back a moan, hands pulling even harder at my hair.

I'll never get enough of how she tastes, I think, groaning as I suck on her clit. She throws her head back as I reach up, squeezing her breasts.

I'll never tire of the sight of her like this. Lost in her bliss, she clenches her jaw tight as she tries to keep her sounds to herself, despite the whines and sighs escaping her. She looks *free*. It's like she's managed to let go of everything else except for what she's feeling and what she wants.

It's breathtaking.

Blair's always worrying about something, and even when she's sleeping, it's like she can't really let go. There's a small frown that mars her face hours after she falls asleep until she ends up clinging to me. It's like she needs to know that I'm right there with her, that I haven't disappeared.

But when I sink two fingers into her core, she isn't worried about anything. Her thighs clamp around my ears as I crook my fingers against her G-spot on each thrust while I flick my tongue against her clit.

Her body draws taut as she moans, cunt clamping down on my hand as she floods my mouth with her release. I let her ride out her orgasm, only pulling away when the aftershocks have ceased.

I click my tongue with false disappointment.

"I thought you were going to be quiet?"

Her eyes fly open in a panic. "No, please, I'm sorry," she whines as I lay a hand on her stomach, holding her in place when she tries to reach for me. She settles for grabbing my forearm. "I'll be good, Andrei! Please, just don't stop." She swallows thickly. "I need you."

I had no intention of stopping, but her words break something inside me.

"*Zolotse*," I grit out. She grabs one of her tits, rolling her nipple with her thumb and snapping the last thread of my self-control. I groan and grab her hips, fingers digging into the soft flesh of her ass. I place the head of my cock at her entrance for a single heartbeat before I sink into her, pulling her down as her wet heat pulses around my length, making me hiss a breath between my teeth.

She inhales sharply, throwing a hand over her mouth to hold back all her hot-as-hell moans as she rolls her hips against me, chasing another orgasm with reckless abandon.

She's so fucking tight, my brain short-circuits while I watch her. From her flushed cheeks to the thin sheen of sweat covering her chest, to how fucking hot she is around me, I don't know what to focus on.

"You were made for my cock, Blair," I grunt, tenderly stroking my thumbs against her hips. *"Fuck."*

I pull her hand away from her mouth. I don't care what I told her, I need to hear her. I need to feel her lips against mine. I need to know that she feels the energy between us. That this isn't just me.

I pull her into a hard kiss, teeth clashing together as my strokes grow sloppy. My balls draw tight, but I'll be damned if I'm going to come before I draw another orgasm out of her.

I shift my hips to a different angle, and her nails rake down my shoulders as she moans against my throat, her voice breaking as her cunt squeezes me like a vise, pleasure flooding her. Watching her come is more than I can bear, and I groan as I pump into her with harsh thrusts, filling her with my cum, needing to get every part of me as deep inside her as I possibly can, until she'll never be able to get rid of me.

I'm still panting as I press open-mouthed kisses against the smooth skin of her shoulder, the weight of her in my arms making me feel complete in a way I didn't know I'd been missing. I listen to the small sounds coming from the back of her throat as I thrust gently, letting her ride out her pleasure, muscles undulating around me.

She feels like heaven.

"I love you," I breathe into her hair, heart pounding in my chest. She tenses, and regret slams into me so fast I'm almost dizzy with it.

So much for waiting.

But now that I've said it, it feels like a dam has burst inside me, and keeping my feelings to myself will slowly suffocate me.

"I've loved you for years."

I kiss her forehead and roll over, my oversensitive cock twitching painfully when I see my cum leaking out of her. Despite how stiff she is, I pull her against me, guiding her to rest her head on my chest.

Maybe if I hold her close, she'll forget I said anything. Maybe she'll go back to being as soft and happy as she was before I opened my stupid mouth.

"Andrei—"

"You don't have to say anything." I smile, though it feels brittle. I smooth a thumb over her cheek. "I just wanted you to know. I don't expect anything else from you." I huff out a breath, wanting to do anything to ease the stricken look from her face.

Sure, I've let myself have moments where I've imagined she might return the sentiment, but I should've known better than to think it would happen this soon.

"What, uh." She clears her throat, hiding her face in my chest, one hand idly playing with my chest hair. "What do you mean, *years?*"

I twist a lock of her hair around my finger, deliberating whether or not I should tell her the truth. It's probably too much, and it'll probably just scare her off, but haven't I already done that? What else is there to lose at this point?

"Since the first time I saw you." I shrug, content to let that lie between us. "We were supposed to get you on our side, get you to leak information to us, but as soon as I saw you, I wanted to throw out the whole damn plan and keep you for myself."

I can still picture the way her hair shone like gold in the sunset as she walked to her car as she left work, looking like the sweetest woman in the world, even with exhaustion weighing down on her shoulders. And when I got her attention, and she smiled at me? It felt like I'd been sucker punched, the way the air was sucked out my lungs. I thought I was going to keel over when her face blanched with fear. And when she realized I was holding a gun, I wanted to.

Then Daniil got to her first.

"I thought you hated me."

Her brows are creased, like she can't figure out how to reconcile her image of me with what I'm saying.

For the first time, I wonder what'll happen if she never can.

My chest squeezes. Maybe she'll always see me as the violent brute who took her at gunpoint and threatened her life.

"Never."

"You threatened to kill me. You kept me locked up until I agreed to work with you."

I stare bleakly at the ceiling, unable to deny it.

"I never would have hurt you. You were never in danger. Not from me."

Chapter 25

Blair

The buzzing in my ears drowns out Andrei's gentle breaths long after he falls asleep. I'm not sure that he's ever fallen asleep before me, but right now, I'm not sure I'll ever be able to sleep again.

The first rays of light break through the curtains, allowing me to watch the steady rise and fall of his chest. His features are softened with sleep, relaxed when he's typically on guard, constantly taking stock of his surroundings and observing everything going on around him.

When he's like this, it's easier to think that he might have been telling the truth, not just blurting out whatever nonsense the post-orgasm endorphins were feeding him. When he's relaxed, he doesn't seem like the same inscrutable figure who upended my life and turned everything upside down to the point that it's unrecognizable.

In hindsight, I'm able to admit none of what he's done has made my life worse.

If anything, him kidnapping me and tearing me away from my boring life probably saved me from spending all my time being miserable, alone, and stuck in a job that stressed me out to the point of having panic attacks.

Even before I got roped into this mess, I was doing a great job of isolating myself and pushing away the few friends I had, and none of those people reached out after I left them behind with little to no warning.

Sure, initially, he pulled me away from everything and everyone I'd ever known and plunged me into the deep end, surrounded by dangerous men with no tools to defend myself, but he's also been the greatest defense I could ask for.

When Andrei's around, I don't have to worry about anyone kicking down the front door and taking me away from my son. He goes out of his way to make sure we're safe and comfortable. He's even helped me make a friend, so I'm not nearly as isolated as I was when I first moved to Chicago. I have people who I can talk to about my life and worries for the first time since... Since ever, probably.

I'm not jumping at shadows and waiting for the next threat to attack me anymore. I know I can rely on Andrei to look after us, and despite my head screaming at me, I know that I can trust him not to go out of his way to hurt me.

Even if having me by his side hurts his standing with Maksim, he won't turn his back on me. That's just not the type of man he is.

He said he loves me.

This man, who I've spent so long thinking hated me, loves me. Has loved me. For years, if he's to be believed, and when

I think about everything he's done for me and Niko these past few weeks, I start to believe he's telling the truth. With every fiber of my being, I believe him.

I've spent most of the night trying to figure out what he has to gain from lying, but I can't find anything.

Telling me he loves me doesn't cover up anything, it doesn't gain him any advantage, and he isn't protecting himself. He's only making himself vulnerable.

Andrei, a man who has never had a moment of weakness in all the time I've known him, made himself vulnerable. To *me*.

Whether he knows it or not, he's given me leverage, something I've never had in our relationship up to now.

Do I even want to use it? I mean, I still occasionally have nightmares about him pressing a gun to my side and forcing me into a car, and when his face is the first thing I see when I wake up, it takes a moment for me to remember where I am, much less that I've *asked* him to be here.

I've spent years keeping my head down and letting people hurt me so I can stay safe, and I'm not sure if I'm even capable of opening myself up to that kind of pain again.

Putting my heart on the line for Daniil nearly broke me, and only now that he's gone am I able to see the full scope of what our relationship took from me.

What if all I'm capable of is hurting Andrei? Maybe I'm too damaged to ever accept his feelings or find it in myself to return them.

It's safer to push him away.

Everything swirls around my head like an unceasing echo, making it impossible to sleep. Still, none of it is dimming the small spark of hope that's taking up residence in my chest, warming me from the inside out.

Andrei Voronov isn't a good man, and I'm under no illusions about it. He's been violent and brutal, and he won't hesitate to do it again if it serves him to.

But when he's home with me, he's patient and kind. I'm never worried that he's going to snap at Niko, because he always takes his time with him and answers his endless questions to the best of his ability. He makes sure to check in with us, even on the days when he spends most of his time out of the house. He comes home with busted knuckles, there's blood staining his clothes, and he carries a gun with him everywhere he goes.

But he could be mine, if I let him.

I smile as I watch him, his hand resting on his chest as it rises and falls.

I fall asleep between one blink and the next, waking up to find the bed beside me empty and cool to the touch. Niko's laughter, clear as a bell, floats up from the kitchen, followed by the low rumble of Andrei's chuckle. It settles the worry that always comes from waking up alone.

I make quick work of getting ready for the day and wander downstairs, pausing in the doorway to watch the two of them. They're sitting side by side at the island, playing with a set of plastic cookie cutters. Niko's arms are flailing around as he shows off what I think is an airplane while Andrei's pretending to evade him with one I think looks like a rose, but I can't really tell. Their backs are to me, but I can still hear the smile in Niko's voice as he talks, oblivious to my presence.

They have such an easy rapport that I'm almost jealous watching them. I can't tell if I'm envious of Niko for how easily he's accepted Andrei into his life, or of Andrei for how effortlessly he's been able to gain Niko's affection. Before I can decide, Andrei peeks over his shoulder and sees me.

He grins, warm and without hesitation, as if he doesn't realize I'm spiraling from his confession.

"Morning." He nods, nudging his shoulder against Niko's. My son's head whips around, cheeks round with his own grin. He wobbles in his stool, but Andrei's hand is firm on his back, helping him keep his balance.

"Good morning, Mama!" Niko drops the cookie cutter and braces his hand on Andrei's arm as he climbs down, rushing over to give me a hug. I kneel down, opening my arms as I wait for him. "Can we make cookies? Andrei and me found the cookie shapes!"

"You did, huh?" I look over the top of his head, and Andrei shrugs, rubbing a hand over the back of his neck. "Are you sure Andrei has something to do with you finding them? It wasn't just you?" I poke his ribs, and he giggles, wiggling away while he keeps a grip on my hand, pulling me further into the kitchen.

"He wanted to use them to make toast, but I wasn't sure if that'd damage them or not," Andrei says as he watches us.

"Andrei said we had to ask first." Niko pouts as he grabs the step stool he uses when he helps in the kitchen, stretching to reach for the upper cabinet where I keep my recipe books.

I shake my head as I watch him, his hand not even close to reaching the handle. He stands on his toes, eyeing the counter like he thinks he'll get away with climbing up.

"Well, for the record, I don't think toast would damage my cookie cutters," I say, keeping an eye on him as I take a quick glance at Andrei. His arms are crossed as he leans on the counter, hair still damp from a shower. He's dressed in a faded black T-shirt and worn jeans that hug his thighs so well I'm almost jealous.

"Good to know," he murmurs, looking perfectly at home, as if keeping a toddler entertained and quiet is as natural as breathing. He looks like he belongs here. He looks like a dad.

I have to swallow the sudden lump in my throat.

It's a good thing they get along. Deep down, I know that.

So why is seeing Andrei like this suddenly putting all thoughts to a halt?

"Careful, buddy." His voice startles me out of my fugue, and I look back at Niko to find him teetering dangerously on his stool. I quickly put a hand on his shoulder to stabilize him, and he settles back onto his feet, huffing with frustration.

"You know, if we make cookies now, you won't be able to eat them until after lunch."

Niko looks at me like I've grown a second head, and it's all I can do to hold back a laugh.

"But if we wait that long, they'll get cold!" His tone is miserable, which I understand.

Is there anything worse in this world than cold cookies?

He looks at Andrei, who chuckles as Niko stomps off the stool, leveling him with his fiercest glare.

"It's not funny!"

Andrei schools his face into a serious mask, but the corners of his mouth are still twitching with restrained laughter. "You're right. It's not funny at all," he answers, sounding just as serious as my ridiculous son. "I guess we have no choice but to wait until after lunch to make cookies, do we?"

With a dramatic huff, Niko nods. "Cookies later, then," he announces with the weight of the world on his shoulders. He looks ready to negotiate world peace as he puts his hands on his hips. "Can we play outside until lunch?"

Andrei doesn't hesitate to nod. He looks like he wants to hand the keys to the castle over to the boy who's looking at him like his word is law.

"Sure thing." He glances at me while he gathers the cookie cutters scattered across the counter. "If you're alright with it, I can go play with him. You can have some time to yourself."

Man, that sounds like exactly what I need.

I nod my permission and he squeezes my hand as he passes me, dutifully tidying the mess and herding Niko toward the door, urging him to put on a jacket.

Just before he darts out the front door, Niko runs back to me and hugs my legs.

"Bye, Mama! Love you!"

I ruffle his hair, and he turns back, bouncing on his feet as he waits for Andrei to open the door for him. Instead, Andrei walks over to me and kisses me, lips moving against mine in a rhythm that makes my knees weak.

I lean into him just as Niko makes a disgusted scoff. Andrei pulls back, lips brushing against mine as he chuckles. It's enough to make me feel dizzy before he rests his forehead against mine, corners of his eyes curling up in a smile.

"Have a good day, Blair. I love you."

Before I can utter a response, they're both out the door, like he didn't just knock my world off its axis.

Again.

Warmth still sparks along my nerves from where Andrei was touching me, lingering even in his absence.

I don't know what to do with his open affection. Or what to make of Niko's casual acceptance of it. Or what to do now that I'm alone.

Without the two of them here, the house feels empty.

Since Niko was born, my time alone has been limited. Before he knew how to talk, Daniil would take him to the office on occasion, but that stopped over the past year and a half or so. And after Andrei moved in, there's always been a background level of noise from him moving around or making phone calls.

But now, there's no cartoons playing on the television. No pretend dinosaurs roaring. No clipped words coming from a makeshift office. I'm the only one here to fill the sudden silence, and I don't even know where to begin.

I pull out an old book, one that I know like the back of my hand, determined to lose myself in the comforting words.

In the time I've known Andrei, he's never been one to do anything without a reason. Either he wants to spend a day with Niko, or he wants me to have the space to work through how I'm feeling after last night. I should appreciate the sentiment, but instead I feel a vague resentment.

I don't *want* to think about what he said. I don't want to try to pin down my feelings for him. I don't want to make anything seem more real or serious than it is right now.

Things are good. We were having fun and getting along. Why did he have to make things more complicated than they have to be?

Ironically, I wish he were here to give me an outside perspective. Talking with Nadya might help, but talking to Andrei is what always makes me feel settled. If I could just talk to him about what I'm feeling, he'd be able to help me sort through everything.

I like him, I realize with a start. It's not just that I miss his presence, or that I want him around because he makes me feel safe: It's because I actually like him. Somehow, he's managed to become my friend, and he's made my life better just by being a part of it.

I blink down at my book, realizing I haven't absorbed a single thing I've read. A glance at my phone tells me that I've been pretending to read for the better part of an hour.

Giving up, I head outside and sit on the porch, wrapping my hands around my knees as I wait for Andrei and Niko to get home like a needy dog. The wind whips through the fabric of my sweater, but I'll be damned before I admit that I need a jacket to anyone, including myself.

Fortunately, I spot them walking down the sidewalk only a few minutes later, hand in hand as Niko grins without a care in the world. The way Andrei looks at him, like what he's saying has the same weight as anything I would say, chases away the chill and brings back the warmth that his kiss instilled in me.

I can tell the moment Niko sees me, pulling on Andrei's hand as he tries to drag him down the sidewalk even faster. I laugh at how his short legs shuffle as quickly as possible while Andrei takes small steps, exaggerating how quickly he's being ushered along.

"Did you two have fun?" I ask when they're close enough.

"Yep!" Niko doesn't hesitate, just keeps marching along with single-minded focus. Andrei grins at me, pausing to kiss me before he opens the door, much to Niko's chagrin. "Now it's later, and it's time for cookies."

He looks at Andrei as he makes a show of pulling his step stool back out, pointing at the cupboard.

"Can you please get the book?" Niko does his best impression of a puppy. "I'm still too little."

"I told you you'll get bigger eventually."

"But I want to be tall now!" He pouts.

Andrei laughs, a full sound that rings through the kitchen, hitting me like a sack of bricks.

I'm in love with him.

The realization slams into me so suddenly I have to take a moment before I remember how to breathe.

I have no clue how or when it happened, but I do. I expect a wave of panic, but instead it's like the tension I didn't know I was carrying around is just... gone.

I allow myself to bask in the feeling as Andrei pulls down a recipe book, putting it on the counter for Niko to look through.

"You know what you're looking for?"

"No," Niko mutters, flipping through several pages before he looks at me. "Mama, I can't read."

I help him find the right page and get out the ingredients, happy to spend an afternoon baking with these two, even if they do spend more time sneaking bites of the dough than they do helping.

While Niko's distracted pressing out shapes with the cookie cutters, I wrap my arms around Andrei's waist. He pulls me against him, smiling softly at me.

Has he always looked at me like that?

How have I missed it?

"I love you," I breathe, and the smile on his face erases any doubts that might have lingered.

"Yeah?"

"Yeah."

"I love you too, *zolotse*."

***

The house is quiet as I stand in front of my vanity, running my fingers over the chain Daniil's rings are on. It's the first time I haven't worn them in some capacity since he slid them on my finger. The diamonds glitter under my thumb.

I've loved and hated these rings in equal measure for years. I loved them for my little family and all the happy moments Daniil and I had together. I hated them for every night I cried myself to sleep, not knowing if he was going to come home, or if he was planning on staying with his mistress all night.

Looking back, I should have seen the engagement ring as a red flag. It's bold, flashy and not my taste at all. If he'd asked me about it, I would have told Daniil I prefer understated jewelry. I would have preferred something more unique, something that didn't scream how expensive it was for everyone to see at a glance.

Something more like Andrei's ring.

Andrei's never said a word about me keeping Daniil's rings. He's noticed them, watching me with a stoic expression when he's caught me fiddling with them, but he never expressed any disapproval or disappointment in me for keeping them close.

Andrei's in love with me, but he let me hold onto these without complaint. And, god, I love him for that, too.

Andrei lets me mourn and heal without making demands, content to be there and let me lean against him when things get hard.

I slip the rings off the chain, turning them over in my hand.

Realistically, they're nothing but precious gems and polished metal.

They don't hold the emotional weight I've given them.

These rings have done nothing to hurt me. They're not the ones who left me. And if I don't wear them anymore, no one will be upset.

I repeat that to myself over and over before I put them in my jewelry box, shutting them away. For some reason, I expected it to feel more final, more like a decision, but nothing happens.

The sky doesn't fall, no one yells, and I have no more closure than I had this morning.

Still, it feels like a weight has been lifted off my shoulders.

When I finally tear my eyes away from my jewelry box, Andrei is leaning against the doorway with his arms crossed, watching me. There's no sign of judgement, no hint as to what he's thinking.

"Did Niko fall asleep?" I ask him, blinking away an unexpected wave of emotions.

"Yeah. He was beat after running around all day."

"That's good."

All I did was put the rings away, but I feel like I've been wrung out and tossed around.

"How long have you been standing there?" I ask, pretending my eyes aren't burning.

Andrei doesn't answer as he crosses the room, wrapping his arms around me. I lean into his embrace, smiling as he searches my face. He moves one hand, silently stroking the bare skin of my neck.

"How are you, *zolotse*?"

With one question, he breaks the dam inside me, and all my feelings rush to the surface. All my lingering hurt, my doubt, my insecurity, my love for Andrei. I hide my tears in his chest, finding strength in his warm embrace.

"I'm okay," I tell him, proud that my voice doesn't shake. "Better with you here."

Chapter 26

Blair

Either Alexei's face always looks like he stepped in dog shit, or he *really* doesn't like me.

He's sneering from the moment I open the front door, trying to shove his way in like he's welcome in my home without any greeting or acknowledgment. I move a step further in front of him, blocking his entrance. As intimidating as his glare is, it doesn't provoke me to move.

"Move, Blair."

"Hello to you, too," I answer with a cloying sweetness that would typically make me cringe but feels appropriate for his attitude. "Is there a reason why you're trying to storm into my house?"

He draws his shoulders back, making him look even broader than he is, but I refuse to back down until I know why he's here.

Andrei doesn't make a habit of bringing his work home, and he certainly doesn't invite anyone over. Though if he was going to, I'm willing to bet he'd at least give me a heads up.

So, Alexei showing up without a word of warning is setting off more than a few alarm bells.

"I need to talk to Andrei. So, you need to move your happy ass and let me in." His hand slams down on the door next to my head, making me flinch.

"Mention my wife's ass again, and you'll lose your ability to speak," Andrei growls from behind me, his tone lethal. He slips a hand around my waist, gently pulling me away so that I'm no longer blocking the doorway.

Alexei's eyes cut to him as he stalks inside, much to my annoyance.

He needs to get over himself. I've never tried to piss him off, I've never tried to bother him, and he needs to find a way to deal with his resentment and find a way to cope with my fucking existence. Luckily for him, I don't like having more of the stupid Bratva in my house at any given time than I need to. One of the few benefits of having everyone who's important hate my guts is that I never had to learn to deal with unexpected visitors.

And maybe I'm being defensive, but his prickly attitude is grating enough to make me want to lash out. Even though that's probably stupid.

Maybe more than probably.

Maybe it's definitely stupid.

I'm safe with Andrei, but I can't let myself forget that the people he surrounds himself with are still dangerous and can make our lives a living hell if they want to.

"Do you have somewhere we can talk?" Alexei asks, looking at me pointedly, and years of resentment and frustration burn down my spine at the unspoken accusation.

I've never said a word to anyone about Bratva business. I mean, hell, the only people I've ever spoken to about it are Andrei and Daniil, and that was because I was fucking *forced* to.

Andrei's grip tightens as he tenses, and it's enough to tell me that I need to calm down.

"You two talk," I bite out with a false smile. "I'll be... literally anywhere else, I guess."

Pulling free of Andrei's grasp, I storm around the corner, trying to talk myself into giving them some privacy. I try, but the anger at Alexei's dismissive attitude won't let me. Maybe if he hadn't acted like an asshole and had treated me like any of his other colleagues' wives, I'd go on my merry way and live in my ignorance.

But he's a dick that can't spare an ounce of respect for me, so I have none for him.

I press myself against the wall, far back enough that I'll have time to retreat if they make it past the entryway, but close enough to still make out their hushed conversation.

"Luca Sotero's dead," Alexei bites out. I rack my brain, trying to think if that's a name I've heard before, and come up empty.

"*Blyad*," Andrei sighs. "He wanted info on him so he'd have a fucking excuse, didn't he?" There's a tense beat of silence that makes me shift from foot to foot. "Did Maksim take credit, or is he letting them figure it out on their own?"

I wish I could see his face and try to figure out what he's thinking. Was this Luca guy important?

"Are you fucking kidding? Of course he took credit." Alexei sounds furious enough to make me flinch.

That, more than anything, tells me I shouldn't be eavesdropping on their conversation. I try to slink away as quietly as possible, my frustration warring with my stubbornness.

I want to be able to understand what's happening, why they both seem upset, but without any context, I know I'll never be able to understand. Sure, if I ask Andrei later, he'll tell me. He's not shy about answering my questions. But what happens if I ask him something that he doesn't want me to know?

If I were to ask him outright if he killed Pavel, would he tell me? I'm sure he did, but would he *confirm* it? Or would he clam up and pull away?

He might love me, but is that enough to convince him I'll keep his secrets?

Maybe it makes me a coward, but I'm not sure I want to find out any time soon. Not when it's so much easier to keep my head buried in the sand and not risk getting hurt.

I duck into Daniil's office, pressing my back against the closed door while I look around the room. There's a thin layer of dust on the shelves and the top of the desk, curtains closed like he just finished working for the night. I pull them open, watching the way the dust floats in the rays of sunlight shining through the windows.

It doesn't add any life to the room. Everything's still empty and dull.

I haven't been in here since before Daniil died. It was always his domain, and I never felt welcome inside it. He preferred that I gave it a wide berth when he was gone, and that I only came in when he invited me.

But he isn't here to get upset anymore.

I haven't been able to work up the nerve to start cleaning in here, and when Mila suggested she do it, I took a page out of her book and pretended she hadn't said anything at all.

My fingers carve a path through the dust as I look at the shelves of books. There are leather-bound hardcovers and fancy notebooks that are filled from cover to cover with his messy notes, jotted down during meetings and hearings. He used to say that they were a police raid waiting to happen, but he trusted them more than keeping digital notes. At least if he burned these, they'd be gone for good.

I entertain the thought of pulling one out and reading it, but can't bring myself to do it.

Giving up, I sink into his chair and run my fingers over a lingering dark blue stain on the desktop, barely visible through the dark stain of the wood. There's a pile of notes stacked on the corner of the desk, tempting me with the sharp angles of his almost illegible handwriting.

I pull one out at random, tracing a fingertip over the scrawled notes and smeared ink without taking in the actual words.

I want to say I can judge Andrei as his own person and assume he won't react the same way Daniil would, but it's hard.

I've let myself love him, but trusting him feels like climbing Mount Everest. If I upset him and he takes off, I'll be right back where I started. Even worse, I'll be heartbroken on top of being alone.

"Shut up and mind your own business," I mutter, resigning myself to being an ostrich for the rest of my life.

It's a shitty strategy, but it's served me well enough so far.

I don't know how long I sit there feeling sorry for myself before the door opens with a creak. I look up, startled to find Andrei looking back at me.

"Did you hear what you wanted?" he asks casually.

He smiles, but it doesn't soften the embarrassment brewing in my gut. I should have known better than to think that he wouldn't know I was eavesdropping. I shake my head, occupying myself tidying the notes, staring at the ink stain.

Part of me is still surprised that Daniil didn't throw out this desk. Or any of the other stained furniture. We hadn't even gotten around to painting over the stains before he died.

Is it even worth trying to cover them anymore?

"I shouldn't have," I admit. "I'm sorry. It won't happen again."

"It probably will. I'm not going to go out of my way to keep secrets from you unless you want me to." I look back at him, bracing myself to see anger. He's leaning against the door, arms crossed loosely over his chest.

He doesn't look mad. He doesn't even look annoyed. If anything, he looks concerned.

"What do you mean?"

"Exactly that." He shrugs. "If you want to know something, ask, and I'll tell you. If you don't want to know anything, that's fine, too." He looks around the room, gaze lingering on the open curtain.

We should be getting ready for another date, but he doesn't seem to be in a rush.

"I know that Daniil kept you in the dark about everything," he says, and again I feel like a child caught with their hand in the cookie jar. "But I also know that you're smart. If you want to know what's going on with my work, then I'll tell you."

He paces across the room, spinning the chair so that I have no choice but to look at him.

"I trust you, Blair." His silver eyes pin me in place, and I couldn't look away if I wanted to. "If you want to know anything, you only have to ask."

I hesitate, but his eyes are sincere. And though it might come back to bite me, I want to trust him, too. I want to trust him so badly.

"Who's Luca Sotero?" I ask quietly, worried this might still be a trick.

"He was a capo for The Outfit. We did arms deals with him," he answers easily, one corner of his lips lifting ruefully. "And apparently Maksim had him killed."

"Why?"

"Probably because he thinks they were behind the hit on Pavel, and he wants revenge." He shrugs again. "Maksim's been making moves to expand into their territory for a few months, though, so maybe he was just looking for an excuse to cause trouble."

Alarm fills me, but Andrei looks as calm as he would if we were discussing the weather.

I take a deep breath.

"But they didn't kill Pavel. You did."

He kisses me and nods, pressing his forehead against mine. "*Da, zolotse*. I did." His face doesn't show any regret or worry. He's just as matter-of-fact about this as he is anything else.

I close my eyes, breathing in the scent of his cologne, and wrap my arms around his shoulders.

"Can we stay home tonight?"

I don't want to share him with anyone else right now. I just want to be close to the man I love. He nods, lifting me effortlessly into his arms.

"Of course we can."

CHAPTER 27

Andrei

"Don't go where I can't see you!" Blair calls as Niko races toward the mass of people crowding the dinosaur exhibit. He looks back at her with a smile, but slows down, remaining in her line of sight.

When I suggested a trip to the Field Museum, he looked at me like I was the sun in the sky, but I'm starting to understand why Blair immediately looked exhausted.

I've never been here before, but I think I realize why they both like it so much. Both of their faces light up when Blair reads Niko the placards in front of the displays, and all his attention is on what's in front of him. I'm mesmerized as I watch them, looking carefree and relaxed as they stroll from exhibit to exhibit, hand in hand.

When Blair told him that he had to wait to see the dinosaurs, and they'd be the last exhibit we'd go to, I thought he would have rushed through everything to get to what he wanted, but it's only taken a little prompting to get him to cooperate.

When he got bored and tried to wander off, I kept an eye on him while we let Blair look at whatever she wanted, sitting on a bench and playing nonsense games until she was ready to move on.

He started to flag when he asked me to tell him about everything in the gem exhibit, but now I'm pretty sure he was just conserving his strength.

His seemingly endless well of energy kicks up to another level the closer we get to the dinosaurs. This whole trip only happened because I was hoping to have a single day without having to hear the *Jurassic Park* theme song, but I think I bit off more than I can chew.

I level a glare at a mother that steps closer to Niko, trying to get a better view for her child, but she quickly heads in a different direction when Blair catches up with him, putting a hand on his shoulder. She looks like she's reaching the point of buying a child leash, and if he runs off again, I'm going to beat her to it.

He smiles at me again, like I've made his whole year just by being here with him, and I wonder how I can talk Blair into coming back more often. Is once a week too much? Maybe she'll settle for once a month. I'd be willing to work with that. Niko deserves to have a fun day that's all about him.

And maybe I just want to enjoy the fact that he likes spending time with me.

I'll never be able to step into his father's role, but I hope he can learn to lean on me. Even if I haven't earned the privilege, I want to have some small part in shaping his life.

When the crowds become too thick for him to shove through, he asks me to carry him so that he can see the fossils, eagerly telling me everything he knows about every single dinosaur species.

By the time we're getting ready to leave, he's practically catatonic and reaching for Blair. She takes him with a smile while we walk back to my car, adjusting his grip on the stuffed brontosaurus that he picked out in the gift shop.

"Thank you for suggesting this." She looks content while she rubs his back, smiling at me. "I'm pretty sure you made his whole week."

"Yeah?"

She tucks a lock of hair behind her ear as she nods, masterfully balancing him on one hip.

"I'm pretty sure you're his favorite person."

I wrap my arm around her, holding tight around her shoulders. I never thought I'd manage to find an actual place in this little family, but her words move something inside me. Her gentle smiles, the way she speaks without any hesitation or resistance. It makes me feel complete. Like I've finally managed to stumble through the dark to exactly where I'm supposed to be.

"*Zolotse...*" My voice trails off as the hair on the back of my neck prickles. I sweep my eyes around us, pushing Blair quickly toward my car.

I can feel her looking at me curiously at the same moment I catch sight of a black SUV rolling down the street toward us. The windows are tinted dark enough that I can't see anything inside, and when one window rolls down just enough for the barrel of a gun to poke out, I shove Blair behind a parked car, keeping my body between her and the SUV.

"Get down!"

No sooner do the words leave my mouth before the sounds of semiautomatic gunfire ring out. Around us, people scream and run away while I pull out my own gun, aiming over the hood of the car with one hand while I push Blair and Niko further down with the other.

Glass showers around us as bullets shatter the bullets shatter the windows and tear through the metal frame with heart-stopping *thunks*.

I return fire, taking no solace when I see their back windshield crack and shatter while they tear off, weaving through traffic and away from the chaos. There are bullet holes in the building behind us, and the sweet smell of coolant invades my nostrils as I pull Blair into my arms.

Her whole body is curled around Niko, who's sobbing into her chest, eyes wide with terror and confusion. I check him over before I look at Blair. I don't see any blood, but it's a small consolation.

My hands are shaking while I run my hands over her cheeks, pulling them into my arms.

Who the fuck did this?

"We're okay," she pants, like she's trying to convince herself just as much as she is Niko. "We're going to be okay."

I rock them back and forth, but my mind's a hundred miles away. They're physically okay, but I can't spend too long here. I can already hear sirens coming, and we need to make ourselves scarce before the cops get here. My heart demands blood, but

I can't afford to let it rule in the heat of the moment. I need to push my feelings aside and make sure my family is safe and never in this position again.

I pull Blair up, scooping up Niko's forgotten toy, and urge her to walk, but she seems numb while we hurry to my car. Thank fuck it's far enough away and didn't get hit by any stray bullets.

I push her into the car, driving off while she holds Niko in the back seat, trying to calm him down.

I should call Maksim. The windows were too dark for me to identify anyone in the SUV, but I'd bet anything that this was retaliation for the hit on Sotero. If The Outfit managed to take me out, they'd have Maksim pinned. He needs me to clean up his messes before the law can get involved, and without me, he'd have to fight against both of them.

But with how he's been acting? There's a real chance this is exactly the sort of ammo he's been looking for to stage an all-out war.

And if this was any indication, he's already been sloppy. If he tries to antagonize the Italians any further, I'm not sure I'll be able to keep my family out of the crosshairs. This was already too fucking close.

Fuck.

Gritting my teeth, I pull out my phone and call Alexei, trying to take a calming breath before he answers.

"What do you—" he asks, immediately shutting up when he hears Niko's panicked wailing. Blair's trying to hush him, but that's not going to happen before his ears stop ringing. *Blyad,* this could have been so much worse than it was. "What's going on?"

"There was a shooting."

"You guys alright?"

I look at Blair and Niko where they're curled up in the back-seat. His face is buried in her neck as he cries, and she still isn't looking at me. My heart lurches in my chest, and for a moment I'm not sure I can breathe.

"Physically, sure. Not sure about the rest of the people out-side the museum."

Honestly, I can't remember if there was blood or bodies around us. I wasn't worried about anyone else.

Just my family.

"Fuck. Any clue who's responsible?" Alexei asks.

I change lanes as I shift through traffic, keeping an eye on the rearview mirror. I don't see a trail, but I'm not going to take the risk of assuming we don't have one.

"I can take a fucking guess," I bite out, cringing when I look at Blair. Niko's too upset to hear a word I'm saying, but I'll still have to make sure to apologize later. "You're my first call."

Hopefully he recognizes the significance of that. If Maksim's in the wrong mood, he might view that alone as treason.

I hesitate, weighing my next words carefully. I can't trust Maksim to handle this. Anything he'd do would probably just lead to further violence, and I refuse to let that touch my family. I only have the vague outline of a plan, but it's more than enough to get me killed if the wrong person were to find out.

Even though our friendship—if you can call it that—is fraught at times, I trust Alexei more than most. Still, I'm not sure I want to put my life in his hands.

I risk another glance at Niko and Blair.

Regardless of the personal risk, I have to make sure they're safe, and if someone's coming after me, they aren't.

I don't have a choice.

"Do you have a number for Marcell Renzuto?"

If I want to keep my family safe, I need to cut a deal with The Outfit. And I don't have time to go through the whole fucking chain of command.

Marcell is only the puppet the actual boss uses to draw heat, but he still holds power. As far as The Outfit's soldiers—as far as the *feds* are concerned, Marcell Renzuto runs the show. He can give me what I need, and he's under too much scrutiny to kill me as soon as I walk into the room.

Hopefully.

Alexei's answering silence is deafening. Niko's sobs have settled into hiccups, muffled against his mother's chest. I tap my thumb against the steering wheel as I take a last-minute exit, cradling my phone against my shoulder.

"Why do you need that?" Alexei eventually asks. I don't answer right away, trying to keep the growing dread in my chest at bay. He sighs. "Why do you need to talk to Renzuto, Andrei?"

His concern isn't misplaced.

I shouldn't have any reason to talk to anyone from The Outfit, especially not after today. I certainly have no damn reason to talk to their front boss. But it feels presumptuous to ask for a meeting with their *actual* boss.

I'm not looking to dodge more bullets today.

And if they really are behind the shooting, I need to do something to get them off my back.

I've just managed to scrape this family together. I'm not going to give them up without a fight.

"Do you really want to know?" I swallow thickly. I've already got a slew of fights set up in front of me. If I have to add Alexei to the list, he might end up being the thing that brings my whole plan crashing down around me.

"No. No, I guess I don't."

"Wonderful. In that case, I'll be at your place in five and you can give me his number in person."

"Are you fucking kidding me, Andrei?" he snarls, but I hang up before he can work himself into a frenzy. If I'm going to do this, I can't worry about Blair's safety right now. As mad as he might be, Alexi will look after them until I come back.

"You're going to be okay," I say, but I'm not sure if I'm trying to convince Blair or myself. She *will* be okay. I'll move heaven and earth if I have to. I'll break everything I've ever worked for and let it burn to the ground. As long as Blair and Niko are safe, nothing else matters.

When I pull up in front of his building, Alexei's waiting for us, arms crossed over his chest. I don't realize until I lay eyes on him that I was half expecting him to be holding a gun, ready to shoot me before I even got out of the car.

Unlike Blair, he hasn't asked me about Pavel's murder, but he's not stupid enough not to have worked out what happened. And he's smart enough to know what I'm planning on doing now, too.

I race around the car, holding the door open for Blair and Niko, who's managed to cry himself to sleep.

Alexei's face is stormy, like he can't figure out whether to start yelling or go straight to throwing punches, but when he takes in our appearances and Blair's red-rimmed eyes, he hurries us into the lobby.

The doors close behind us with a gust of wind as he shoves a piece of paper into my hands.

"I take it I'm looking after these guys tonight?"

I nod. "You keep them safe, and we're even. You won't owe me a damn thing."

Blair presses herself into my side, her weight a welcome comfort that I don't deserve.

I wrap an arm around them both, kissing the tops of their heads. This whole fiasco is even more miserable to bear after such a wonderful day, and I only hope I'll be able to have more days like it in the future to make up for it.

"You're going to come back?" There's a hitch in her voice that sounds like she's holding back tears, and I clench my jaw hard enough that my teeth hurt.

"If I can." Her watery eyes meet mine, and I wish that I could reassure her.

I want to promise her that everything will be alright. That I'm going to come home and hold her while she sleeps. But even if everything goes according to plan, I'm probably still walking straight into a trap.

I can't promise her that I'll be able to walk away at the end. But I'm sure as hell going to try.

I grip the back of her neck and pull her into a searing kiss, desperate to feel her against me for as long as I can.

"I love you," I murmur against her lips.

Alexei guides her away from me, herding them toward the elevator, and, crucially, away from the massive glass windows that offer no privacy or protection from the street. I smile at her, taking in every detail of her face as the elevator doors slide shut behind them.

In the next heartbeat, I'm pulling out my phone.

The sooner this is done and over with, the sooner I can come back to them.

***

I've never had the pleasure of meeting Marcell Renzuto before, and I also can't say I've ever wanted to.

He has a reputation for being as charming as he is calculating, the kind of man who will do anything to get a new car or another source of cash. He's treacherous, but no more than any other man around him.

He stands to greet me as his gold rings glint in the dim lighting. The smile on his face is as welcoming as a shark's. It does nothing to distract me from the five men placed strategically around the room, each standing with their hands clasped in front of them, a firearm displayed prominently on their hips.

Yeah, I've never felt more welcome anywhere in my life.

"Andrei Voronov, in the flesh." His eyes glint with malice, and I feel the absence of my gun like a physical ache. I'm not making the smartest choices today, but I don't have a death wish. When his man searched me at the door, I didn't hesitate to surrender my weapons.

If Renzuto wants me dead, there's nothing I can do to prevent it. My weapons would do nothing but accelerate how quickly he'd make it happen.

"What brings you to our part of town? You don't strike me as the sort of man to offer condolences for our fallen friend."

"I'm not." I shrug as I take the seat across from him. "Especially not for a man that was so inclined to bring trouble on himself."

The private room of his restaurant is flooded with dark red and black accents, the gold lights and candle holders sparkling in the low lighting. If there were less guns around and the air wasn't filled with a malevolence that promises harm to anyone who dares to linger, hell, it might even look romantic.

Each man is dressed in a tailored suit, not a hair out of place. It only serves to show exactly how out of place I am in my jeans and the hoodie I had to steal back from Blair.

Something tells me that no other man in this room would dare to be caught dressed in anything but their Sunday best.

A lot of things can be said about the Russian brand of organized crime, mostly that it doesn't have much organization going for it. It's chaotic and messy, which can be a strength just as much as it can be a vulnerability. It's hard to attack something that has no real structure, but it's also hard to control.

The Outfit, though less organized than some crime families, is far too rigid in their roles. Even in this display of manpower, Marcell's showing both them and me that he has solders who would die for him. Men that would fall for someone who doesn't even truly hold the reins of their operation, for nothing but smoke and mirrors.

It's nothing but a disgusting performance.

The formality that is entrenched in every moment of this show is enough to make any man want to start throwing punches. No one can live within The Outfit's strict lines and remain themselves. Not really. They'll always end up boiled down to a machine that exists solely to follow orders.

"And yet, here you are. Why bother gracing me with your presence?" Marcell's still smiling, but he no longer looks amused.

Heaven forbid I don't play his fucking game.

"I was shot at earlier while I was out with my wife and her son." It's a fight to keep my tone even, and the subtle shift in his posture tells me he can hear my simmering rage.

"That's unfortunate, but I fail to see how it should concern me." He waves a dismissive hand in front of him, and it hits me all over again that I could have lost them.

In the blink of an eye, Blair and Niko could've been nothing but stains on the sidewalk. Not because of this man, but because of the whims of his boss. Just because of who *my* boss is.

If I were to lose them, it'd break me.

"You and yours want revenge for what happened to Sotero, yes?" I ask. He raises a single dark brow, his expression bored.

I lost my chance to back out of this when I called him, and I've never been one to beat around the bush, so I simply say, "I will kill Maksim Maslov. He'll cease to live, and without him there will be no one to push the Bratva further into your territories."

Renzuto leans forward, tapping his index finger against his thumb while he considers it.

"And why would you do that?"

"The bloodshed is going to continue. Things have gone too far for it not to, and we both know it. But leave my family out of it."

"Just like that?" He leans back in his chair, and I wonder if he even has the authority to make the call on this. "I give you my word, and Maksim's gone? You won't come after us in the future?"

I shake my head, well aware that if he dismisses me, I'm either going to die in this room and be marked as a traitor, or they'll sell me out and let the rest of the Bratva take care of me. I'm loyal to our cause, but no one else will see it that way. They'll just see what I've offered to do.

I'm not loyal to Maksim, though. He isn't worthy of it. He never was.

But Blair and Niko? They're worth everything.

Nothing will sway me from doing everything I can to protect them.

"I don't control the Bratva, and I have no interest in trying to," I tell him. "But you won't have to worry about whoever takes over killing off your men because the wind has changed direction."

His eyes watch me with an intensity that matches what I'm feeling.

It doesn't take a genius to see that we're already heading toward war. The dominoes have been set into motion, and nothing that happens in this room will be able to stop them. All we can do is try to mitigate the losses.

War is expensive, both in money and blood. To pretend otherwise would be beyond foolish, and for a man who's been presented with the chance to stem the bleeding, it would be suicidal. My eyes flick to the guard closest to the door and back again, watching as Marcell runs the numbers.

I'm not surprised he brought so many men with him. It's crucial to their operations that he does everything in his power to protect himself, to give off the illusion of power.

But it's also more mouths who will know exactly what is said in this room. It's more men that may lose someone further down the line. And if they do, there's no amount of threats he'll be able to issue that will keep the details of this conversation confidential.

All the structure and formality may be able to buy a man's soul, but they can't buy his loyalty.

When he meets my eye, his cutting glare tells me he's come to the same conclusion.

Marcell's only in his role to be the boss for the men on the streets, someone to distract the feds while the real boss works behind the scenes. If he loses his men, he's nothing.

He's completely powerless.

For men like us, it's a fate worse than death.

"As I said, the only thing I want is assurance that your family won't put mine in harm's way again."

He rolls his neck, like he's trying to fight demons off his back, and I know I've got him.

"Fine," he bites out, jaw tight, like I've talked him into selling himself out instead of making a reasonable offer. "But only after he's dead. Until then, they're fair game."

Trusting his word is tortuous, but I have no choice.

"Deal."

CHAPTER 28

Andrei

The last time Maksim summoned me, he'd pulled back on his amount of security significantly, which means I just need to find a way to get the remaining men to look the other way when I show up.

The sun has set, but I don't like the odds of trying to sneak onto the property unnoticed.

I need to get this done and over with as soon as possible. Blair and Niko are safe with Alexei for now, but I can't discount the possibility that Marcell won't have me followed just so he can strike before I get a chance to hold up my end of the deal.

Which means I'm not going back to Blair until Maksim is dead.

One of the few upsides to having a paranoid, increasingly unstable pakhan is that he'll need me to clean up a mess for him soon enough. I just need to be patient and find a way to keep his security from knowing I'm there.

His calls are daily, bordering on hourly over the past couple weeks, and for once, I'm glad when my phone rings, turning toward his house before I even hang up on him. His words are slurred, barely comprehensible as he screams through the line. If circumstances were different, I'd add it to the list of things Maksim's done to piss me off.

Right now, I hope he's fucking wasted. Hell, I hope he's gone on such a rampage, made such a mess, that no one will notice another body added to the pile.

I pull up to the gate, but the gatehouse is dark. With rising suspicion, I drive along the driveway, but there are no guards wandering around, no men watching the front door. The bottom floor is dark. Half expecting to walk into carnage, I'm pleasantly surprised to find the inside clean, all the way until I find Maksim in his office.

Maybe it's my lucky day after all.

There's only a single corpse on the floor, and for the first time in weeks, I don't recognize them. Maksim's slumped forward at his desk, glass forgotten as he takes a swig straight from the bottle, pressing it against a spot where his eye is starting to swell shut with a bruise. He doesn't react to my presence, doesn't even seem to realize that we're alone.

Whoever this was, at least they put up a fight. Even if they were only brave enough because Maksim smells like a distillery, it's better than the sea of bodies that were too frightened to defend themselves that I've cleaned up over the years.

Every inch of space Maksim's ever consumed has been a waste. He's only ever been a spoiled, angry child who face-planted into power and never learned to be content with it. His constant struggle for more money and glory will be what defines his life.

His legacy will be bloodshed.

As long as Maksim is alive, he'll never cease to ruin everything and everyone he perceives as a threat to his ego. And through my association with him, he'll always be a threat to me.

"Are you just going to stand there, or are you going to *do* something?" His voice is slurred, barely coherent in his drunken haze. I've been standing here for several minutes, but he's acting like I've just arrived, his bleary eyes watching me as I take in the destruction.

The remains of a vase lie in front of one of the broken bookshelves, shattered in a hundred beautifully decorated, ornate pieces. There's blood spattered across the crushed velvet chairs, already drying and ruining the fabric. Everything is in ruins, a shell of what it once was.

"I'm curious about what happened," I say with a shrug, picking one of the shards up.

"I'm not paying you to be curious," he wheezes through his broken nose as he takes another swig. He's swaying from side to side, even while sitting.

"How the hell did you manage to take him down?" I can't stop myself from asking as I tilt my head toward the body on the floor. Decorum is wasted at this point, and I'm not going to force myself to bother with it. "You're blind drunk, and he looks like he was a healthy young man. So, how'd you do it?"

He drops the bottle to the ground and places his hands weakly on the desk, chest heaving like he's run a marathon as he pushes himself up. Even then, he still sways, like a stiff breeze could push him over.

"Are you so numb that you don't feel anything?" I continue. The body's neck is twisted at an unnatural angle, limbs akimbo. "Wait, let me guess. You didn't kill him at all, did you? He fell, hit his head, and you snapped his neck when he passed out."

He takes a couple of shuffling steps toward me, clinging to the edge of the desk for support. "Want to try that again, *pizda?*"

The single lamp illuminates his sagging frame, his clothes just as rumpled as the rest of the room, the fine fabric of his shirt a reflection of the broken debris and the opulence of the furniture.

I can't help but smirk as I circle away from him, keeping my distance. He might be so drunk he's barely standing, but he's still a wildcard. He has nothing left to lose, and that makes him dangerous.

"You couldn't get the job done on your own, could you? That's pathetic, even for you."

I turn the piece of broken vase over in my hand, running my thumb along the jagged edge.

The room, like the rest of the house, is draped in ubiquitous luxury. Yet he's reduced it all to nothing but gilded garbage.

"Take a look at how far you've fallen, Maksim. You expect me to believe you're the feared pakhan? You can't even stand on your own two feet anymore. How long has your drinking problem been out of your control? Or are you just so choked up over the waste of space that you called a son?"

I step to the side as he lunges for me, nearly tripping over his own feet.

Any hope I had of tonight being satisfying is long gone. He's nothing but a shadow of the man who used to loom over the rest of us. He's never deserved his power, and it's never been more apparent than it is now.

"What do you know about my son?"

I shrug, thick porcelain cracking under my shoes as I walk away, keeping an eye on him the whole time.

"I know he was drunk when I killed him. I suppose he got that from you." I let my words sink in, and I can see the moment they click, his chest heaving and face stricken. His eyes flare as I move around the room.

Maybe my confession gave him the jolt he needs to sober up a hair, because he seems to find his feet beneath him in slow, shuffling steps.

"I know Pavel was a threat to my wife. I know that he was harder to kill than you'll be. I know that his death was far more satisfying."

The rapidly cooling body lies on the ground between us, his blood soaking into the rug. When Maksim lurches toward me, his fists swim blindly. I grab his shoulders, catching him before he falls face-first into me, unable to keep the grin off my face.

"What did you do?" he seethes, the vein in his forehead pounding rapidly beneath his weathered skin.

"You saw his body at the morgue, right? You know exactly what I did."

"I will fucking end you, Voronov!"

"I'd like to see you try."

He moves quicker than I thought he'd be able to, a series of wild blows coming at me faster than I expected. One clips me on the chin, the sting throwing me off balance for just a moment, long enough for his other hand to reach out and grab my face. His nails claw into my cheek, drawing blood.

If he weren't drunk, he would've gone straight for my eye. I almost let out an inappropriate huff of laughter at the thought. *Almost.*

Instead, I shift my grip, pressing the point of the broken vase against the side of his neck. I apply enough pressure to get his attention, and he stills, even as his nails stay embedded in my cheek, gouging against my flesh.

"You kill me, and they'll come after you. Your *wife,*" he spits the word, as if the very idea is poisonous, "still won't be safe."

"No one's been loyal enough to die for you for a long fucking time." I press harder, a bead of blood dripping down his neck.

"And you're planning on taking over?"

"Fuck no. And I don't give a fuck who does. Until it's a man who isn't a threat to my family, I'll kill them, too."

I stab into the delicate skin and muscle that protects his carotid artery, immediately calmed by the warm blood that rushes around the rough edges of the porcelain.

He lets out a shocked gasp and I pull back, refusing to react even when his blood splatters against the wall.

It isn't long before he collapses to his knees, hovering over the other body.

I crouch next to him, grabbing his chin in my bloodied hand, forcing him to look at me as he bleeds out. "I give my loyalty to those who deserve it. And that has never been you," I snarl, forcing the shard into his neck once again, letting it make a home in his rotting flesh.

Maksim crumples unceremoniously, soaking both him and the corpse in red. Lifting the cold hand of the dead man, I put it on the shard still in Maksim's neck, using his hand to hold the shard in place until Maksim's blood stops flowing.

Only after the dead man's hand is covered in Maksim's blood do I drop it, doing my best to make it look like whoever this man was is the one who killed Maksim.

It won't be enough to convince any cops that there wasn't another person here, but it'll give me deniability if I'm asked.

But, realistically, no one's going to care who really killed Maksim Maslov, anyway. The Outfit and I will know the truth, and that's all I care about.

For Maksim to die alone in a tattered room, with no one to care, would be the ultimate failure in his eyes. I hope this corpse enjoys the notoriety of being the one to do the honor.

At least on paper.

I linger only long enough to wash the blood off my hands and face before I head home to change my clothes and tend to the scratches on my face. They won't scar, but they won't look great while they heal, either.

Then again, I probably have a few days before anyone even knows anything's happened.

All I want is to have Blair and Niko home with me. I shoot a text off to Renzuto, letting him know my end of the deal is done. Even if he doesn't believe me until someone exposes the body, he won't try to do anything to me again until he knows for sure.

Once I no longer look like an extra from a slasher flick, I speed toward Alexei's condo.

The need to have my family back in my arms is incessant, making it hard to breathe, and I don't feel settled again until I'm carrying a sleeping Niko upstairs. I help him change into his pajamas while he's half asleep, then carry him to our bedroom.

Blair's already under the comforter, curling herself around my pillow when I lay him down next to her. She wraps an arm around him, pulling him to her chest as she looks at me with big, scared eyes. I give her a reassuring smile as I slip in next to them, laying a hand on her hip.

"Did you take care of it?" she whispers, looking worried even as her eyes are involuntarily fluttering shut. I nod, but she doesn't see.

"Yeah. It's not going to happen again."

She nods, rubbing her face against the pillowcase.

I watch the two of them long after they fall asleep. I don't want to turn off the light, though I know I should.

If there's a heaven, I know that I'll never see it. I've done too much shit for any God to even consider it. But knowing that these two, who mean more to me than I can ever express, trust me to keep them safe feels as close to it as a man like me could ever get.

CHAPTER 29

Andrei

Nikita stands at the head of the room swirling a glass of cognac, working hard to give off an air of inflated self-importance. He seems to think that because he was Maksim's right hand, he deserves to be showered with respect and has a right to the power and position of pakhan.

He's oblivious to the fact that he lacks both the charm and the authority required to lead anyone. Without Maksim here, he's nothing but another ego in a suit.

Alexei takes another long drink from his glass, feigning boredom as he watches the room. Outwardly, he looks just like everyone else. Black suit. Drink in hand. Not a tear to spare for our fallen leader as his eyes shift from man to man, inspecting them each in turn.

The only thing giving away his irritation is how tightly he holds his shoulders, refusing to let his guard down.

He always was smarter than he let on.

The women and children left the funeral over an hour ago, and the crowd is starting to get restless. They no longer appear to be content to reminisce and pretend to talk shop. They're waiting for someone to take charge and turn this into a proper meeting, but no one's stepping up.

So many of the men here think they can lead, but none of them have the balls to actually take the first step and seize the crown.

Nikita takes another look around, clearly expecting someone else to do the work while he reaps the glory and steps up to declare himself the new pakhan.

Beside me, Alexei subtly tenses, unable to keep from boring holes into the side of Nikita's head. His expression has fallen out of his neutral mask, lip ticking up in a snarl.

I nudge him with my elbow before he can act on his sudden anger. The intensity in his eyes doesn't ease, but he does look away from Nikita long enough to shift his glare to me. It only lasts a moment before he goes back to his silent vigil.

"You know, if you really want to let him hang himself with his own noose, you'll take whatever power he thinks he has for yourself."

Out of everyone here, Alexei's the best man to take over, something I was hoping he'd figure out in his own time, but he needs to get over whatever his hang ups are before he does.

I'm not afraid to give him a nudge if that's what it takes.

His eyes snap to mine, finally breaking up the monopoly Nikita has had on his attention.

"You already have weight to throw around with how much money you earn," I point out. "At least you know how to manage something. That's more than he can say."

Really, what's so different between running nearly a half dozen clubs and a criminal syndicate? It's all about knowing how to manage people. Alexei's more than proven himself capable in that regard.

He nods idly, like he's only half listening to me, but it's enough.

"I could also let him flounder. He'll crash and burn in his own time." His tone is bland, like he doesn't care either way, but the tick in his jaw betrays him.

I watch curiously as he resumes scanning the room.

Nikita Dyomin isn't popular among the men. He's slimy and standoffish, but I can't figure out why Alexei is focusing his ire onto him. He has the means to make hell for anyone in this room, so why Nikita?

"You could," I concede, "but we're already fighting one war. Is his failure worth risking another?"

The mess with The Outfit quickly spiraled out of control when the police made a show of investigating Maksim's death. It's turned into something that will take time to clean up. It'll tie up time, money, men, and firepower that, frankly, we aren't in a good place to lose. Not without someone with a plan pulling strings behind the scenes.

Without a level head in charge, we'll end up shedding every resource we think we have faster than we have any hope of replenishing them.

Add an internal power struggle on top of everything else, and we'll be left with a shit show that will have no other outcome than catastrophic disaster.

I'd rather we not try to fight a war on two fronts, but if Alexei's going to refuse to step up, I won't force him to. I can only hope that he doesn't let Nikita bury us all before he gets a chance to start digging us out.

"Perhaps." The corner of Alexei's lip twitches into a smirk that he quickly conceals behind his glass.

"Do I even want to know why you're focusing on him?" I ask. He lifts a single shoulder in a shrug, and I know that that's as much of an answer as he's likely to give me for now. "Then pull your head out of your ass and stop looking at him like you're plotting his death."

He looks at me, eyes cutting.

"And how am I supposed to look at him, Andrei? Like I respect him? Like he has my undying loyalty? Should I put on a show before I stab him in the back?" I meet his stare, not blinking. "Or, wait, it was the throat, wasn't it?"

His look around the room is pointed, making the unspoken threat more than clear.

"Isn't it better to be straightforward? Why bother with the underhandedness?"

The men in this room are already a loaded powder keg. A single spark, and they'll turn on me faster than I can come up with a defense. In their need for revenge, it wouldn't matter who I am to them or what I've done, only what they think happened.

They'd gladly make me another casualty.

I squint, trying to figure Alexei out.

I don't think he wants to turn on me. I think he's trying to deflect, to keep me from prying into whatever his deal with Nikita is. I just don't know why he's being so forceful about it.

"Loyalty is earned," I say with a shrug. "As you know."

I've never been one to back down from a challenge, and he knows it. If he's serious, then I'll make sure he's the first one I take down. I won't be able to make it out of this room alive, but I can guarantee he won't, either.

He nods to himself, and I force my shoulders to fall.

"Relax. My sister would take great joy in skinning me alive if I let anything happen to you."

"If you let anything happen that would upset her friend, you mean."

Nadya and Blair have been as thick as thieves lately. If something were to happen that would upset Blair, Alexei would have Nadya breathing down his neck, and if something upset Nadya, I'd have the same from Blair.

Clearly, he isn't happy about it, but I'm thrilled that Blair has someone in her corner. It's the first time I've been able to see what she's like with someone she calls a friend. And seeing her happiness is something I'll never sacrifice, no matter how annoying it makes Alexei.

"For the record, being discreet and being manipulative are very different things."

He scoffs. "Still doesn't feel right."

"Doesn't have to. It's kept me kicking so far, hasn't it?"

"I guess I can't argue with the results." He shrugs, looking more relaxed than he has in weeks.

"By the way," I say as I lean against the wall. Now that I know he isn't going to try to have me killed, I might as well have a little fun with him. "Did you lose a fight with a street cat? Or were you mauled by a different type of beast?"

His hand goes to the back of his neck, covering the red scrapes that peek out over the edge of his collar.

"Fuck off, Andrei."

I smirk into my glass, trying not to chuckle.

Alexei's normally so composed and put together that whenever there's a single thread of his appearance out of place, it throws him off.

"I'll tell her to put away the claws next time," he mutters.

I take a sip of my drink to drown the huff of laughter, trying not to draw any attention to myself.

No one's looked at me twice today, and if it stays that way, I'll be able to leave happy.

I don't know exactly what Blair's been rubbing on the scratches on my face. It smells like honey, and she says that it helps small wounds heal faster. To be fair, it seems to have worked. Between the ointment and growing out my facial hair, the remains of Maksim's attempts to defend himself are difficult to see.

Then again, most people tend to be so caught up in their own heads that they don't notice much about anyone else in the first place. Not even men who should know how to be observant. If it doesn't affect them, they dismiss it without a second thought.

Every man here is too busy looking over their own shoulder to see the red flags that are practically dancing in a conga line down the center of the room.

They don't notice that all the older men have gathered around Nikita, quietly arranging themselves around the man they assume will lead. They don't notice that most of the other men are scattered, watching warily as the booze flows freely.

They don't notice that the thin threads that have tied us all together are fraying at both ends.

It's only a matter of time before it all comes to a breaking point, and only those who can keep their heads up will manage to dodge the shrapnel.

"Gentlemen," Nikita drawls, bringing all eyes to him. He pauses as if to savor his time in the spotlight. I hold back an eye roll, while Alexei is as stiff as a board. His shoulders are drawn back, fists held tight.

If I didn't know any better, I'd think he was looking for a fight.

"How about we deal with those Italians?"

Epilogue 1

ANDREI

The radio drones quietly in the background while I drive, allowing the sun to warm my face. It's unseasonably warm today, so I'm far from surprised when I pull into the driveway and see Niko running around the front yard, laughing as he kicks a ball and chases after it.

What I *am* surprised to see is Blair standing in the open doorway wearing one of my old sweatshirts over a pair of leggings, paintbrush in hand.

I lock the car as she smiles at me, and only then do I see a bucket of paint and a tray at her feet. She cracks open the lid and takes her time stirring the contents before she pours it out, revealing bright yellow paint that makes me pause in my steps.

When she said she was going to look at paint colors for the front door, I figured she'd take her time before she settled on one.

And I thought she'd settle on something more muted. A nice blue. A soft green. Or maybe a bold red, even. Not the obnoxious ray of sunshine that she's currently loading her brush with.

Forcing my feet back into motion, I stop at the bottom of the stairs, while she beams at me. "Do you like it?"

A hundred answers fly through my head, and none of them are flattering.

"It's very... cheerful," I settle on, shoving away all my protests and disparaging thoughts. "It looks like springtime."

And I'm pretty sure The Beatles had a submarine in that exact color.

"I helped pick it!" Niko calls across the yard, oblivious to my many plans to strip the paint and beg her to pick another color. He sounds proud, like he can't believe that he got to make such a big decision. One he gets to look at every day.

He runs over, throwing his arms around my legs, his smile matching his mother's and erasing my remaining reservations.

I guess we'll have a yellow door.

So what?

It's different from every other house on the street, and if Niko ever complains about it when he's a teenager, we'll get to remind him that he's the one responsible for it.

Now that I'm thinking about it, I can't fucking wait.

"You did a good job, kiddo. It's a great color."

Blair's eyes sparkle with poorly concealed laughter, and I only feel a little bad for how obvious my feelings apparently are. I ruffle Niko's hair as he watches her carefully painting around the edges of the door.

"Can I help?" he asks, twisting away from me as he starts reaching for a spare paintbrush. "I can do the top!" He reaches above his head to prove his point, knees knocking against the wet paint as he reaches a few inches above the doorknob. He teeters on his feet, and Blair and I both scramble to keep him upright so that he doesn't fall into the paint tray.

"How about this? We'll go inside and change into clothes that we don't mind messing up, and I'll hold you so you can reach the top. That way we won't step on your mama while we help." He nods and takes off like a shot, sprinting up the stairs while Blair laughs.

"He's going to get paint everywhere, isn't he?" I chuckle.

"He's three. Of course he is."

"You say that like the moment he turns four, he'll instantly be coordinated." I press a kiss to the top of her head. "And I suspect that won't be the case."

"Probably not," she concedes. "But let's withhold judgment. He might prove us wrong."

I shake my head as I shuffle past her, quickly heading upstairs and changing into a pair of sweats and one of my old T-shirts that I dig out of Blair's drawers. Niko beats me back downstairs, waiting impatiently as Blair shows him how to move the paintbrush so he doesn't leave streaks everywhere.

I can almost see every word she says going in one ear and right out the other when he spots me, jumping to his feet and raising his arms until I pick him up. He squeals when I twist him around so that he's sitting tall on my shoulders.

Blair hands him a loaded paintbrush while he lurches forward in his eagerness to get to the door, nearly tumbling over my head.

They both quickly lose themselves in their painting, Blair working efficiently while Niko and I end up covered in streaks of yellow while most of the top of the door is still white, with only a few messy globs of paint covering the primer. When Blair stands, her hair is splattered the same color, globs of yellow soaking the strands and dripping down her face.

She glares at Niko's loaded brush while he laughs, hiding his face behind messy hands.

"Alright, let's get you cleaned up before you end up stuck this color," I suggest when he gets bored, slapping the brush against the door more than he is actually painting it.

"But I like being a sunshine!" he pouts, crossing his arms over my head and letting the wet paintbrush smack me in the face. I try to flinch away, but the damage is done.

Blair starts laughing, falling out of the squat she was in and landing right on her ass, sending Niko into a matching fit of hysterics. He wiggles as I lift him off my shoulders, slipping the brush out of his hand as I put him on his feet.

"Yeah, yeah. Laugh it up now," I mutter. "I'll get even later."

My warning does nothing to deter them. If anything, they just laugh harder, falling into each other for support while I scrape my hand over my face, trying to remove as much of the paint as I can. It comes away soaked in the awful color, and my attempts to wipe it off on the drop cloth under the door only smear it around more.

Great.

"Now we both need to get cleaned up before we're stuck this way."

Blair wipes a tear from the corner of her eye, face flushed while she catches her breath.

"You two go clean up." She grins, patting Niko's shoulder. "I'll finish up here. Then we can order a pizza for dinner. That sound like a plan?"

Like she said a magic word, Niko turns and heads upstairs without a word of protest, leaving a trail of yellow footprints behind him.

I sigh and follow, doing my best to limit the damage.

He stands on a step stool, scrubbing his hands diligently while I use a washcloth to scrub at the paint that's drying on my face. He leans forward, trying to scrub at the paint that's all the way up to his elbows, humming to himself while he nearly faceplants into the sink.

"Careful, little man," I say, putting a hand on his shoulder and pulling him back to his feet. "We don't want your mama to think I tried to drown you."

"You wouldn't do that," he giggles. He points at my reflection in the mirror. "You have more paint there."

"Where? Here?" I ask, swiping the wet cloth against his cheek, smearing more paint. "Or here?" I rub it over his chin. He squeals, pushing my hand way.

"Not me! You!"

"Are you sure? Because from where I'm standing, it looks like you've got it worse."

He narrows his eyes and, faster than I can anticipate, turns and rubs his face on my shirt like a cat, turning it into a collage of dirty water and saffron yellow. Then he takes off, giggling as he runs down the hallway while I turn off the sink and rush to clean off as much of my hands as possible.

"I'll get you for that!" I shout after him, smiling.

What a little jerk.

I chase after him, knowing that he's probably making a mess on every corner and wall as he goes. His giggles stop when he ducks behind the door to my office, trying to be sneaky, like he hasn't just left a trail leading straight to him.

I slow down, deliberately keeping my steps quiet as I approach. If he wants to escape me, he's going to have to do better than that.

I pull the door open in a rush, picking him up when he falls backward without it to support his weight, tickling him while he screams, and does his best to wiggle free as I cage him against me.

He squirms the whole time I carry him back to the bathroom, only settling when I set him on the counter, determined to get us clean. As clean as we can get, anyway. He doesn't fight, resigned to his fate. It takes ages, constantly having to stop and rinse off the cloth between attempts, wringing it out before I try again. Despite my best efforts, we're both soaked by the time we're clean.

He's smiling when I help him down, tossing the washcloth into the sink to deal with later.

His tiny arms wrap around me, keeping me from pulling away.

"I love you, Andrei."

Everything in me stills, unsure how to process that. I've been content knowing that he likes having me around, that he sees me as a friend. I figured I'd be able to milk that until he got old enough to start lashing out at me, and I was willing to cross the bridge when we got there.

Him telling me he loves me? I kind of want to cry.

"I love you too, Niko." My voice is thick, but he doesn't notice and just slips past me, like nothing out of the ordinary happened. I look at my reflection, startled when I see Blair standing behind me, a gentle smile on her face while she ruffles Niko's hair as he passes by.

"Hey."

"Hi. You mind telling me why the hallway is yellow?"

I shrug. "Niko and I liked the color so much, we thought we should spread it out. Doesn't it make everything look so cheery?"

I put a hand on her hip, urging her closer to me so that I can hold her, breathing in the floral smell of her shampoo while I try to find more stable ground.

"Take your time," she murmurs against my chest. "But just so you know, I love you just as much as he does."

"I love you too, *zolotse*."

I kiss her, pouring every ounce of my gratitude into it, hoping that it'll convey exactly how much she means to me. I will her to understand as my tongue moves against her, only stopping when Niko calls down the hall asking when dinner will get here.

Then we sit on the porch, her hand in mine while we wait next to the open door so that the delivery man doesn't smear the still-wet paint.

Epilogue 2

BLAIR

I'm pretty sure shopping at Christmas time is one of the higher levels of hell.

Parking is impossible, people take up whole aisles just so they can stare at their phones, and Niko wants to stop and look at every light and decoration on display. It's been fifteen minutes, and I'm already cursing myself for deciding that *today* was going to be the day that I picked up the tools the internet has assured me will get paint off hardwood flooring.

I should've waited. Until March, probably. When everyone's gone home and decided to only go outside in reasonable numbers instead of forcing me to contend with the most inconsiderate, selfish humans alive while I'm trying to wrangle an excited toddler.

I wasn't feeling well this morning, and navigating through the crowds isn't helping. And if the guy at the end of the aisle wearing a cloud of cologne takes a single step closer to me, I'm going to puke on his shoes.

Maybe it would be easier if the store kept all the Christmas decorations to one part of the store, but to get where I need to, I have to dance through the light displays, navigate both the real and plastic trees, and resist the lure of the yard decorations.

Now, finally, the promised land is in sight.

Twenty feet away, the cleaning supplies beckon, calling my name. I just need to get through the sea of people staring at the inflatable lawn decorations, and I'll be able to escape this place relatively unscathed. I consider using my hands as blinders to keep Niko focused on the task at hand, but as someone carelessly walks into my shoulder, jostling me, I decide that it's smarter to keep his hand tight in mine so he can't wander off.

"Mama, look!"

Biting back a sigh, I stop, trying to figure out what Niko's so excited about this time. It doesn't take long.

Right at his eye level is an inflatable stegosaurus wearing a jolly scarf. It isn't big, maybe the size of a corgi, but Niko's face is bright; it's as if he just saw Santa Claus in the flesh. My gut drops, already trying to figure out how to negotiate my way out of a temper tantrum before he even asks.

"Can we get it?"

I start making a sympathetic but non-committal noise when it hits me.

I want to buy him the damn dinosaur, and there's no one to stop me.

The only reason I instinctively wanted to say no was because Daniil would've made a big deal about how tacky and classless he found it, like he did every other time Niko asked for one.

If I bought it when he was still alive, he would've thrown it out and washed his hands of the whole thing when Niko cried because his new favorite yard decoration was gone.

He wouldn't have cared that it made Niko happy; the only thing that would have mattered to him would be how other people viewed it.

But Daniil's opinion never should have mattered when it comes to making Niko happy, and it definitely doesn't matter now. I eye the shelf before I sigh, looking toward the front of the store, already dreading the trek back to the entrance. Resigned, I pick up Nikolai to make it a little bit easier.

When I turn around, he turns his watery eyes to me, cracking my heart in two. For a moment, I want to cry, too.

"We aren't getting him?"

I almost laugh at how quickly he switches from calling the dinosaur an *it* to a *he*. Like in the minute since he realized it was a thing he could have, he's created a whole backstory and personality for it.

"We are. But we're going to need a cart."

With my luck, I'm going to have to find a way to not make that dinosaur seasonal, because he's going to throw a fit when I try to pack it away after the holidays.

***

I'm impressed by Niko's ability to stay out of the way as I work another spike into the ground, shoulders aching from the effort of making sure each one is planted so it can keep the inflatable in place. I'm about to call him over to help me turn on the electric pump when we both spot Andrei's car rolling into the driveway.

Niko waits by the patio, bouncing on his feet until the car turns off, only then sprinting toward it, arms wide and voice loud as he launches himself into Andrei's arms. His mouth works hard to keep up with his brain as he regurgitates everything that happened while Andrei was out.

I almost laugh at Andrei's bewildered face as he half listens, looking across the yard at the new additions.

Two of our new decorations are positioned face-to-face, grinning at each other just like Niko wanted. Two more are on either side of the mailbox, keeping watch for passersby. One is set up half behind the tree as if it's hiding, and when I turn on the pump, the last one will be set up near the patio, ready to greet anyone who happens to stop by.

They're ridiculous, but seeing Niko's excitement for each one is worth it. I can't wait to see what they look like after the sun goes down.

Andrei holds Niko's hand as they head toward the door, and I fiddle with the cuff of my sweater, unease curling down my spine. Andrei won't make a scene in front of Nikolai, but what if he hates them?

I won't let him throw them out, and part of me knows he won't make a fuss over something as minor as what the yard looks like.

But the worry still persists.

"Is she ready yet, Mama?"

I tug on the spike, making sure that it's secure in the ground before I nod, Niko's smile bright in the fading sunlight. "Seems like it. You want to turn on the fan?" He runs beside me, eagerly pressing the button and backing off so he can watch as it fills with air.

It's identical to the other five, but you wouldn't know it from looking at him. He's talked my ear off the whole time we've been in the yard, telling me all about each one, and what they think about the others in the yard.

Apparently, this one is named Ana, and she doesn't play well with the others.

Andrei waits patiently until it's standing at attention. It's a little lopsided, but otherwise it's a bright and cheery addition to the yard. We just need to wait for snow to complete the look. Only when Niko's giggling to himself does Andrei crouch down.

"Why don't you go get cleaned up while I talk to your mama?" he tells him. The anxiety comes back before Niko is even up the stairs, tightening my stomach. "We'll join you in a bit. Then you can introduce me to your new dino armada."

I want to call Niko back and keep him glued to my side so that Andrei doesn't say anything untoward about our new lawn decorations. He was kind enough when I painted the door, even though I'm sure he would've picked virtually any other color, but what if this crosses a line that I didn't know existed?

"Please tell me these are the only ones you bought."

He sounds resigned, and the tension in my spine notches even tighter.

"The store only had six, so," I shrug. "I was only going to get two, but then Niko asked if the others were going to miss their friends. And he's only going to be little once, you know? So, we bought all of them."

He nods, rolling his neck.

"Thank fuck. Were they a pain to get set up?"

He doesn't look mad. He looks more curious than anything else. "It wasn't that bad. They're short, so I didn't have to work too hard to get them secure. Why?"

"I, uh, might have bought a blow-up T. rex from a store across town." He looks like he's awaiting a scolding, and I almost laugh. "And I was hoping you could help me set it up after he goes to bed on Christmas Eve so we can tell him that Santa brought it. But if you've already bought one, I'll need to return it. And if I have to deal with another store before the new year, I'm going to get arrested for assault."

Unable to help myself, I laugh. I fall out of my crouch, laughing as I sit on the cold ground.

"Well, if you do, I'll make sure to pay your bail."

"If you would, I'd appreciate it. I really don't want to miss Christmas."

God, Andrei's sweet. He's such a good husband. He's incredible with Niko. And I'm so glad that I get to keep him. Because every time I think I can't love this man more, he does something like this. He's so thoughtful and caring that I feel like I'm going to melt.

I love him. I love the way he loves Niko. I love the way he waltzed into our lives and didn't give us a choice but to let him love and take care of us.

He sits next to me, pulling me into his arms until my laughter dies down.

"I love you," I say as I rest my head against his chest.

"I love you too, *zolotse*."

His heartbeat is steady under my ear, echoing my own as it sings for him.

"I have to tell you something," I admit, trying to focus on his heart until it drowns out my anxiety.

"What's that?"

"My period's late."

He freezes, arms squeezing tighter as he cages me against him. "What?"

"I picked up a few pregnancy tests. But I wanted to tell you before I took them."

We haven't talked about having more kids. I'd like more, eventually, and he's never even blinked when it comes to taking care of Niko, but I don't know how he'd feel about having one *now*. We haven't been married long. And so many things are still up in the air as far as his work goes, but still.

I didn't rush into marrying him with bright, shiny hopes, but being with Andrei feels like a task that I'm willing to take on. Not just willing, but excited for. I'm not under any illusion that being with him is going to be a walk in the park, or that we'll never have rough patches, but I *want* to be with him. I *want* to work through those things.

And I hope that he might think this is a good thing, too.

"You're going to have my baby?"

"Maybe. I don't know for sure, but..." I shrug, stomach flipping with tenuous excitement. "I might be." He presses his lips against my hair, holding me tight against his chest. "Would that be okay? If we had a baby?" He pulls back, twisting me until I'm looking at the awestruck expression on his face.

"Blair, I'd fucking love that."

"Yeah?"

"Yeah."

We're smiling as we kiss, laughing when Niko comes back outside to whine impatiently, asking when dinner's going to be ready.

My relationship with Andrei might not have started in the typical way, but I wouldn't change this moment for the world.

Acknowledgements

Where to begin?

First of all, Yvette, without you this story wouldn't have been what it is! I don't know what I would have done if you hadn't held my hand and guided me through the editing process.

To Dad, your endless patience when I made you listen to me rant about things you had no context for, trying to help even when I was too stubborn to listen, was invaluable. I love you, and I couldn't have done this without you.

To Carlos, for figuring out which notebook you were not allowed to mess with. You were invaluable when it came to bouncing ideas back and forth, even if you're constantly rooting for a Pavel zombie arc that will never happen.

And last, but certainly not least, thank *you* for taking the time to read Plaintive Vow! It means the world to me that you took the time out of your day to listen to these characters and share their world. If you enjoyed it, please consider leaving a review!

About the author

E rin Robinson writes dark romance for readers who like complicated men and the women who make them fall to their knees.

When she isn't writing, she can be found digging around in her garden, herding her ridiculous cat, or curled up with a book in hand. She hopes that in time, she'll be able to pursue writing full time.

For updates on future releases, including sneak peeks, sign up for her newsletter on her website, authorerinrobinson.com.